COVENANT KEPT

VICTORIA GARAFOLA

ISBN 978-1-68197-999-1 (Paperback)
ISBN 978-1-63525-004-6 (Digital)

Copyright © 2016 by Victoria Garafola

All rights reserved. No part of this publication may be reproduced, distributed, or transmitted in any form or by any means, including photocopying, recording, or other electronic or mechanical methods without the prior written permission of the publisher. For permission requests, solicit the publisher via the address below.

Christian Faith Publishing, Inc.
296 Chestnut Street
Meadville, PA 16335
www.christianfaithpublishing.com

Printed in the United States of America

Thanks and love to my mom and dad for all they've done. Love to Denise, James, and Jimmy. A special thanks and love to Fran, Herman, Pauline, Richard, and Lynda for your friendship, prayers, teaching and encouragement. And thanks to all my Christian brothers and sisters for your support.

To the One who is and always will be. Thank you, Lord, for granting me a second chance at life.

PREFACE

I would like to offer special thanks to you for reading this book. This fictional story was *inspired* by the biblical prophecies written in the book of Revelation. To understand biblical end-times, I encourage you to read your Bible and seek a spiritual leader if you have questions.

As Christians living in this broken world, we need to spread the warning that Christ Jesus left for us long ago. Many people will scoff at this message, but it must be shared nonetheless.

I would like to recount my testimony and the reason I wrote this book. I've always believed in the Lord but not as fervently as I should have. I dealt with a multitude of serious family problems. I experienced terrible and inexcusable events that ate away at my love for family, life, and myself. I fell away from God. I wrestled with his existence because I could not see how there could be any god in the midst of the chaos.

Lost and unsure what to do, I enlisted in the navy at just twenty years old. The time in the military was good for me, but it came at a heavy price. I received a crushing injury to my leg that kept me from returning to active duty.

The years passed by swiftly as they often do. Realizing I was another ten years older and still lacking direction, I enrolled in college. Finding a church to fit into seemed nearly impossible. I was empty and lonely, and I still had the feeling that something was missing in my life. After graduating with my bachelor's degree, I kept working because I still lacked purpose. Several years later, I made the plunge and returned for my master's in psychology.

My injury continued to get worse until the Department of Veterans Affairs (VA) had no choice but to acknowledge it. After many years of arguing with them, they recognized something was wrong. They found avascular necrosis in my leg. Put simply, a bone was dying, and I needed another surgery.

I underwent the procedure the day after graduation. The surgeon attempted a bone fusion with an external fixator. Even though it was a tremendous surgery, my doctor insisted it be an outpatient procedure. They began my discharge as soon as I woke up from the anesthetic. The pain from the surgery was immense, and my family questioned why they were sending me home, but the nurse only said, "You don't want her to stay here."

I spent most of the next two weeks hallucinating from the medication. The VA insisted that I wasn't experiencing anything out of the ordinary. Two weeks later, while I was transferring from my couch to my wheelchair, everything spun.

I only had time to say, "Mom, something is wrong." I woke up with her beating on my chest, and all we could do was wait for the ambulance.

When I arrived at the emergency room, the doctors sent me in for a CT scan to see what was rattling in my chest. As soon as the test was completed, the sensation of spinning began again. A petite CT tech threw her arms around me and held on for dear life.

The ER nurse instructed me not to move but to stay calm and still. She explained there was a significant blood clot lodged in my chest. Before I understood what was happening, a tall thoracic surgeon stood at the foot of my bed. He explained how he would open my chest, crack my ribs, and remove the clot before it moved into my lungs.

There wasn't much time to act. The surgeon called in his team. The anesthesiologist and surgery nurse had to prep me while running down the hall at two thirty in the morning. Frightened and with just a moment to say good-bye, I thought about what would happen to my mom if I died and wondered if God would forgive me.

I woke up on a ventilator, unsure if I would recover. Doctors explained that I had less than one percent chance of survival. "No one survives something like this" was the consensus. I spent the next ten days in cardiac intensive care. Each day, doctors came close to shake my hand. Over and over, they would ask if I understood what happened.

The surgeon showed me a picture of the blood clot. It was an unbelievable seventeen inches long and in one continuous thick strand. It traveled through my heart and became lodged in the ascending aorta, which put me in cardiac arrest.

As time went on, I didn't get better. Fluid collected around my heart, my heartbeat was irregular; my body wasn't healing; and I had to have another bone-fusion surgery. As a final insult, I developed multiple lifelong debilitating illnesses.

Depression became a serious issue for me over the following few months until I finally gave in and reached out to God. I prayed every day for guidance and gained a renewed strength. I was so thankful that Christ heard my cries and answered. I had always felt I was going the wrong direction, and I knew that I was not as close to God as I should have been. While he did not cause the trials in my life, he did use them to get my attention.

From out of the blue, this story came to me. I felt compelled to write this book and write about the glory of God. The story is harsh at times, but these are harsh times we live in. There will come a time in all of our lives in which we will have to decide. Will we accept the truth about the one and only God, or will we accept the consequences of our unwillingness to believe?

My testimony shows the grace of the Lord and how he loves us even when we stray. My survival was not luck or good timing. If I had gone to bed earlier that night, if I had not gone to the hospital, or if the blood clot had broken loose again, I would not be here. I had an awesome surgeon, but even he had to admit there's no medical explanation why I'm alive today.

God is amazing and so is his Son. Christ blessed me that night with a second chance at life, and it's my job to honor him. Thank you for reading my story.

> *For the message of the cross is foolishness to those who are perishing, but to us who are being saved it is the power of God.*
>
> —*1 Corinthians 1:18*

PROLOGUE

Life's only true constant is that it is inconsistent. No matter how much we believe we know, life is an uncertain journey. Sometimes it's filled with wonder and joy, but it can also be filled with sadness and pain. Starting in our early years, we have hopes, dreams, and aspirations for our future. Whether or not we accomplish those desires, most of us count on having another tomorrow. We believe we will have another day, another chance to do all the things we hope to do. We feel there will be another opportunity to right our wrongs.

Many of us lose direction throughout our journey. We easily become distracted and lose sight of what is truly important in our lives. Our days are hectic, and we're always running to catch up. Exhausted from the demands of work and life, we just go through the motions of existing.

Distraction is only part of it. The human race lacks control. Therefore, everywhere we turn, we see anguish. Crime consumes the world. Almost weekly, we hear new stories of parents murdering their children. People torture animals, and pedophiles kidnap, molest, and murder defenseless children. Rape, arson, theft, and despicable behaviors are happening all around us. With never-ending wars and an incredible lack of morality in people today, it is difficult to find hope for the human race.

Furthermore, many seek to convince the faithful that there is no God and that Christ was nothing more than a mythical figure. Keeping faith in God is hard when we are bombarded every day of our lives with such negativity. Many who do believe in God often blame him for the wrongs in their lives. Maybe they are angry with him because they failed to achieve something they'd hoped for. Perhaps, they blame him for the loss of their loved ones or for the pain caused by the sins of man. They become disillusioned in him and lose their faith.

The world has become an egocentric, narcissistic copy of what it once was. The very soul of humanity has been corrupted and fades slowly like a dying tree struggling to draw the tiniest bit of nutrients from soil that is dead and empty. People's faith in God is fleeting, much like the heart of humanity.

A gifted humanitarian, minister, and Nobel Peace Prize winner by the name of Martin Luther King Jr. once stated, "Our scientific power has outrun our spiritual power. We have guided missiles and misguided men." This statement is as true today as it was then.

Scholars, often with the help of mainstream media, try to convince the faithful that the idea of an all-powerful being is foolishness. Indoctrination into this faithless society begins early in our lives. In the United States, prayers have long been banished from secular schools for fear of offending nonbelievers. Instead, children are taught subjects like evolutionary theory as fact. The system teaches the belief that we can only understand what we can touch, taste, hear, or see. And even though this country's very foundation was built on Christianity, any references to God are systematically being eliminated.

Many seek out their own reasons for our creation and our very existence, even if it means the facts have to be manipulated to reach their desired results. Many well-known atheists and agnostics refer to those who have faith in God as incapable of being logical. Therefore, they believe the faithful cannot be reasoned with. The accusers believe Christians use the idea of God as a crutch or a means to hide from reality. Furthermore, some people in the world claim to be devoted to God but exhibit appalling behavior and perform atrocities in his name.

We need to remember that religion was created by people and can therefore be manipulated and abused. Many nonbelievers choose to ignore the fact that there is a difference between religion and faith. Similarly, there is a difference between those who are faithful, living righteous and respectful lives and those who manipulate God's Word for their own desires. Ultimately, abusing God's commandments alienates nonbelievers and steals away any hope of bringing them to his light. In the end, much of society has convinced itself there is absolutely no God, and to many, that makes perfect sense.

But what if we choose not to believe and later discover that all the things we've convinced ourselves of being true were ultimately wrong? What if God is real? What if he has lost his faith in humanity? What if he has decided the time has come to judge us and make us answer for our transgressions? What if we have to make choices that we never imagined having to make? But what if help is coming from the most unlikely of beings?

My name is Alijah. God has judged humanity. The time has come.

* * * * *

Angels are the oldest children of Elohim (God). Many of my kind have traveled the earth since the human race was created. They seamlessly come and go in mortals' lives, attempting to guide them to God's merciful light. Many angels come to greet souls departing from the earth. Some will make themselves visible to comfort those who need it most. For whatever reason, they most often impact lives in the slightest of ways.

My brothers and I can only wait for the day we are called upon. We have observed the earth through the ages and have witnessed its changes. Since the time of my creation, I have watched its inhabitants, the humans, as they grew and progressed.

They are an intriguing species. Humans are the youngest of his children, yet they are the most complicated. Many of us have been called upon to guide humanity and aid them as they grow. However, no matter how angels have tried, humans continue to allow themselves to be corrupted. Through observation, we have never fully understood the human race, and I have always wondered why creatures who have the sempiternal love of Elohim could so easily, without question or consideration, squander it.

Since the humans' conception, they have demonstrated how they can adapt, develop, and rise to brilliant heights. But despite all their diligent work, they destroy not only their accomplishments but also each other. It is their willingness, even blatant eagerness, to bring desolation to one another that astounds me. They have been granted ample opportunities to correct their mistakes.

Oddly enough, humanity's only assigned tasks were to take care of the earth while they inhabited it, be kind to one another, follow the commandments of Elohim, and have faith in his glory. They were to remember he is the Alpha and the Omega and worship none other than him.

Elohim saw early that humanity was faltering. It did not take long before they constructed idols to worship. They so quickly forgot our Creator, forsaking his name and his goodness. They fashioned beings in their minds, believing them to be the architects of the earth and the designers of humanity itself. They did not remember there is only one true Creator of all.

While many faithful servants live under his commandments, many more do not. Destruction, death, and torture are commonplace to them. These… creatures… afflict one another with pain. They abuse, torment, and destroy one another for little reason other than sport and greed.

The land was only lent to them, yet they destroy it. They believe it is theirs with which to do as they please, scarring and abusing it—such a tragedy. Humans were allowed to inhabit and share the earth, and even though it is theirs to share, they seek to conquer each other.

We have known for some time Elohim was losing his faith in the humans. He has spent centuries weeping for them, saddened by what his children have done and deeply troubled by what they have become. He is angered by their savagery, confused as to why they do such abhorrent things. He offered his Son, who was sacrificed for their salvation, and yet they did not learn.

Not all angels have the same purpose. Some, like myself, are warriors in a great army who will fight for a divine purpose for the most divine of beings when called forth. When my brothers and I were summoned, we knew the time of retribution and glory was at hand.

We are bound by honor, bound by the Holy Spirit, bound by Elohim to bring his glory and cleanse the earth of evil. There are none who know the time of reckoning. However, when the Lamb breaks the seals, Elohim will command us to do his bidding. We will ride into the human realm and deliver his judgments to the disciples of the Great Deceiver. For we are the horsemen of the Apocalypse… and it is death I bring.

> *Now, brothers and sisters, about times and dates we do not need to write to you, for you know very well that the day of the Lord will come like a thief in the night. While people are saying, "Peace and safety," destruction will come on them...they will not escape.*
>
> —*1 Thessalonians 5:1–3*

Chapter 1

The horsemen were forbidden to walk the earth. Their existence was to be unknown to humans until the time set for them to bring God's wrath upon the wicked and begin the cleansing of the earth. However, a light, an unbearable light, drew one of them down to earth.

He did his best to disregard it, turning his eyes from the radiance. "Why can I not forget it? What draws me to it?" He was consumed by the light and could think of nothing other than descending to earth to search for it.

"Brother," a voice boomed out from behind.

He shifted his gaze from earth and looked over his shoulder. "Yes, brother. I hear you."

The angel's brother, known as Kovesh, was a powerful creature. His skin was pale and tinged slightly gray. His long white hair framed a chiseled face that appeared to be as strong as his prominent frame. His nearly translucent wings had shades of charcoal grey and midnight blue. They loomed over his shoulders, and when fully extended, they were long enough to reach far past his fingertips. Each feather on his wings was flawlessly positioned, and although they looked beautiful all together, each was rough and came to a sharp point. Kovesh wore snow-white armor that was perfectly tailored to his body. A long black bow was securely attached to the back of his armor.

"I see something troubles you. Explain," Kovesh demanded.

The horseman questioned, "Do you see the earth below?"

Kovesh furrowed his brow. "Of course. The earth has been overcome by the darkness."

"Yes, but within the darkness, there is light." The horseman returned his gaze back to the earth.

With a sigh, Kovesh turned his eyes downward. "I see no light, brother. I see only the darkness the humans have created. Do you not see that?"

He raised his voice and entreated, "You must look deeper. There is still a light. A soul needs to be saved. How can you not see it?"

Kovesh peered down, shook his head slowly, and looked back at his brother. "Mortal souls are filled with the Holy Spirit of El Shaddai. It is his Spirit that illuminates the human souls, causing them to shine brightly, but his faithful children have been called." He drew in a breath before adding, "It is such a pity how they have desecrated earth's realm… again. They have forgotten the sacrifice of Christ. They do not seek to understand it, and worse yet, they do not desire his gift of eternal life. Why would they not wish to reside by the side of Christ? They unquestionably gave no thought to the commandments of El Shaddai, God Almighty himself. They have forgotten all they were taught and are now as immoral as their ancestors were before the first cleansing. No, I no longer see their light. Are you sure your eyes do not deceive you?" He turned his eyes to meet his brother's. "There is little light to be seen. Far too few believers remain."

The horseman could see the concern in Kovesh's gaze. He lowered his eyes and spoke slowly, "Forgive my agitation. I am disheartened for the forsaken. They will experience fear and pain unlike any they have ever known. If only more could have been saved."

Kovesh placed his hand on his brother's shoulder and replied, "Nothing to forgive. We all are troubled by what they will face. However, do not despair. When the Lamb returns to earth, the faithful will arise in his glory, and light will conquer darkness once again." Kovesh bowed his head as he walked away.

The horseman stayed behind to watch the earth below. When he knew he was alone once again, he descended.

"I know the soul is there. I feel its pull. I beg your forgiveness, Lord Jesus, but I am compelled to seek the soul, the one who was left behind."

The light grew brighter as he searched the mountain pass. Every moment, a new and strange feeling grew stronger. The forest was getting dark. The burnt-orange sun was setting, slowly creeping below the horizon. Droplets of dew quivered on the tips of deep-green leaves. A misty haze hovered low to the ground, hiding the tiny branches and leaves that had long fallen away from the mighty trees.

Suddenly, the light emerged from the darkness. A woman was walking through the night alone. He listened to her fierce and strong heartbeat as she came closer to him. He desired to reach out to her and ask many questions, but that was forbidden.

"No, it is not my purpose," the angel said to himself, slowly shifting his body to the right so he could place her clearly in his line of sight. "I do not understand why El Shaddai did not usher her into heaven. Does she doubt?"

The woman stopped abruptly in her tracks. She stood quietly in the center of the dirt path with her eyes wide open. She jerked her body around and then faced north again. The rapid movement caused her to lose her footing and stumble backward into a large boulder. After regaining her balance, she grasped her flashlight and notebook and squeezed them tightly against her chest. She mumbled something softly under her breath while the horseman stood in silence.

"Dr. Harden? Doc, are you there? Oh please, please be you!" she whispered frantically into the night air.

The gloomy night only responded with the sound of leaves rustling in the soft breeze. The horseman watched her silently and waited to see what she would do next. He listened to the depth of her respirations and the sound of her heartbeat. Her life force was exhilarating and made him feel close to heaven. He pondered why she was there alone, whom she was searching for, and whom she feared.

Through the silence of the night, the deafening sound of a breaking branch echoed loudly to their ears. Startled, the woman jumped backward to duck behind the rock she nearly crashed into earlier. She scrambled quickly to turn off her flashlight, but her hands trembled so violently that she could not hold the button down long enough to shut it off. She pushed it into her bosom to muffle the light, but she yelped as it dug into her sternum.

The angel leaned forward in a smooth motion, watching anxiously. He moved as silently as a leopard stalking its prey. He held tight to a knot on the side of a young but large Western red cedar. His grip was so tight that it crushed the knot and left an indentation of his fingers in the side of the tree.

The breeze carried a soft voice from up the path. The leaves in the trees were restless as the thin brown branches rhythmically swayed. Throughout the forest, an amazing cedar scent permeated the evening air. The pallid moon was high and almost full. It seemed to be closer to the earth than it had ever been. Its light glared down onto the woman as if it too was watching her. As the voice grew closer, the woman crouched lower.

Then the voice that was once barely audible was now clear as the night. "Alijah, Alijah, where are you?"

The woman raised her head just high enough to peek over the boulder. With a deep sigh, she got back on her feet and softly said, "Dr. Harden. Oh heavens, Doc, you scared the life out of me."

Hunched over, the man trotted out from between the trees. He rushed to her side with his knees bent, staying low. "Sweetheart, are you okay? Did anyone see you?" he questioned as he gently brushed her long hair back.

The horseman curiously studied their interactions and became more intrigued by the moment. He softly repeated her name. "Alijah...Alijah...Alijahhh."

She and Dr. Harden swung their heads to the side and observed the woods. "Are you sure you weren't followed, honey?"

She grabbed his right forearm and leaned into him. "I wasn't followed. I was very careful, but do you feel like we're being watched?"

He pulled her closer, whispering, "Yeah. This is getting creepy. I think we need to go now. It's dangerous out here anyhow. We cannot get caught or followed. Just stay low and stay close. Let's make this quick."

The two ran up the north pass and disappeared into the night. Even though the horseman was tempted to follow the woman, he knew he had to resist. He had disobeyed the commands of God already by going to the earth before he was called. The mighty angel ascended to the heavens but felt compelled more than ever to seek the light.

> *Then I heard [a] voice from heaven say: "Come out of her, my people, so that you will not share in her sins, so that you will not receive any of her [judgments]; for her sins are piled up to heaven, and God has remembered her crimes."*
>
> —*Revelation 18:4–5*

CHAPTER 2

It had been about six months since it all happened. Alijah was chatting with her mom in the living room. Her parents' house was a lovely split-level brick home that was warmly filled with Tuscan countryside décor. The Italian design always helped them feel like they were back in Italy. While they often traveled to Tuscany to visit relatives, the family called Washington State home.

Mother and daughter had been discussing the usual things. Every time they talked, Alijah's mom would change the conversation to how she had found the perfect guy for Alijah. The gentleman her mom had in mind this time was a divorced forty-five-year-old man named Karl who had no children. He was a kind and handsome man, but he just wasn't what Alijah wanted.

Education was far too important to Alijah. When she knew enough to be placed in a laboratory, she began working, and that was her life from then on. Education and career was all that mattered; after all, she figured she could build the rest of her life later. "Many women focus on career first," she'd say to herself. She was only forty years old. "Forty...," Alijah would snicker when she said that. "If I had only known decades ago what I know now, I would have done many things differently."

After going through the usual "Sweetheart, I'm simply trying to make sure you don't spend your life alone" and "Mom, stop trying to set me up—I can find my own dates when I'm ready" dialogue, Alijah sunk deep into the old white couch and looked out a window that had a chipped gray trim. Her mom was humming a popular rock-and-roll tune from the early 1950s, pausing to chuckle at Alijah's dad. He was telling off an uncooperative cooked chicken in the background as he prepared dinner.

In an instant, everything darkened as if a black shroud engulfed the sky. Eerie dark clouds formed low and moved swiftly through the atmosphere. When they suddenly stopped, they completely eclipsed the sun, and darkness consumed the sky. From the blackness, a blinding golden light beamed. Then a defining sound filled the thick afternoon air. To Alijah, it sounded as if the sun had collided with the moon. She swung her hands to her ears to muffle the painfully loud, odd, trumpetlike sounds that echoed through the atmosphere. An indescribably beautiful and powerful voice filled the sky and shook the earth. It spoke only one word, "Come." Then the blinding light faded into the midafternoon sky.

"Mom? What was that? Did you hear it? Mom?" Alijah stood up and walked closer to the window. "What was that? Mom, didn't you hear it?" She turned around to check on her mother, but she wasn't there. The clothes her mom had been wearing sat in a messy pile on the floor. A wave of heat engulfed Alijah. She felt her body tense up, and she unconsciously contracted her fingers. She felt the fabric of her mother's orange throw pillow rumple and separate from the stuffing inside. "Mom... Momma," she murmured.

"Dad!" Alijah shouted as she sprinted toward the kitchen. What she saw next made her stop in her tracks. She peered into the kitchen, terrified to discover that he was no longer there either. The chicken that once gave him such a problem was there on the counter, alone. The knife he was using sat precariously beside the rough white-and-blue-striped kitchen towel that was dangling off the edge of the speckled Corian counter. Numbness rushed through her body. She looked around for some sign of them but saw nothing.

Her heartbeat grew excruciatingly louder. She hoped with all of her heart that it was a joke. She hoped that somehow, her mother had run back to the kitchen and ducked behind the counter with Alijah's dad. For a moment, she imagined them both huddled around the corner, rubbing their arthritic knees while giggling too loudly to maintain the ruse.

Alijah managed to muster enough strength to pull her body forward. Her eyes were fixed on the counter and stung from the air-conditioning that was blowing on her face. She still had the little embroidered pillow placed firmly against her stomach. She dragged her feet as she made her way around the center island. As her eyes shifted to the floor, the little pillow slid out of her hands and dropped to her feet, landing on a pile of her dad's clothes. Fear paralyzed her for what seemed like hours until she was startled by the sound and smell of a burning pot. Her father had been boiling potatoes in it, but the water spilled onto the burner and caused a pungent smell.

She quickly turned the stove off, and chills crept over her while a feeling of sharp needles penetrated her skin. As she gazed into the kitchen, her eyes blurred, and tears fell uncontrollably.

She thought, *Where'd they go?* She tried hard to rationalize what had happened, but in the end, only one thought repeated in her mind. *Oh no. Oh heavens, no! What if it's true? What if—no, no, it can't be…the rapture? No, that's just an old tale. It's not true.*

Suddenly, she felt as if the wind had been knocked out of her. The feeling was so intense that her knees buckled, dropping her to the creamy marbled ceramic tiles. Her ankles twisted beneath her, causing her to smack her tailbone on the cold, hard tile. Severe pain shuddered up her spine.

She sat on the kitchen floor for a few minutes, trying to rationalize what had happened, but nothing made sense. *No! It's all just an old tale. It can't be true. I only turned my head for a minute. No, it's all a bad joke. No one at all could just disappear, especially Mom and Dad. Don't be stupid, Alijah. You're a scientist, a rational human being. Pull yourself together, and look for them. Get up!* She stood too quickly, lost her balance, and fell against the counter.

She hobbled around the house desperately searching for them. Ending up in the lonely living room, Alijah picked up her mother's necklace. A silver locket, no bigger than a quarter, hung from a delicate choker. The locket was a Mother's Day gift and safely housed a tiny picture of Alijah and her dad.

The silence was broken by screams coming from outside. From the window, Alijah could see several people running up and down the street. One of them was Mrs. Franco. She and her husband came over to play poker for pennies every Saturday night. She was a cantankerous, aging woman whose favorite pastime was to find fault with almost everyone and everything. Lately, she was most consumed with her thirty-one-year-old daughter and family. The daughter, her husband, and their two toddlers had moved in with Mrs. Franco after her son-in-law lost his job. She could never say enough bad things about him.

Alijah secured her mom's necklace around her neck in anticipation of finding her parents. She limped back to the kitchen to collect her dad's keys and then headed out the front door. When she stepped out onto the porch, a creepy silence permeated the air. It was almost as if the screams filling the streets a few moments prior were suddenly silenced. No dogs were barking, no birds were chirping, not even the wind was blowing. One of the neighbors had a big German shepherd named Louie. He loved to bark at anything that moved, but it seemed he too was gone.

In the distance, the sounds of Mrs. Franco's terror tore violently through the air. "Elizabeth! Elizabeth, you answer me now! Howard, Lilly, Taylor! Oh please, answer me!" Her hair was in a frazzled bun, and she was barefoot and wearing a pale-green T-shirt with white linen shorts. When she spotted Alijah, she abruptly stopped screaming and stared. She charged toward Alijah, who had no time to react, and threw her arms around her, slamming her against the front door. Pain once again seared through Alijah's spine when the doorknob dug into her back.

"Where are they, Alijah? Have you seen them? Have you seen my family, my grandbabies...," she trailed off amid shrieks and gasps. "I was playing with Lilly and then she was...she was...that horrible noise...she wasn't there, Alijah. She was gone!" In Mrs. Franco's hysteria, she pulled down on Alijah's arm so hard that neither woman could stand up straight anymore.

Alijah tried to pry out of her grip. "I don't know where your family is, Mrs. Franco. I can't even find mine. Let go of me."

The woman pulled tighter and whispered, "How could they just disappear? Lilly was right in front of me. I didn't even close my eyes." She repeated herself while she shook Alijah harder.

"Please, Mrs. Franco, you're hurting me!" Alijah tried to break free, but each time she moved, the hysterical woman coiled tighter like a boa constrictor contracting around a limb. Panicked, Alijah commanded, "Let go of me, now!" and wedged her knee between the woman and herself, but it caused them both to fall to the unforgiving concrete. Pain blazed once again throughout her already-sore back. She hit her head when she fell, and lightheadedness overtook her.

When she came to, Alijah thought she heard her mom. "Mom? Oh gosh, Mom! I had the worst nightmare." She rubbed her eyes, trying to regain her sight.

"What's wrong with you?" the woman demanded. "Why are you calling me that? I'm not your mother! Stupid, stupid girl, where are my grandbabies? Where is my daughter and my husband? Alijah, where are they?"

Panic set in as Alijah realized it was Mrs. Franco kneeling and hovering above her. She had Alijah by the shoulders of her shirt and was shaking her violently. The chill of the concrete seeped through Alijah's clothes. With both hands, she grabbed the woman's face. "Mrs. Franco…Ann…I don't know where they are. I don't know where my own family is. Let me go, and I will help you look for them."

The woman began screaming again and shook Alijah harder. "Shut up, you dumb girl! I don't care about you or your stupid family. I want my daughter! Where is she?"

Alijah could no longer bear it, so she pulled her left arm back and smacked Mrs. Franco across the face. Her hand stung from the blow, but it shocked her oppressor long enough to push her off. She struggled to get to her feet while Mrs. Franco stumbled backward and glared at her with hateful eyes.

"Mrs. Franco, I'm sorry, but you were hurting me. Let's work together," Alijah pleaded.

"You brat! You horrible, miserable girl, how dare you. I don't need your help!" She called Alijah a filthy name and ran off.

Alijah spent hours wandering the streets, finding no signs of her family. Exhausted, she finally dropped to the dirty curb and stared at her parents' house as twilight fell. Deep inside, she wished that the booming voice from the darkness would return for her. She watched others—mothers, fathers, brothers, and sisters—wandering the streets and crying out for their loved ones.

The day was forever seared into Alijah's mind. The pain of believing her family was gone and knowing no one could save her, overwhelmed her. She knew she was left behind.

For many weeks, people debated whether it was the rapture of the church. Some people claimed it was some tremendous government plot to strike fear in the American people. Others claimed it was mass hypnosis. Some even claimed it was a mass alien abduction.

Alijah knew the truth, and it wasn't a government conspiracy or some extraterrestrial old-fashioned roundup for rustling in the human herd. The simple and painful truth was that God was real, and he had taken his believers home. Her parents were saved because they had faith, but Alijah's heart had strayed, and she would have to suffer the consequences.

She believed she would never know peace or heaven; she'd only experience damnation for her choice. The emotional pain seemed too much to bear. She prayed for death, but if she believed anything to be true, she knew death would not save her.

Many, including Alijah, had dedicated their lives to persuading others that the Holy Bible was nothing more than the church's method of controlling its people. Many faithful servants of God had to fight every day to preserve their faith and sometimes their very lives. But for every believer of God in the world, many more existed who denied him.

Many dared to question why God would send his Son back. By the time the rapture had come, people had lost their minds. Children killed children, people bombed sacred institutions and beheaded others based on religious beliefs. Hate crimes and violence filled the country. More than a quarter of the American people were living on the streets. Children were starving, and at least half of the population didn't care.

Sexual immorality was at an all-time high. Most people didn't care whom they slept with or how many sexual partners they had. Everything was about personal gratification. Television and movies promoted the "I don't care whom my actions hurt" generation. The worse you behaved on television and stage, the bigger the paycheck you received. Every commandment that God had given humanity had long gone out the window. The earth as a whole had become a modern-day Sodom and Gomorrah. One honest look at everything that had been happening in the world would erase any question of why God chose to pass judgment.

The big question has always been, "Is there a God?" When more than a third of the world's population simultaneously disappeared in the blink of an eye, that question was answered.

> *I am the resurrection and the life. The one who believes in me will live, even though they die; and whoever lives by believing in me will never die. Do you believe this?*
>
> —*John 11:25–26*

Chapter 3

Since she was a child, Alijah wanted to be a medicinal chemist. She desired nothing more than to find the cures for diseases so she could save people. She had committed much time to learning to manipulate chemicals, twisting deadly compositions into lifesaving compounds. Her desire started when her little sister became ill. Angela was a sweet child who loved just about everyone. Like her big sister, she had long, straight black hair. The love of the family reflected in her sweet little face. She had always been small and underweight. Born at four pounds nine ounces, she struggled to gain weight during her short seven years of life. Alijah was only ten years old when Angela passed away.

Even though little Angela was sick, life in her family's household was good. Her parents learned early that her time on earth would be short. She was diagnosed with cancer at six years old. Alijah would always remember the day they learned of Angela's fate. Though she was young, she was old enough to understand something terrible was happening.

The family of four was sitting in the pediatrician's office, waiting for the diagnosis. Her parents had thought Angela was only feeling growing pains. Before the diagnosis, they always tried to make light of the situation and told her the aches and pains were just her body playing catch up to where she should be. In addition to being born very small, she wasn't growing anywhere near as fast as they knew she should be. Her parents weren't sure if there was a problem, but they became worried when the pediatrician had Angela repeat the blood test several times.

Alijah was entertaining her sister with a little redheaded doll dressed in a sunflower-covered summer jumpsuit. Their parents sat holding hands on a small bench while waiting nervously for the doctor to return. The office was sparsely decorated, but it was warm nonetheless. The counter kept all the normal supplies along with a good stock of low-sugar treats. Pictures hung on the pale-yellow walls, making the room bright and cheerful. A number of toys sat in each corner. It was a room that would make most youngsters feel at home.

Angela's pediatrician was a tall African-American male with a well-tailored beard. His lab coat was white and had cartoon puppies embroidered on the pockets. He was wearing a yellow dress shirt with a black-and-white polka-dot bow tie. He always went by the name of Dr. Reggie and had a kind and caring personality. He greeted all of his patients with a big smile. On this day though, he was different.

As he entered the room, he glanced down at the girls. His face was sullen, and his shoulders were drooping as if they were laden with the weight of the world. His eyes were red and looked as if he'd been crying. He quietly took a seat in front of the family on a short rolling stool, pushing himself close enough to touch the parents' hands.

He took a deep breath as he leaned in close. "I'm so, so sorry. Annabel, Jonathan, it's...the labs. I've had the test run several times, and I've conferred with my colleagues."

While the doctor drew in another gulp of air, the girls' father interrupted sharply. "What is it? Just say it, say it out loud, and tell us what we have to do to make her better! I don't care what it costs. I'll work three jobs, four jobs, *five* if I have to. I don't care about the cost. Just tell us!"

Dr. Reggie met his eyes. "There are only a few medications that can help her. Jonathan, Annabel, your baby…it's cancer, and it's advanced." He spoke rapidly, fighting back his tears, "I have the names of a couple outstanding oncologists who work in our local children's hospital. They will do everything they can for her. They'll do everything they can to extend her life."

He continued explaining that the lab workup confirmed that Angela didn't have just any cancer; it was osteosarcoma. After reviewing all the labs and x-rays, he and his colleagues determined that little Angela was already at a stage two. It had metastasized, spreading into her spine and rib cage. Alijah watched her mom slide out of the chair and onto her knees, choking out, "Oh God, no, not my baby. Please, Lord, take me, not my baby!" and she looked at her father with his hands covering his face. Dr. Reggie, Jonathan, and Annabel held each other in a huddle, crying. Alijah didn't know what was wrong, but she understood that it was bad.

Angela didn't understand it all at first. They sheltered her from the truth for the first few months until one day, Angela looked at her mom and asked, "Mommy, am I going to heaven soon?" Jonathan and Annabel sat both girls down and explained what was happening. Alijah could never forget that conversation. To her, it was surreal. She didn't understand why her sister had to die. She didn't understand why the doctors couldn't save her.

The doctors gave aggressive treatments, hoping they would at least slow down the cancer, but as quickly as it was spreading, they weren't hopeful. The specialist estimated her life span to be about a year. Jonathan and Annabel took leave from their jobs to spend every moment they could with Angela. They wanted to make her as comfortable and happy as they could. The pain of knowing their baby was dying was excruciating. Although they put on smiles and laughter whenever the girls were near, Alijah could hear them weeping through the wall at night.

Only a few months in, the chemotherapy, radiation, and medications only served to make her weaker. Angela was a tough little cookie and did her best to find the energy to play as hard as she could. Once in a while though, it was too much for her to bear.

One day, she threw a bottle of chocolate milk across the living room. It hit a wooden shelf and shattered, sending milk dripping down eggshell-colored walls. Terrifying screams filled the living room. Angela dropped to the floor, kicking her legs and swinging her arms. Her mom and dad reached down to grab her, but she was swinging so hard she hit her dad right on his temple and knocked him to the floor. She continued to scream until her face was crimson red and all the oxygen was expelled from her lungs.

Her parents were stunned and watched her in sadness. But what followed the outburst was a moment Alijah carried with her every day of her life. She ran to Angela's side, scooped her up into her own little arms, and held Angela's head to her chest. "I'm here, Angie. I won't let you go," she repeated in a sweet voice.

Angela snapped her arms and legs toward Alijah and latched on. The girls held tightly to one another, crying.

"Why do I have to go to heaven now? Why do I have to go alone, Ali?" Fear quickly consumed her. "Will I be in the dark? Will…will I be alone in the dark?" She screamed again.

"No, Angie, heaven is bright. It's really bright. All the angels will be there, and guess what? Grandma and Grampy are going to be there too. They'll be there when you get to heaven, and they'll take good care of you until Mommy and Daddy get there. And when I grow up, I'll come too. Oh, and Jesus! Don't forget Jesus. He'll be there too. See? You shouldn't be scared, 'cause heaven's a good place, and you won't be alone." Alijah tried her best to console and reassure her sister while fighting back her own tears.

Angela whispered, "I love you, Ali. I'm gonna miss you."

No longer able to control herself, Alijah replied, "I love you too, little poop, and I promise, when I grow up, I'll find medicine that can cure all kinds of cancer." She erupted into tears. Jonathan and Annabel dropped to their knees and engulfed the girls in a hug. The family stayed huddled tightly until both girls fell asleep.

Seven months later, little Angela died. Her passing took away a piece of everyone in the family. As for Alijah, not only did a piece of her die, but her faith died as well. At such a young age, Alijah couldn't understand why her sister's life had to end. She didn't understand why God would allow a little child to perish. She didn't understand why her Angie had to die slowly and painfully.

As she grew older, Alijah grew further from God and turned her grief into anger and doubt. By the age of eighteen, she had completely lost faith. The sole thing she did believe in was science. She believed this was her only life, and she was the solitary master of it. She believed that science would be the only way to stop others from going through what she and her family had gone through.

She had sworn to Angela that she would do everything she could to find a cure for cancer. So she spent all her school years learning everything she could about medicine. Her efforts earned her early admission into one of the top medical schools in the country. She graduated from high school ahead of time and went straight into her doctoral program.

> *If anyone says to you, "Look, here is the Messiah!"... do not believe it. For false messiahs and false prophets will appear and perform great signs and wonders to deceive.*
>
> —Matthew 24:23–24

CHAPTER 4

The American economy plummeted, and the rest of the world soon followed. Poverty was at an all-time high, affecting nearly ninety million people. Before the rapture, a man by the name of Emil was running for president of the United States. He promised that he would fix the housing crisis, fix the economic mess the American people were facing, bring calm to the quickly growing civil unrest, and most importantly, facilitate the end of the numerous worldwide wars. His campaign was massive—the largest in history—and he relied on the super wealthy for all of his financial backing.

During the elections, he chastised the wealthy for not doing their part to rebuild the economy, and he promised to place heavy tax burdens on them. To help strengthen his hold on the desperate American people, he required, with the exception of his supporters, anyone making over two million dollars a year to bear his new tax burden. Then the excess money would be redistributed in the form of gifts to anyone at or below the poverty level. With the overabundance of poverty-stricken people, Emil would not lose the election.

However, once elected, the hopeless citizens never saw the money. Emil continued to wage his own private war against anyone over a certain financial bracket, which now included all who had supported him. The excess taxes collected never surfaced. Using the people's money, President Emil purchased a 10.2-million-dollar home he called "modest and necessary." He was sure to live exceptionally well, even though most of the country was suffering and on the verge of a devastating nationwide financial collapse.

His biggest supporters were outraged by the betrayal. Then word leaked out on how funds had been misappropriated. All of the financial backers turned on him publicly, declaring that he was a fraud and a thief and demanding his impeachment. Emil quickly regained control when the most vocal detractor was found dead. The other critics were arrested, along with their families, for suspicions of treason. Many were never heard from again.

Emil had been caught in lie after lie. He flooded the world with new unbacked currency that caused further economic decay across the world. Even though people were irate, they clung to every word he spoke and every promise he made, including his promise to end poverty in the United States. People cried with excitement, exclaiming that Emil was going to fix everything, and he would save them all. The strange mass devotion took many people of faith by surprise; they were stunned by the blindness of the others. It was as if they were all asleep, not wanting to awake from the dream.

Emil had a strong build and stood at six feet five inches tall. He claimed to be a devout man of God. His hair was black, and his eyes were blue. His facial features were proportionate and well balanced. The color of his skin did not give much away as he appeared to be of multiple cultures. He was an extremely charismatic speaker and a handsome man.

The president said that he would ensure no poverty and no hunger. While everyone knew his promises were lofty, most people paid no mind. Those who chose not to subscribe to his lies knew that even if half of his intentions were altruistic, the majority of his promises coming to fruition was simply not possible. Some people, however, suspected his motives were everything except altruistic, but they felt powerless to do anything about it.

During his first year of service, Emil sold out the United States on several occasions. He chose to surrender to the enemy of a nineteen-year war. He provided sanctuary to those who were convicted of war crimes against the United States. People were outraged when they heard, but as usual, the collective "head" of the people ducked back down into the dirt, pretending nothing was happening.

As the president continued to plunge the country further into decay, people pointlessly went about their daily activities. Instead of paying attention to world events, they focused their energies into nonsensical things. They worried more about beauty, success, money, and celebrities than about what was happening around them. The government-regulated media slowly desensitized them to everything that was going on. The United States was being dismantled slowly and systematically.

After the rapture, violence escalated beyond control. Emil responded with his first big proposition, which called for the launch of facial-recognition cameras throughout the United States to help combat crime. Small groups of people protested, demanding that lawmakers reconsider the idea because of the numerous possibilities of the technology being misused.

After the facial-recognition cameras were put into place, President Emil offered the citizenry card. It came with the promise of offering a new way of helping with common-sense things such as gun control and immigration. He pledged that anyone registered in the national database would be eligible for government assistance. Then came the time for the government to introduce the new quantum computer. This super computer was the only way for the government to keep track of all the necessary information. Even though the idea of Big Brother watching people and storing all of their information on this system sent the conspiracy theorists and antigovernment groups into a tailspin, the majority of people didn't mind. In fact, the promises of free government help with food, housing, and medical supplies made registered citizens rejoice. Some desperately needed the assistance, but many citizens just wanted someone to take care of them. The general consensus was, "Why should I work for it when the government will give it to me for free?"

By the time his second term came, President Emil had set in motion plans that would forever change the course of the world. The economy had plummeted to a low far worse than that of the Great Depression. The United States had been devastated, but now, countries all over the world were collapsing.

Hunger, homelessness, and uncontrollable violence were worldwide pandemics devouring the human race. World leaders, even between allied nations, were at odds and were provoking irrational global violence. North Korea attacked South Korea; England was fighting France; Russia and Israel bombed each other; Iran and Germany fought; China and the United States were threatening each other; and Japan and Australia were on the verge of war.

Emil convinced the people of the United States that it would take years to correct the damages, but he would raise the country to greatness if the American people would lift the two-term limit. The majority foolishly agreed.

President Emil petitioned his ideas worldwide of a "unified economy" as well as a "unified community." His one-world monetary system made perfect sense to all who listened. By what should have been the end of his second term, he had convinced almost all of the world leaders to join his unified community and to share wealth and resources.

The final victory came with a global disarmament. The agreement was supposed to bring about peace to all nations—all nations but Israel. The Israeli government refused this global unity and begged for other countries to stand against Emil. They warned that allowing him to take complete control would be the beginning of the end. No one heard them; Israel stood alone, and President Emil was elected and named Sovereign Overseer Emil. His title reflected his grand accomplishment of obtaining, for once in human history, so-called world peace. Together, the world blindly elected a totalitarian.

Emil had every country destroy its flag, and only fly the flag of the new unified community under his new world order. The massive chaos the world had been plunged into was suddenly stopped, but what was left was a world sitting in limbo. Using this to his advantage, the overseer tightened his grip on nations across the earth. The citizenry card, which once was only an offering of goodwill, was turned into a requirement. The card was no longer just for gun control or a little government aid; it was for necessary services such as medical care and food.

Emil was separating people from his unified community. If you were not a part of the community, you were against it. If you were against it, you were the enemy. He flooded the media with propaganda, targeting unregistered people. He claimed they were the ones wanting to dismantle all that was good in the world, all that he had created. Those who had registered for the card enjoyed newfound freedom with the government giving them everything they desired. None of them lacked for food, housing, and medical care. Many of his followers called it Shangri-La.

Those who had never believed in God suddenly found themselves worshiping a self-proclaimed god. People cried out his name, calling Emil the messiah who was thought to have returned to them from God. Emil embraced the opportunity. The growing number of people joining the community was astounding. He reached out to all world leaders, demanding they convince the "lost ones" to unite with the unified community so that all people would coalesce under one savior—Emil.

He sought to accelerate his control by asking everyone to offer a tribute to him. He called it a simple symbol of faithfulness, a symbol of dedication to him. People were asked to pledge their loyalty by also accepting a token of that faith: a tattoo representing the new global nation. The symbol on it was a single snake crossing over the earth.

Not too long after the tattoo was introduced, Emil demanded all citizens have a microchip implanted beneath the skin just under the tattoo. Once the microchip was inserted, citizens slid their hands underneath scanners to verify proper placement and then had a current picture taken. With each pass of a hand, monitors revealed the final piece of the puzzle. The screens not only revealed the microchip but also exposed the glow of two additional snakes. Just as the first snake, each tail formed a single circle. The three snakes together formed a perfect trio of elegantly scribed numbers—666—covering the earth.

Protest poured out from most of the faithful, who took to the streets, begging people to wake up from the lie. They warned that willingness to accept the mark was the same as renouncing the one and only God and accepting the beast, Satan. The few religious programs still remaining on television were quickly shut down as authorities claimed the programs were spreading antigovernment lies. All protests were met with violent reprisal. Soldiers for the overseer marched into what were peaceful protests and rallies, beating people ferociously and taking them to prison. Most of those people—Christians, Jews, Catholics, and many of other faiths—were never seen again.

The overseer met the accusations of being the Antichrist with laughter, claiming in a global speech, "Change is always frightening, and a change of this magnitude is no different. The peace I have brought is a gift to the entire world. I offer all people everything they need and desire. All I ask in return is for you to demonstrate your faithfulness with a simple mark. The mark is of our grand republic, and the implant carries your information to provide swift identification and medical care. For you, nonbelievers, this is nothing more than a silly little mark. I find it quite amusing that it torments you who still believe in your false gods. Those who offer their allegiance to my unified community will need to accept the simple tattoo. It is only a demonstration of your devotion to the new world I've created, to what I've gifted to you. The number, which is revealed only under a specially crafted machine, is not the number of the beast as religious fanatics are claiming."

He paused to laugh before continuing, "The number does represent the number of sins of the human race. It represents the lawless disgrace I have saved you from. For I am not some invisible being who allowed this to happen, I am not the one who allowed the chaos that engulfed this world, and I am certainly not an unseen being who would abandon you in your most desperate hours. I am here, flesh and blood, for you to touch and see and hear. You see, I did not leave you, my children. It was not I who stood by idly while you deceived and destroyed one another. I came to your aid when you needed me the most and saved you from yourselves. I am your savior, and I ask—no, I demand—a symbol of your loyalty."

Churches, temples, synagogues, and other religious institutions were closed. The overseer deemed the practice of any religion a transgression against the government. He labeled all religious institutions as terrorist groups. Emil ordered every government office throughout the world to erect a statue of him holding the symbol of the unified community.

He ordered all people to worship at only government-sanctioned churches. Those who were caught in the worship of any other gods were arrested. Raids into religious assemblies were televised. Many who were unsure about the sovereign overseer became terrified and accepted his symbol of unity. Those who denied him ran into hiding, while others sat in disbelief and waited. Anyone who wished to worship God had to do so in silence and in hiding.

In one swift move, the freedom of religion was completely vanquished. Freedom of speech was crushed. Freedom itself was taken away. People were frightened of being labeled a deviant, so they accepted the citizenry card, the mark, and the implant.

Still, Emil was not satisfied. Too many people had independence from the government. For his unified community to work efficiently, he demanded that everyone be a part. He had to find a way to make people need to be a part of his program. What quicker way would there be to make people need governmental support than by removing their income?

Rumors circulated that the government was placing sanctions on all employers. The new laws being imposed would include the removal of any employee not willing to join the unified community. Regardless of tenure or effectiveness, any employee who refused was fired. The rumors came true; companies quickly began firing employees, and mass layoffs began. All over the world, people were suddenly without work and with no prospect of income. Even though there was a glorious world peace leaving many with a feeling of wonderment, desperation continued to grow. It didn't stop there. Many hospitals and medical facilities were closed down. A controlled number of medical centers were reopened, using only the overseer's programs. Soon after that, the government deemed certain foods as luxury and forced grocers to only sell selected items to unregistered people.

Social programs such as social security and welfare were stopped. The programs were rebuilt, grouping people into categories of usefulness. According to the overseer, far too many benefits were being paid out to citizens who did not put back into the community. Retirees and the disabled saw drastic reductions in their benefits, with the greatest cut being to medical care. The overseer deemed it necessary to give them only basic human rights. As long as they were registered, they would continue to have small salaries to aid with living expenses, but no medical care was offered. He considered them a burden in his new healthcare system. People who were unable to support themselves were left to die.

Continuing to tighten his grip, the overseer enforced new laws for the housing industry. Only those who were registered and had the mark were able to purchase housing or rent apartments. In another act—what he deemed a gesture of goodwill—he allowed people who were already renters or homeowners to stay where they lived. But that didn't last long either.

Countries that were once proud and strong were now completely divided. Sovereign Overseer Emil used the media to convince his followers that anyone not willing to take the mark and join the community was against them; they were the nonbelievers, and they were a threat. Emil was growing more and more powerful. The more control he had over the people, the easier it was to manipulate them. But to him, it was not enough nor was it fast enough. One day, the media announced that he had signed into law three new bills.

He began his speech with his typical smile and enthusiasm, "My fine people of our great unified community, we have watched as our world was devastated by war. We have had to endure the ravages of disease and hunger, but despite it all, we have risen like a phoenix from the pit. The inferno of tragedy and suffering has built a better and stronger world."

As his smile faded, his words turned sharp and hostile. "Yet we have a blight, an infestation of those who would see us fall to our knees. They would destroy the very foundation of our hard work. These… people… are nothing more than a cancer, eating at our very souls. They lie, trying to convince you good people that I am some sort of monster, when in fact, I am your savior. I have ushered in a new and better era." His face twisted and became distorted in his anger.

He then continued his speech with a mirage of heartfelt kindness. "So today, in an effort to protect all my good citizens, I offer these gifts to you. Number one, it is now a global law that all people must be registered members of the community. For now, I will allow you to come to the community willingly. However, there will come a time when I will issue the order for arrests. Number two, for anyone to own a home or rent any type of property, you must be registered. All of you who still refuse to obey the law will be evicted and moved into central housing units. And finally, I would never starve my people, even those who seek to destroy me. I am, however, going to deem all fresh foods as premium items reserved only for registered citizens. Only the faithful shall have luxury."

> *Everyone who wants to live a godly life in Christ Jesus will be persecuted, while evildoers and impostors will go from bad to worse, deceiving and being deceived.*
>
> —2 Timothy 3:12–13

CHAPTER 5

It took only a few short days before the overseer gave the order to evict all noncitizens from their dwellings. They were given ten days to vacate their homes. Families who had spent generations in their homes were forced to move into dormitories. Only one room was allowed per household, which meant entire families were tightly packed into efficiency apartments.

Those who made the mistake of waiting until the last minute were removed by force. Soldiers stormed into their homes and apartments at all hours of the night. Some people were woken up and dragged out of their beds. They were given ten minutes to gather whatever they could and leave. Most people ran out of their homes with just some clothes and personal items. Anything left behind was considered abandoned and was stolen by soldiers or destroyed.

Alijah had signed up for the housing but waited as long as she could before moving. It broke her heart to give up the house. It had been passed down from her grandmother, and when Alijah's parents disappeared, she moved into it so she could feel close to them. She took as many family pictures as she could. She spent days studying each hallway, each room, and each crack in the walls to remember every sight, every smell.

She believed that what had happened was the rapture, but she still struggled with her belief in Christ. With no job anymore, she could not possibly afford a moving van. She had hoarded as many dry foods and supplies as she could in her car. When she saw soldiers evicting people one block north of her, she packed whatever else she could into the car and left. Her heart raced as she drove down the road. Her body trembled, her eyes welled up with tears, and she began to hyperventilate.

She pulled over to the side of the road and screamed out, "Why? Why *me*? Was I that bad of a person? Really, really, God, if you are there, how could you see me as a bad person? Sure, I didn't believe in you, but I gave of myself. I dedicated my life to finding cures to illnesses to save people—yes, even your people. I saved *your* people. How can I be that bad in your eyes? So I didn't know, I doubted that you were real. I'm sorry. I messed up, but aren't you supposed to be a forgiving God? That's what you want everyone to believe. So why, why, God? Why could you not have forgiven me? I'm sorry, okay? All right? I'm s...s...sorry!"

She pivoted in the driver's seat to look back. She sat on her right knee and held tight to the headrest as she looked out the back window in horror. The screams she heard sent shivers down her spine. They came from inside the houses as soldiers forced their way into each home. They moved brutally and swiftly down the block.

People of all walks of life were being dragged from their homes. Alijah watched in terror as she witnessed Sarah Bennett, a member of her mother's ladies club, being pulled out of her home by her hair. Alijah gasped as she watched Sarah being pulled into the middle of the street and dumped onto the asphalt like a bag of trash. She was in a thin lace-trimmed nightgown, and her legs were bare. During the scuffle she had kicked her legs, scratching them badly and causing her left slipper to fall off. She was instructed to get into the truck to be relocated, but she refused the soldiers' demands. She sprang to her feet and ran to her husband, Alan, who was being forced out of the house as well.

As she leapt into his arms, a piercing sound echoed through the night. Sarah's head fell back as her shoulders spasmed backward, and her knees buckled under her. Her muscles tightened throughout her body. It was clear she had been shot in the back. Alan dropped to the street with her in his arms. He lifted her head, gently placing her cheek on his left shoulder, and squeezed her tight to his chest. He let out an enormous shout, "No!" with a raspy voice. His cry filled the air with a thick, sickening feeling. Then silence fell.

For a single moment, time ceased to exist, and everyone could hear Alan's whispers. "Dear God, please forgive us. We doubt no longer. Oh please, take her, take my Sarah far from here, away from this nightmare. We pledge our souls to you. Sarah, say it, baby. Ask for forgiveness." He wept as he leaned his head against hers and rocked softly.

A putrid scent of suffering saturated the night air. Terrified people looked on from large open-bed trucks and from alongside the road. Alan's eyes shifted to the sidewalk, where he noticed a little girl with long, curly black hair standing on the curb. She was a small African-American child dressed in a pink nightgown with little ducks lining the bottom. Her feet were bare, and she appeared to be only about eight years old. The child moved toward the couple quietly as people watched in confusion. No one knew who she was or where she had come from, but she was alone in the middle of a war zone.

When she reached Alan and Sarah, she knelt down on the blacktop and stretched out her arms. In a soft and sweet voice, she said to them, "You needn't fear any longer. He has kept his covenant, and you are both welcome in his house." As she laid her hands on their heads, wings of blinding light came from behind her and surrounded the couple.

As if in slow motion, a soldier stepped back, pulled his gun from his belt, and shot Alan through the right temple. The child looked up at the soldier, smiled, and then disappeared. Alan and Sarah lay dead in the middle of the street in a pool of dark-red blood. The soldier stood there, shaking, while people all around him dropped to their knees.

A soldier whose red nametag read Alex Rodriguez asked, "Did you see that?" He looked at the commanding officer. The officer in the midnight-blue uniform smacked Alex across the face and ordered him to continue the executions, but Alex ran into the darkness.

People knelt down and loudly denounced Emil while singing praises to God. The other troops sprang into action and continued the street-side executions. The screams of anguish rang painfully in Alijah's ears. She struggled for breath as she trembled, unable to turn her head from the horror. She sobbed as she watched so many people she had known for years—good people being beaten and forced into trucks. The last family to be loaded into the trucks was the Azary family. They were a young couple who had adopted a two-month-old baby girl who was found in a trash can just six months prior to the rapture. They stood at the back of the truck. Mr. Azary had a few of their possessions in his arms, and his wife held a single picture. Other families huddled together, watching everything they owned being stripped away from them.

Alijah watched each of the trucks as they turned and rumbled past her car. Each one turned in time for her to see many families go off into the night. She untwisted herself in her seat and looked down at the steering wheel. She rubbed her hands along the wheel, examining every stitch on the leather, and then suddenly looked up and exploded into a violent fit. She began to punch the ceiling of the car repeatedly. With rage in her eyes, she looked toward the sky and accused God. "This is your doing, your creation, and these monsters are your people! You dare punish us for our sins, our disbelief? Weren't you the one who gave us reason to doubt? Yeah you, you gave the reasons to doubt. Look at the world! We're in the gutter because the people you created are bad. Look at them, look at Sarah and Alan." She screamed until her voice cracked, and then she took in a deep, painful breath and cried out, "I hate you!"

When she had recovered from her emotional outburst, she drove to her designated dormitory and moved her things inside. Each trip she made between the car and the room was slow and painful. Her hands were sore and bleeding from her fit in the car. She felt as if everything was some type of surreal nightmare she couldn't wake up from. Her eyes were swollen from tears, and her head ached. And she wasn't the only one. One by one, people slowly dragged their personal belongings into their new rooms. There was no fighting or anger; there was nothing but the cries of men and women echoing in the night. Husbands and wives held on to one another and fought back tears. Some elderly people who could barely walk struggled to make their way up the stairs.

At the entrance to the dormitory, Alijah dropped a box of her belongings on the cold cement and fell to the ground. She cupped her hands over her face and sobbed. "Why, oh why?" Warmth overcame her as she felt soft hands caress her shoulders.

"Sweetheart, it will be okay," a gentle voice spoke to her. She looked up and focused. The face belonged to a middle-aged, dark-skinned male whose eyes were bloodshot red and looked tired. At his side was his wife, a beautiful mahogany-skinned woman who looked as if she too had been crying forever. With a soft Southern accent, she said, "Oh baby, I know, I do know. It looks so bleak right now, but we can still be saved. You mustn't lose hope. Are you alone?"

Looking down, Alijah mumbled, "They're gone, they're all gone. They were all I had in the world, and now, they're gone."

The man reached down, gathered Alijah's things, and helped her to her feet. "You are not alone. My name is Michel, and this is my wife, Chante. We're in room 301. If you need us, you just let us know. And don't you dare despair because you see, we are only damned if we haven't learned from our mistakes here. Jesus told us what we needed to do, and we didn't listen then, but there is still one more chance. If you choose to believe, you too can be saved."

The couple helped Alijah upstairs to her dorm room. "We'll talk more, but for now, let's get you settled, hon. Get a good-night's sleep, and you come see us tomorrow. Michel and I are going to start a fellowship, and we want you to join us. You'll join us, won't ya, hon?"

"I just sat and watched as they killed her. I couldn't do anything but watch. They shot her in the back. The soldiers killed them both," Alijah repeated herself as the couple set her boxes on the counter. Alijah was in room 323, not too far from Chante and Michel.

"Hon, promise me you'll stop by tomorrow?" Michel asked with his hand on Alijah's chin. He helped her onto the bed and wrote down their room number before locking her door behind them.

Alijah woke up in the middle of the night. It was hard to see anything because it was far too dark. There were voices coming from down the hallway—nothing frightening, no screams or cries, just low voices. She slid out of her hard bed and onto the floor. Exhaustion had overtaken her to the point where she could no longer stand up. She crawled on her hands and knees to the door and then leaned her ear against it. She slowly shifted her weight until she was seated on the cold floor.

Soft, calm voices said, "Dear precious Lord, we beg for your forgiveness. In our blindness, in our foolish pride, we doubted you, oh Lord. We kept our eyes closed and tried our best not to see. We were weak and too afraid to embrace your glory. We lacked trust in your Word, and now, we suffer by our own hands. We know that what we now reap is what we have sown. What we beg of you, almighty God, is that you forgive us—forgive our weak hearts. We kneel before you, asking for your tender mercy. We know you are our one and only Savior, and we give our souls to you and you alone. We beg for redemption and await your glorious return to this cursed world. Praise your name and your Spirit. Praise you, the divine. We pray for your strength for the days to come, for we will surely weaken and fall like little children. In your sweet, glorious name we pray, amen."

Alijah listened to their prayers and wondered if they were right that it was not too late. She laid against the door in a fetal position and rocked gently. Her eyes were heavy, and her mind was filled with questions as she slowly drifted off to sleep.

"Pumpkin, what are you doing on the floor?" her mother's voice asked from behind.

"Momma?" Alijah replied as if she was in a drunken state. "Momma? Is that you?" She turned her head. Her mom stood beside her. She was wearing her favorite housecoat and her furry pink slippers. Her hair was in a messy bun, and she had no makeup on, which was unusual for her. She loved her blush.

Alijah sprung up from the floor and threw her arms around her. "Oh my gosh, Mom, you're here! You're not gone. You're here with me! Oh, thank you, God!" she cried out.

"Pumpkin, I'm here. I'll always be with you." Her mom gently pushed Alijah's hair behind her ears.

"It must've been a terrible nightmare." Alijah laughed through the tears. "You and Daddy had gone, had been raptured to heaven, and I was left behind because I doubted. I was all alone in a strange apartment, all alone in the whole world, and you both were...oh, it doesn't matter now. I'm just so happy it was a bad dream." She hugged her mom as tight as she could.

"Oh sweetheart," her mom interrupted, "my sweet little girl. Daddy and I love you so much, but I only have a short time, so you must listen. The Antichrist will come, and the beast will follow, but the Messiah will come as well. Your future, your very salvation, depends on your choices now. It's going to be up to you. We will not be able to help you with what is to come. There will be many trials, and you must face them, but reach out to the others to learn all you can. Build your faith. Be strong in it, baby. No matter what happens, do not take the mark. Do you understand me?"

Panicked, she shouted out, "No, Mom, no! No, no, please no, it wasn't real! You're here with me. You have to be. I can't do this alone!" Alijah sobbed and squeezed her mom as tight as she could.

Her mother raised her voice. "Alijah Anna Maria Rossi, do you understand what I'm saying?"

Alijah frantically grabbed her mom as she slid away from her. "Mom, please don't go, don't leave me." She hurled her hands toward her mom's nightgown.

"Baby, please! Please, did you hear me? Do you understand what you must do? Believe, don't give in, and we will see you again. Fight, hold on to your faith. Christ will come back for you. We love you so much...," her voice trailed off as her image faded.

Alijah heard a thumping noise and felt a sharp, drumming pain fill her head. In her panic to reach out to her mom, she had fallen forward and hit her head on the floor. She cupped her forehead with her hand, trying to hold back the pain. She took in a deep, raspy breath. She wrapped her right arm around her stomach and rolled her body on the floor. Each beat of her heart was a booming sound. The night crept away from her.

> *Whoever acknowledges me before others, I will also acknowledge before my Father in heaven. But whoever disowns me before others, I will disown before my Father in heaven.*
>
> —*Matthew 10:32–33*

CHAPTER 6

It was hard for her to simply rise from bed. After another sleepless night, she lay on the rigid mattress, staring at the dusty ceiling. She made an effort to strike up a conversation with the ivory popcorn ceiling, but it had no interest in engaging in chitchat. Dawn was near, and Alijah knew that getting up would acknowledge the start of another day filled with dread and grief.

She rolled onto her side and stared at the plain little brown lamp. It was attached to a cheap white alarm clock that was bolted to the nightstand. The lamp was on a timer, and it was always followed by a hatefully loud alarm. "Why do I do this? It's half past four, and here I am, awake once again. Why do I even try? It's not like anyone cares if I live or die anymore," Alijah grumbled to herself. The annoying clock taunted her as it wailed its alarm to unceremoniously ring in the new day.

Her mind began to wander as she sat up. As she thought of what faced her, she acknowledged that most days were too much for her to bear. This day would be no different.

It had been almost two weeks since they moved the clinic deep into the woods. The small sanctuary was unlikely to be found. Being farther into the woods, the new location was beyond any soldier's patrol route.

Sovereign Overseer Emil mandated that no one, especially medical personnel, could practice medicine outside of designated healthcare facilities. Anyone caught doing so was subject to incarceration. Imprisonment was a more frightening thought than ever before. Many who went into the prison system did not come out. There were rumors of summary executions prior to any trials being given. But Dr. Harden refused to quit.

Alijah met Andrew Harden at a seminar just before the rapture. From their conversations, she learned that he was a gifted internist prior to the overseer's rise to power. Before then, most hospitals, while having their share of problems, had been operating efficiently. People without healthcare insurance were still able to receive emergency treatment, but when Emil implemented his Community Health Program or CHP, the whole system changed. CHP was a global healthcare program for anyone who had the card. The problem was that people could only have the card if they were willing to accept the mark.

Dr. Harden saw so many people in pain, suffering because of the lack of medical treatment available to them without the card. He petitioned his local CHP office in an attempt to get some leniency but was turned down. He pleaded with the governor of the CHP office to seek approval for basic care. In his last attempt, he chased outside help by seeking an old friend who was a high-up government official. The friend betrayed Dr. Harden, who was reported, arrested, beaten, and thrown to the side of the road when it was all over. During his captivity, an official from the sovereign overseer's office spoke to him. Dr. Harden was told that if he were to go any further in his protests, or if he were caught practicing medicine outside the overseer's programs, he would be killed. The official promised that Dr. Harden's wife would be tortured and put to death as well. The doctor took his wife and ran, leaving their home and lives behind. As much as he wanted to help the hospital, he could never set foot in there again.

Many people had run deep into the forest and up in the mountains to hide. These people who lived off the grid were those who refused to take the mark. Dr. Harden and his wife had sought out these communities and opened a roaming clinic. But they had too many close calls with soldiers, so he and his wife joined a budding off-the-grid community that resided in the dense, remote forest. There they were able to create a permanent clinic that quickly became a highly sought-out destination for unregistered people. They certainly didn't offer the best medical care, but it was better than nothing.

Alijah still lived in the city. Not everyone had the mark yet, but for those who didn't, it was getting impossible to buy healthy foods of any kind. It had come to the point that the only things available to unregistered citizens were canned foods and a few types of powdered drinks. Roaming military patrols randomly stopped people to check for citizenry cards. It had become frightening to go out. The tattoo was still voluntary, but rumors circulated that people were beginning to be forced to get it. Most individuals, like Alijah, traveled in the early-morning hours, when the number of on-duty soldiers was limited.

The dormitories only had three or four unisex bathroom stalls and just as few showers for each floor. They usually had long waiting lines, so Alijah made a point of hitting them early every day. After her shower, she consumed a small amount of leftover food from the night before.

"Oh, I'm so hungry," she whispered as she tossed out the can. She forced a laugh. "At least I've lost all that weight and then some." She sighed. "I never thought I'd be starving, though."

She was hungry for food and hungry for companionship. She was both saddened and terrified by what each day could bring. She could barely find any joy in life or even any life left in the world. Outside her little dorm room was only hate, greed, anger, and death.

The sun would rise soon, and Alijah had to hurry through the mountain pass before the soldiers made their rounds. She held tight to her small flashlight and ran down the darkened stairwell and out the back door of the building.

"Oh gosh," she uttered in a whisper. She stopped in her tracks and ducked behind the filthy large green garbage cans. Two tall slightly overweight guards were standing by the back of the building, smoking cigarettes. She was terrified as she waited silently for them to walk away.

Please go away, please go away, she thought. Sweat dripped into her eyes, and her breathing was labored as she peered through a small gap between the piles of garbage. A putrid smell filled her nostrils. The trash hadn't been picked up in weeks. She felt a wave of nausea overtake her while she squatted in a pile of unrecognizable trash. She took several big gulps of air in an attempt to control the feeling in her stomach. She knew if she threw up, they would know she was there.

Something scurried up her leg. She swiped her pant leg quickly and a disgusting fat brown roach slipped out. Instinctively, she panicked and fell forward onto her hands, landing in a pile of mushy goo. She slid forward, almost landing face first in it. The goo slid slowly into the beds of her nails, between her fingers, and up to her wrists.

She shuddered as she wiped her hands against the concrete-block wall. She leaned her back against the wall to rest for a moment while she continued to pick the filth from her nails. She became overwhelmed by fear as her heartbeat grew deafeningly loud.

"Did you hear about the new law the overseer just passed down?" one of the soldiers asked.

The other snickered and replied, "Which law? He's been issuing new ones virtually every day." He cleared his throat. "I mean, his laws are always good for the people. Everyone knows that, right?"

"Yeah, sure, of course," the soldier agreed, looking down at his feet. "It's just, this one means there will be no food at all to be sold to unregistered residents. There's going to be a lot of hungry people." He paused for a moment. "And it's good that he does it, right? I mean, all these people have to do is just get a lousy tattoo on the hand. They're bringing the misery on themselves, right?" He glanced over his shoulder.

"No food at all? But—" the other soldier stopped. "Do you hear that?"

Alijah, insecure of her position, looked down to be sure she wasn't moving. *Is it me? How do they hear me?* she thought as her panic increased. Then she heard it; a loud wheezing sound came from close by. She quickly turned her head from side to side to search for the noise, intending to swiftly shoo away whatever was making it, but then it dawned on her. *Oh no...it's me!* At some point her asthma had flared, and she was wheezing loud enough for them to hear. She took controlled deep breaths to calm her breathing down and quiet the raspy rattling in her lungs.

She leaned forward to peek through another hole in the garbage, but when she did, she slid in the rubbish and knocked over a box of trash. The mess rolled down her body and landed with a crashing sound.

"Please, no, no, no," she mumbled softly. She squatted as low to the ground as she could, but the rattling grew again. Her body betrayed her.

"What's that?" the guard shouted as he started toward the trash.

On her hands and knees, she leaned low in something disgusting, and a feeling of terror completely overtook her. Her hands and feet were numb, and she felt something pinching and inching its way up her spine.

Her mind was racing. *They're coming. They're coming. Oh no, they know I'm here.* Just then, something squeaked loudly in her ear. With her peripheral vision, she spotted a large gray rat that had made its way up her back and stopped on her shoulder. The rat's coarse fur rubbed against her cheek. It glanced at her and then dug its little claws into her sweater and made its way down her arm.

"Come out with your hands raised, and those hands best be empty, or we're going to open fire," one of the soldiers ordered in a sharp Northern accent.

Alijah leaned her head back and looked toward the sky. She rolled her right shoulder forward and held her breath, and with a squint of her eyes, she shook her arm as hard as she could and sent the rat flying in the air. It landed at the end of the trash pile with a loud squeak and scurried off.

Laughter erupted from the guards as they watched the rat run away. "Holy—that rat almost gave me a stroke! I hate those things. I hate working these disgusting dormitories. Filth everywhere. Since the overseer cut back services, the dormitories have gone downhill."

The other looked at him and whispered, "It's gonna get real bad once the last of the food is taken from them. A lot of people would rather die than pledge allegiance to Emil. Some really think he's the… well, you know. You've heard the rumors, right?"

"Shut it, rookie," the soldier snapped. "You talk too much, and people who talk too much disappear. It doesn't matter what we think. It doesn't matter what those people think. We have a clean place to live. We have food, and we've got a job for the small price of allegiance to Emil. So what if he wants us to tattoo a number on our hands? It's just a tattoo. It doesn't cost a thing. They could take it and lie. Anyhow, I don't ask questions, and neither should you, if you value your life. Let's move. Time to check in."

Nothing but a tattoo? It doesn't cost us anything, huh? Just your flippin' soul, you heartless jerks! she wanted to shout. Alijah watched as the soldiers walked around the building and out of sight. She felt relief but also disbelief that they hadn't found her. "I don't believe it," she whispered to herself. "Oh, this is gross, disgusting, and definitely a perfect start to another perfectly lousy day." She worked to clear the nasty garbage residue off herself with a dirty old towel she found lying on the curb. Hunching over, she jogged quietly across the pale dead grass and through the back courtyard and entered the dark long mountain pass.

For it is by grace you have been saved, through faith—and this is not from yourselves, it is the gift of God—not by works, so that no one can boast. For we are God's handiwork, created in Christ Jesus to do good works, which God prepared in advance for us to do.

—Ephesians 2:8–10

Chapter 7

He had been watching Alijah's movements for months. The horseman normally waited for her in the morning alongside the mountain path she traveled. She passed him each day on her way to the where she rendezvoused with Dr. Harden. Alijah's soul had become brighter and had grown stronger over the past months.

One day, from his dwelling in the heavens, the angel watched the earth. The horseman who would bring war, Mil'chamah, stood behind him. "Brother, you have been consumed by this human for far too long. What is it that draws you to her?"

He turned to Mil'chamah. "How do you know of her? Can you also see her?"

"No, Kovesh spoke of this and of his concern. The light of the faithful is far too dim to pierce the darkness, and it is most certainly not as bright as you perceive it to be. It is still early. The Lamb has yet to break the first seal. The new believers are growing in the Holy Spirit and in their numbers. The human souls will only be bright enough to reach the heavens after the first four seals have been broken."

The angel continued to observe Mil'chamah. His skin was pale, and his hair was as white as falling snow. Like his brothers, he carried his weapon in preparation for what was to come. His sheathed sword was plainly decorated but grand. Mil'chamah had already donned his crimson armor in anticipation of events to come. He appeared to have grown impatient with his brother's lack of explanation.

The horseman continued, "She has a strong soul—"

"How do you know this?"

"I know because I have seen her. I suppose you are aware of that as well." The angel became annoyed by his brother's lack of enthusiasm. "You must understand, I have not forgotten my place. I do not forget what is to come. I do see the light, and I know the child has a good soul. She seeks him, but she is merely lost and confused."

"You must stay the course, brother!" Mil'chamah shook his head. "You are losing your way over a single soul, a soul that does not fully acknowledge the Creator or his Son."

"But do you not think there are others? Have you grown callous toward his children? Was it not we, the angels, who failed to complete our tasks? We did not help the Father's children keep on the path of righteousness, and now, many of them will suffer the utmost of horrors. How can you deny heaven its faithful children when they have only lost their way?"

Mil'chamah's voice softened, and he said, "I do not wish to deny his children. However, it is not for you to decide which soul is worthy and which is not. You have one purpose and one purpose alone. You are the harbinger of death. You will bring forth the purest of evil. We were designed not to save the humans but to bring cleansing upon the earth. If you must continue this, do so only with the blessing of Christ Jesus, for it is only by his authority that you may make this journey." He walked away but uttered, "Have strength, my brother, and know we shall always stand with you."

A feeling of warmth and peace overcame the angel. A loving and calm voice from afar called him to the great hall. He knew it was time to answer to Almighty God and Lord Jesus for his transgression.

As he entered the great hall, he saw the seven apostles sitting beside Jesus, who wore a majestic gold crown. To the Left was God, the Creator of all. The thrones were not adorned with gold and jewels like many humans would believe. God does not care for the riches humans place such value on. If heavenly wealth could be measured, it would be measured by the faithful children of God.

Even the angels have difficulty fully viewing God, for his light is as bright as the sun. They can, however, see an outline of his face and hear his voice. To any angel, the voice of God is home. While Jesus also shines as bright as the sun, the angels are able to view him more clearly. They crave his voice and light as much as they crave that of his Father's. It is the light of Christ that keeps them strong and guides their way.

When the angel arrived at the throne, he knelt and lowered his head.

"Why are you ashamed? Raise your eyes, and say what troubles you, my son. Speak it and be free," Lord Jesus commanded in an authoritative but gentle voice.

He lifted his head slowly and looked up to meet the gaze of the Lord. "Lord Jesus." He quickly glanced over to acknowledge Elohim. "Yahweh, Father, you are the Alpha and the Omega. I kneel before you on this blessed day to plead for your mercy."

"Speak."

"Since Elohim, the eternal God, created me, I have waited to be called upon. My purpose is clear, and I shall carry out my duties with unswerving loyalty. But shamefully, I have violated your commandment and entered the human world. While they do not know of my presence, there is one whom I...one who needs to be saved. Please, Lord Jesus, her soul is strong, and I know, I know she can be saved.

I have heard her cry out to you. I believe she seeks redemption. She merely needs your grace."

Christ stood slowly and stepped toward the horseman. He circled him before stopping behind him and looking toward Elohim. "I hear the faithful cry out for redemption, but sadly, this is not the cry that I hear from her."

The angel looked confused. "Lord, you know her? Though you do not hear her, can you not see her light? How—"

"Of course, I know her. I know them all." He smiled before proceeding. "I knew them before they were born." He brushed the angel's wing and then walked in front of him. "Come forward, my horseman."

"Yes, my Lord, of course you do. Forgive my thoughtless words." In shame, he bent forward and laid his head and hands near the feet of Christ. His brothers came beside him. They knelt to the floor and bowed their heads.

"You are the fourth horseman who will bring the most bitter of consequences to the youngest of my Father's children. Yet, my son, you have devotion to this soul. You say you have heard her cries as well?"

"When I traveled to the earth, I heard her, my Lord."

"You see her light while your brothers do not. Why do you believe it draws you?"

"I know not, Lord Jesus. I am certain though, her heart yearns for your love. When I...descend to...destroy your child, even though—"

"Tell me, horsemen, what is your purpose?" Christ commanded the others to reply.

Mil'chamah raised his eyes and said, "Father, my Lord, there are none above you. We are your humble servants and are destined to usher in the punishment of the wicked and to cleanse the earth. My brother knows, this and—"

"My angel, explain to me. Why do you feel such shame?" Christ ordered the transgressor to speak.

"Forgive me, I meant no wrong. I am confused why I would see her soul while others do not. She is only beginning to understand, but like many of them, she is confused and afraid. The girl is frightened every day of her mortal existence." He abruptly lowered his head and hands at the feet of Christ again. "My Lord, I am conflicted. My purpose is to bring evil to the world. The angel who was once cast out will ride in my wake as I bring suffering and death to your children. Why would a creature such as I feel an eager need to protect any soul?"

Christ knelt down and touched the back of his head. "Look at me. My Father created you for a perfect purpose with a perfect love. While you will bring forth suffering to the wicked, you will bring a time of joy and goodness to the righteous. You are an angel, my Father's creation, and shall forever serve my will. Feel no shame because you find a light among the wicked. If you are able to guide my precious child back to me, I will forgive her and grant her a place by my side."

More angels came forward, bowing and then raising their heads to listen to the Son of God.

"My angels, faithful servants of Elohim, the all-powerful Creator. Soon, my Father will command the seals to be broken, and his judgment will rain upon the earth as my apostles foretold. I desire for my wayward children to find the Father's light. Therefore, I proclaim to you, go forward to the earth, and guide my lost children. I will open heaven's gate to all whom you reach, but remember, their journey is their own. Teach them. Help them understand that even though the human race calls him by many names, there is only one Creator, and I am his Son. Let them bear the mark of my Father, and let them be spared from his judgments. Help their light shine to the heavens, but only let those to whom you convey the good Word know you." And with that, Christ walked back to his Father's side.

> *Have mercy on me, O God, according to your unfailing love; according to your great compassion blot out my transgressions. Wash away all my iniquity and cleanse me from my sin.*
>
> —Psalms 51:1–2

Chapter 8

Distinct silence awoke Alijah from her troubled sleep. Three o'clock in the morning was far too early to even prepare to leave. If people heard her in the showers that early, they might be suspicious. No one in the dormitory knew she was helping in a medical clinic, not even Chante and Michel.

During the course of the year, Alijah had grown close to the kind couple. They, along with a few other residents, had become a surrogate family to her. Chante met with her for daily devotional studies. Alijah deeply appreciated the fellowship and friendship that ensued. The companionship helped soothe the sting of loneliness and hopelessness she often struggled with.

Alijah had spent all her teenage years as an agnostic and all her adult life as an atheist. Up until the rapture occurred, she was positive there were no gods at all. She lived her days thinking that she was the master of her own life, that death was the end, and that logic ruled. She poked fun at the idea of God and the notion of anyone knowing her before she was born. However, in a single moment, her world turned upside down.

The rapture propelled Alijah into the world of God, the direct opposite of the very core of who she had become. For months, she wrestled with her belief in God. She was angry with him and blamed him for all the sins of mankind. She felt fear, loneliness, frustration, and doubt. It took her many months to come to terms with all that had happened, but over time, she accepted her new reality and experienced deep spiritual growth. She became excited to learn more about the Lord and prayed he not only would forgive her but also would use her life in a mighty way. Day after day, she woke up excited about Christ and eagerly awaited his return.

Chante loved to teach Alijah, whose enthusiasm made Chante excited about her own faith again. The two women shared their stories, both the triumphs and the failures, and talked about the valued people in their lives. Multiple times during the week, Michel and the ladies held makeshift church services and Bible studies for everyone in the dorm. Alijah was surprised by how many people had spent their lives believing that living a good life was enough and that they didn't need to go to church or commit to any one religion.

Michel always told his little congregation, "I have heard of people being turned away from God because they question why they should believe in a god who thinks he's above other gods. It's an understatement to say they were confused, but if any of you are of that mind-set, then let me explain. There is only one God, the God of Abraham, Isaac, and Jacob. He is the one who should be revered, feared, and worshiped. No one before the rapture understood that God was never about a man-made religion. Religion should have always been about God. Instead, as humans often do, we built religions and squeezed God into it. People everywhere abused the name of God and used his name to justify their actions and to glorify and deify themselves. People have spent centuries twisting his words. By those actions, many were turned away from God."

Alijah believed, for whatever his reason was, the Lord led Chante and Michel to cross her path, and she was most grateful for every day they had together. As she continued to think about her new family, the alarm clock went off. It was time to start her day.

* * * * *

Andrew Harden, otherwise known as Doc, was a short man, standing only at five feet three inches. His hair was very short and looked as if someone had sprinkled salt and pepper onto his head. His beard had grown scruffy and unkempt. His eyebrows were thick with a slight separation in the middle and became animated when he spoke. He wore a tattered thick black sweatshirt with dark jeans. His white sneakers, which looked like they were expensive at one time, were dingy and worn down. Even though Alijah had only known him a short time, she felt safe with him.

At the end of the tent, Doc had crafted a makeshift desk out of a collapsed dusty box and a thirty-two-gallon trash can. He dragged two small metal patio chairs to the desk and invited Alijah to sit with him. As she chatted away about the day's events, he pulled out a bag of food. He pointed the opening toward Alijah, who stopped in the middle of her sentence and stared down at the table.

She looked up with her eyebrows raised. "Is that—"

"It's beef stew." He opened the bag, filled up an aluminum cup, and insisted that she eat. "Go on. That's real beef and fresh potatoes, carrots, and onions. Enjoy!"

"Where did you get it? Fresh beef! I haven't had fresh beef in forever. We only get that disgusting preserved ball of animal by-product in a can but never real beef." She gobbled down the first bite.

"Is it good?"

"Good? It's a little slice of heaven." She proceeded to all but inhale it.

"Honey, slow down. You're gonna make yourself sick from eating so fast! My dear Lord in heaven, sweetheart, when was your last meal?" He looked at her with pity in his eyes. "And don't you dare tell me another lie about getting plenty of food."

"They're only issuing those wretched cans of beef or chicken. I can't even get bottled water anymore. Emil has deemed it a luxury item and won't sell it to us. He also cut back the supplies allowed on one ration card. I usually am allowed a can or two of creamed corn or green beans, but what I actually get depends on what's left in the trucks."

Doc gasped. "Alijah, those cans are only enough for two or three small servings. That's not nearly enough food."

"You worry too much," she replied. "Anyway, I have a rockin' skinny body now!" Her attempt to make light of the situation failed.

"Skinny? You're nearly anorexic. Look at yourself! You're skin and bones, and sometimes, you can barely stand up straight because you're so weak. Your eyes are sunken in and have dark circles. Your hair is falling out. You have trouble concentrating." He touched her hand. "Your skin is dry, and look at your nails."

"Come on, Doc, I can deal with it."

"Don't be stubborn! You're going to deal with it right into an early grave. I've been talking to my wife, and we know it's not an easy life here, but we want you to come stay with us. Now, now, before you say no, we want you to just think about it and consider all the positives. Our little community has cattle for fresh meat, and we grow vegetables, so while we don't have feasts, we have enough to keep us all healthy. We have shelter and fellowship, and for the most part, we're fairly safe here. And your being here would be far less risky than us having to meet in the middle of the dark woods before dawn. You've been invaluable at the clinic. Please, Meg and I really want you to come. Think about it."

Alijah finished her cup of stew and offered her thanks. She looked down at the table and was unsure how to respond to his offer. She cared for Doc and his wife, but she understood that another mouth to feed would bring hardship on them.

"I love you both for caring, but I don't know. The last thing I want to be is a burden. The truth is, I have a couple friends back at the dorm that I just can't abandon. They've looked after me since I got there."

"What do you know of these friends? Are they trustworthy? Are they intending to get the mark or the citizenry card? Maybe, if you know for sure they're safe, I'll make arrangements so they can come too."

"Oh, they have no love for Emil, that's for sure!" She cleaned up the little table. "Chante and Michel believe wholeheartedly that he's the Antichrist. They're just as afraid and hungry as me, but I don't know, there are so many people I could help there."

"Please think about it, and remember, you're family, not a burden. For now, take this." Doc handed her a large brown paper bag. "There's fresh food in there. The veggies can sit out for a few days if you can't get them in that mini fridge of yours. Just keep that meat cold until you're ready to eat it. I'll give you more when I see you next week, and don't tell me no. You take it."

He hugged her tightly, and she squeezed him back, thinking about how badly she wanted to stay with them. But she knew if she were going to move to their community, she'd have to bring the others. She couldn't bring herself to leave them behind. "I promise I will consider it. I just want to be careful." She stared at the canvas tent wall for a moment before looking back at him with a smile. "I can't begin to thank you enough for this. Tell Meg her stew was phenomenal! I haven't had anything like that since Mom...," she couldn't finish the sentence without tearing up. "It's getting late. I should go."

He helped her get her heavy backpack on. Every time she left the settlement, Doc sent her home with a doggie bag of some sort. As he helped her onto a horse, he said, "Take care, sweetie, and remember to go straight home. I pray Christ will protect you on your journey."

Transportation to and from the settlement was only by horseback. A gentleman by the name of Robert had a full working ranch prior to Emil's rise. The first four years of Emil's presidency frightened the entire family and prompted Robert to build a small settlement high in the mountains, where he and his family became survivalists. With the help of ranch hands, he had been stocking supplies for years. When Emil crowned himself sovereign overseer, Robert took his family and friends permanently into the mountains. He founded the off-the-grid community where Doc created his clinic.

Alijah always rode in tandem with Robert because she never felt comfortable on a horse. Usually, the two would engage in stimulating conversation, but that night, they rode in silence. When they finally arrived at the pick-up and drop-off point, Alijah climbed down in a most ungraceful manner. Robert chuckled briefly, but his smile did not last long.

"Alijah, I've got a bad feelin' about tonight. Why don't I just take you the rest of the way?"

"No, Robert, I'll be fine. No one's in the forest, especially at this time of night."

He climbed down and attempted to convince her, but she insisted on going it alone.

> *For I am the Lord your God who takes hold of your right hand and says to you, Do not fear; I will help you.*
>
> —Isaiah 41:13

Chapter 9

"I really hate running late. It's dark enough in the forest when it's high noon," Alijah said out loud as she walked down the pass. Under the canopy of giant trees, she could barely make out the moon that had risen to the center of the sky. She usually enjoyed her walks through the forest, but that night, she felt on edge.

The forest came alive in the evening. Each sight, sound, and smell filled her senses. In the darkness, the sound of the nearby stream echoed throughout the forest. It reminded her of tiny raindrops falling to the earth, each drop sounding distinct from the others. The dew of the night air lay gently on the leaves and branches. The fresh scent of the great western red cedars filled her nostrils. The trees were tremendous and looked as if they could touch the moon. Alijah always viewed them with a sense of amazement. Some of them had been growing in the forest for hundreds of years. The cedar giants had always been home to an assortment of wildlife, but after the rapture, only beasts of burden and those most commonly used for food remained on earth.

The forest was lonely at night. The few animals that still resided there watched Alijah carefully as she walked by. The soft howling of the wind combined with the various animal sounds formed a magnificent and unusual symphony that almost sounded like a multitude of alien instruments being played in perfect, peaceful harmony.

The pleasant walk home from the drop-off site always took about an hour. This meeting point had to be far enough away from the dormitory that neither Alijah nor the people of the settlement would be spotted by anyone. Emil's rise to power kept most people from traveling, and very few went into the woods anymore. For the most part, the only people who explored there were the local residents and those who had something to hide. They certainly never traveled into the woods at night after the curfew was implemented. Alijah was the only one from the dormitory to travel to the settlement, which meant she had to walk alone. While she knew there was always a chance she would be caught, she felt relatively safe traveling the forest at night.

"Ouch!" she cried out as she fell to her left knee. "Great, just what I need—to break my leg in the middle of nowhere." The moon had peeked out enough for her to see that in the middle of the path was a small rock. In the darkness, she had not seen it, and it had tripped her and caused her to twist her ankle. She removed her sock and shoe to examine her leg. It didn't appear to be swelling, and she was able to still move her foot, though her sore ankle required her to sit still for a few minutes.

There was no reason not to breathe in and enjoy the beauty of the forest. Alijah leaned back onto the palms of her hands, tilting her head back just far enough to gaze at the moon, which brightly illuminated the night sky and cast shadows in the thick forest. Each and every star she could see between the trees looked close enough for her to reach out and touch. Her mind wandered as she played over and over in her head the dream she had about her mother the first night in the dormitory. It had felt real enough to her to smell her mother's perfume. She wondered if any part of the dream had been real.

"Maybe all of this is just a dream, just some awful nightmare. Then again, maybe it's not," Alijah muttered with a forced laugh. She shifted her weight forward on her hips and stretched her arms over her head. It was time to get moving. She couldn't risk falling asleep out there and dawn coming before she could return to the dorms.

She had just gotten to her feet when a wave of silence overtook the forest floor. She suddenly felt a rush of terror resonate throughout her body as she realized something was watching her. She quickly slid on her backpack and looked back up the path where she had come from.

"Well, well, what do we have here? Whatcha doin' out here all by your li'l lonesome, sweet thang?" The menacing voice, which had a bit of a raspy Tennessee accent, came from a man who leered from within the shadows. Alijah couldn't make out his face, but she could see something shiny by his side. As she quickly sized him up from the outline of his figure, she could see he was short and appeared overweight. She wasn't sure if he was a soldier, but even if he wasn't, he wasn't anyone she wanted to be within grabbing distance of.

She instinctively stepped backward when the figure stepped forward and became visible by the moonlight. He had a rather large gut and was holding some kind of bottle in his right hand and what looked like a knife in his left hand. The man was definitely not a soldier, and judging by the size of his stomach, Alijah suspected he was a community citizen.

Her suspicions were confirmed when he dropped the bottle and brought his right hand up to unbuckle his belt. The glow of his watch shined a hint of light over the unified community tattoo prominently displayed on his hand. His breathing became rapid while he stood there for a moment and watched her.

Without a thought, Alijah jumped back a step before she turned to run down the path. Thoughts of not only outrunning him but also losing him plagued her mind. He couldn't see where she lived or what she looked like in the light. If he did, he might be able to identify her to soldiers.

Terrified by the thought of what he was planning, she ran faster than she ever thought she could. Skinny, jagged branches whisked by her face as she dodged each one in her path. The more she had to duck around the foliage, the more ground the man gained. She rapidly calculated each step so she wouldn't trip over another rock or root protruding from the soil. Her mind was filled with the horrible things that could happen with no one around to help her.

She kept checking back to see where he was, but in her haste to keep track of him, she did not see a sharp branch jutting out over the path. As it caught her arm, it tore through her skin and caused terrible pain. She stumbled briefly but managed to regain her footing. She had the instinct to scream out loud for anyone to save her, but she couldn't.

"Got ya, witch!" He grabbed a handful of her hair and pulled his arm back. Alijah's head swung back violently, causing her legs to go out from under her. For a fraction of a second, she lost her breath. The man pulled her back, trying to push her to the ground, but she had no intention of giving up. She swung her arms to give herself the momentum to turn her body around. On her knees, she straightened her back and prepared for a fight.

"Run from me, will ya? Well, guess what? I win." He snickered. "I got somethin' special for ya," he added in a vulgar tone. His breathing was deep and heavy—so heavy that it almost sounded like he was congested.

"Yeah, well, guess what? If I'm going to die, it sure isn't going to be at the hands of some revolting pig like you!" With crushing force, she grabbed him between his legs and squeezed with every ounce of strength she had. She was fighting for her life.

He let out an ear-piercing scream before he released her. Alijah sprang to her feet and shoved the large man backward to knock him off his feet. The pain from her open wound seared through her arm. Her body was aching, and it had become difficult to control her breathing. Fear had triggered an asthma attack, but she knew she couldn't stop running. She was still at least fifteen minutes from civilization and did not know how she was going to make it.

The moon once again ducked behind the tree canopy. The only light Alijah had was the vague moonlight reflecting off the dank leaves. She couldn't tell if the man was still behind her, but she was too afraid to stop. Out of nowhere, something grabbed her foot, and her entire body slammed onto the forest floor. She screamed out as pain soared up her leg like electricity. She was face down on the ground and withered in pain. It took all of her strength to push herself up. She could feel blood seeping from her arm down to her hand.

She pushed up to her knees to look back and see what had grabbed her leg. The culprit was a thick root from a neighboring tree that had grown out from the soil and arched several inches off the forest floor. It was in the perfect position to catch her foot while she was running. When the root tripped her, her shoe must have popped off because it was now trapped where her foot had gotten caught.

The moon snuck out from the canopy again. She lifted her pant leg to rapidly survey the damage. Her ankle was clearly broken; the bone was protruding out of her skin. Alijah held her breath and listened to every sound in the forest. "Please be gone, please be gone," she whispered. From up the path, she heard rustling in the trees followed by the awful raspy breathing sound. "Oh Lord, help me please," she pleaded as she tried to stand up. But the pain was excruciating and made it impossible to put any weight on her right ankle. Swiftly, she contemplated where she could hide in the thick vegetation that surrounded the tree. She wiggled her shoe out from the root and crawled into the flora. She leaned against a tree, closed her eyes, and hugged her shoe with all of her might.

"Oh man, where did she go? She best not run to no soldier." He was quiet for a few seconds before mumbling, "Nah, she ain't got no business out here neither." He glimpsed down.

The smell of the damp vegetation filled Alijah's nostrils while her heart thundered in her ears. She suddenly was overcome by the feeling of being watched. Alarmed, she instinctively held her breath and opened her eyes. Above her stood a dark figure. She could see his face but not his eyes. The figure put his finger across his lips and uttered a single, "Shhh."

The citizen bent down to examine the ground. He touched patches of ground until he felt something wet. As he lifted his hand, a cloud passed, and the moon exposed the blood on his finger. "Well, lookie here!"

The man stood up and fought to stuff his belly back into his sliding pants. Alijah's heart sank with the knowledge of being discovered. She tried to rise up and scoot back, but the dark figure gently placed his hand on her shoulder. He bent low and leaned forward into the vegetation. Alijah was frozen in place. She had no idea who or what the figure was, but she didn't feel fear when she looked at him.

The vulgar man stepped into the brush and pushed his way toward the tree. He pushed back the last bit of thick brush and froze in place. He met the eyes of the dark figure. He saw the creature's face almost nose to nose and gasped.

"What the heck?" He fell backward over a tree root and scrambled to grasp his knife. The figure followed closely. Panicked, the man squirmed his way backward and tore the skin on his elbows. "What—whatever ya are, stay away from me. Ya hear me? Stay away!"

The figure ignored his commands and straddled his body. The creature tilted its head slowly to the left and, in a low, deep voice, spoke, "Wicked one, you take allegiance with the beast." It continued with a smile. "The time of judgment comes."

The man coughed heavily and, as panic set in, dropped his knife to shield his face with his hands. His voice shook as he muttered, "Judgment?"

"Foolish sinners think your deeds go unseen. He knows the evil that consumes your soul. Only eternal damnation awaits you. Now leave this place, never to return." The man let out another ear-piercing scream, struggled to his feet and fled, leaving his large serrated knife on the ground.

Alijah sat up with her back against the large tree. She watched as the figure returned to her side and spoke to her, "Do not fear, child. I shall not harm you."

She studied his face that was now visible in the moonlight. His skin was pale, almost gray. He wore armor that was a blend of dark gray and green. It wasn't any kind of armor she had ever seen before; it was thin and appeared light. There were strange symbols down the plate protecting his chest. She could not read the words and had no idea what language it was in. His hair went down the length of his back and was the color of freshly fallen snow. What drew her attention the most was that his eyes looked completely black. His nose and lips were proportional to his hardened face. He looked as if he was scarred from some great battle he had once fought. He wore a sash around his waist that was neatly tied in a knot with the ends dangling down each leg.

"Alijah, why do you not speak? Are you afraid? I promise that I will not harm you." He knelt down and sat beside her.

Unsure what to say, she stumbled over each word, "No...I mean, I don't...I don't think I am...I believe you. I don't know why, I mean, I know I should be, and...how do you know my name?"

He raised a gentle smile. "I have seen you before."

"What are you?" She quickly became embarrassed by her own question. "I mean, who are you? I'm sorry." She lowered her head before she looked back up at him.

With a short but hardy laugh, he returned her gaze. "What are you seems to be the appropriate question. Feel no shame in that."

"What is your name?"

"To your people, I have many names. I am an angel, a faithful servant of El Shaddai."

"El Sha—who?" Alijah raised her eyebrows high.

"El Shaddai, child. He is known to you as the almighty God. The one true Creator of the heavens, the earth, and all that spans the universe."

"So...so you're an...an...angel? Ohhhk."

He lifted his wings high and wide. Their span was great, and like the wings of his brothers, they were nearly translucent but had shades of charcoal gray and midnight blue elegantly intertwined. "I am," he said quietly.

After he relaxed his wings behind him, Alijah leaned forward and reached out to touch them. Slowly, she stroked them, feeling the feathers as they rose up to a natural arch that peaked just above his head. The feathers seemed to emanate their own light and felt soft but rough at the same time. Each one came to a sharp point but did not cut her. She leaned back and placed her hand on his chest plate to feel the embossed symbols.

Confused, afraid, and excited all at the same time, she whispered, "You're an angel."

> *For the grace of God has appeared that offers salvation to all people. It teaches us to say "No" to ungodliness and worldly passions, and to live self-controlled, upright and godly lives in this present age, while we wait for the blessed hope—the appearing of the glory of our great God and Savior, Jesus Christ.*
>
> —*Titus 2:11–13*

Chapter 10

"God is real? It's all real?"

He took her hand from his chest plate and gently raised it to his cheek. A warm tingling sensation overcame him. It was the first time he had ever felt a human being. "Yes, he is real."

Tears filled her eyes and cascaded down her cheeks while she laughed uncontrollably. "I don't believe it!"

He blinked his eyes slowly and looked back at her. "That is why you were left behind."

Alijah's smile drifted away. "I suppose in the back of my mind, I have always known he was real." She took a deep breath. "I certainly get it now. Is the rest of it...is it all true? Was Jesus the Son of God? Will he return for others?"

He lowered her hand. "Yes, Alijah, the Lamb of God comes."

"Who's the Lamb?"

"The Son of the Father—Christ Jesus, the Lamb of God."

"Can I still be saved? I believe now. Will he take me too? Do I have a chance?" she asked with an anxious and frenzied voice.

He released her hand and sighed. "Living a good and just life alone is not enough. It is up to you to open your heart to him. It is up to you to have faith. It is then and only then that he will shower his perfect love upon you."

She examined a blade of grass. "I've been angry and scared. I've said such terrible things, but they were just in anger." She swiftly looked up and gasped. "No, oh no, what have I done? I've blamed God for everything and said such horrible things to him! Have I damned myself? Am I lost? Have I...can't you help me? Can't you tell him...tell him that I didn't mean it, any of it! Can't you save me?"

He leaned to the side and placed his hand on her broken ankle. "He knows your heart and will forgive all, child. You need only ask. Neither the Creator nor his Son has ever wished to condemn your kind. The Creator has longed for this world's spiritual awakening. It pains him deeply to watch his children suffer, but the time of cleansing has come. But do not fear. Embrace his light, and return to him. It is all he asks."

"But can't you teach me what to do? Maybe if you help me, he'll hear me."

A simple smile rose from his lips. "Your salvation is why I have come. I will lead you to the path, but you must walk it alone."

"I'm afraid, and I don't have a clue where to begin."

"Trust in the Creator. Speak to the Lamb of God, and his light will come to you."

"With all that is happening, trust is something not easily given."

"I have faith in you."

Alijah returned her gaze to the blade of grass. She could feel the dew of the night landing gently on her skin.

"May I ask you a question?"

"Yes."

"I'm wondering, I mean no disrespect to you, but if you are an angel, why are you dressed like a warrior? And how is it that you know who I am?"

He let out a short chuckle. "Young one, so full of enthusiasm, so full of excitement for the truth, yet like many of your people, you dispelled truth for the sake of logic. Yes, I am both angel and soldier."

She couldn't rein in her snarky reply. "That sounds like a bit of a contradiction in terms."

The angel considered her question before replying, "El Shaddai has a mighty army that is poised to fight the evil that now consumes your world. I am a soldier for the Creator and his Son, Christ Jesus."

"I thought that was only true in the movies." She snickered nervously.

"Movies? I know not what you refer to, the Messiah spoke to his apostles about the things I am telling you. Those disciples created the Scriptures, which were to be passed down to all of their descendants."

Alijah could not stop herself from staring at the angel. She remembered that not less than ten minutes prior, her life was close to ending. She no longer felt the immense fear that fueled her body while she ran and fought to escape the citizen. She had so much to ask the angel but did not know where to begin. The very sight of him, the thought of what he was and all that he represented amazed her. Jumbled thoughts filled her mind and made it difficult for her to form a complete and logical sentence. Her heartbeat was mellow and smooth. She felt an incredible peace soar through her with each breath she took.

The angel tilted his head back down toward her ankle. "I saw your light shining to the heavens. I came to see why you were still here on earth." He continued to study her ankle while he said, "I have seen you in this place before. I have heard others speak your name."

"You've been watching me?"

He quickly met her gaze. "I mean you no harm. I only wish to help. I wonder though, why do you walk these woods alone?"

"Tell me what your name is first. You've watched me. You know about me. I want to know something about you. What is your name? Please tell me."

"You may call me Mavet."

"Mavet?"

He replied, "Of a language from El Shaddai."

"Mavet?" she whispered to herself. "Where have I heard that before? Is that like a Hebrew word?"

"It is."

"Is that the language of God?"

"He speaks all languages."

"What is Mavet? What does your name mean?"

The angel hesitated. "A simple translation is death."

Alijah stared at him, unsure of what to say or do. The very thought of the name made her shiver. "Death? Are you like the grim reaper?"

"Grim reaper? I am one of four who are destined to usher in the judgments of El Shaddai."

Alijah tried to explain her question without sounding so foolish. "Well, my people, the humans, we, I guess we came up with this idea of a creature who comes to escort the living into the afterlife." She looked down, feeling silly.

"I know nothing of such a creature. However, angels do greet souls as the Lord calls them home. As for me, I am a harbinger of sorts, the fourth horseman as foretold in the Holy Scriptures. My brothers and I shall bring the first judgments."

"The fourth horseman? I thought all of that was just a metaphorical way to describe the judgments. But you're no metaphor!" She shook in excitement. "Oh, this is just too incredible. So wait, if you are one of the horsemen, has it started yet? When will—"

"The Lamb has not broken the first seal, but the time of judgment is at hand."

"But—"

"I know you have many questions, young one, but we must wait to speak more of this at another time." Mavet sighed. "Tell me, why do you travel these woods alone?" The angel had watched her many times in the past, but he had never been this close. Her soul was beautiful, and her scent was unlike anything he had ever known. He listened to her heart beating swiftly within her body.

Alijah looked up toward the heavens. "I help in a clinic. Emil doesn't allow medical treatments outside the unified community anymore. He doesn't want anyone who won't become a member of his society to have medical treatment, so we have to help people in secret."

"Emil? You refer to the one who comes before?"

Alijah looked at him with confusion "Yeah, him. When you look at him, he looks kind and smart, so charismatic. When he speaks, he convinces just about everyone that his right is the only right."

Mavet smiled subtly. "Servants of the deceiver are always quite convincing. That is how they turn the Creator's people from him. The exiled angel will work through the false prophets and the anti-Messiah so that he may rule the Creator's children."

"I have so many questions, I just don't know where to begin."

"Time for your people is short, but we will speak again. Daylight approaches. You should return to your dwelling."

"I'm not quite sure how," Alijah said, looking down at her ankle. "I took a pretty bad fall, and my ankle is definitely broken."

"Your bone is not."

Alijah looked down toward her ankle. Mavet's large and strong hand was still lying on top of it. "It's broken. I saw the bone sticking out of my skin."

He lifted his hand gently and smiled in her direction. "It is not broken, child."

"What?" Alijah bent her knee and pulled her leg toward her with both hands. Her skin looked as if the bone had never torn through it. Not so much as a bruise or a scratch was anywhere on her ankle or lower leg. The only trace of a problem was blood on her white sock. "Wait, how did you…"

Mavet offered another friendly smile. "We are not without our, how would your kind say, talents. The Creator has blessed some of his angels with certain abilities, even one such as I. Tell me, do you feel pain?"

"No. I don't believe it! How"—Alijah cupped her hands over her face and breathed deeply—"I feel good. It feels good. I can't believe this is all happening. I know I'm a sinner, but meeting you, I feel so blessed."

Mavet watched her curiously, not understanding why she hid her face. For a moment, he studied each of her fingers. They were thin, delicate, and gentle. He slowly reached out his hands to touch her, but he quickly retracted them when she suddenly dropped her hands to her lap.

"Thank you," Alijah said with tears in her eyes once again. "Thank you for this night."

Mavet bowed his head slowly and then rose to his feet and reached down to her. He wondered if she truly understood what his place was and if she was ready to face all that was coming. Being in her presence, he questioned if he was wise enough to guide her to Christ.

"Come, I will walk with you."

She held tight to his arm. "I would love that, Mavet." They walked the remaining miles in no hurry. Her smooth hand wrapped tightly around his forearm.

Mavet was tall, nearly eight feet. His frame was quite large and imposing with broad, strong shoulders. Alijah stood at only five foot six and suffered from the effects of malnutrition. To Mavet's eyes, she appeared tiny and frail.

The angel walked her to the edge of the forest. They waited silently for the soldiers to disappear into the distance.

He peered down at her. "This is your dwelling, is it not?"

"Unfortunately, yes. You won't come any farther, will you?" Alijah asked as she looked up at him.

He glanced back at the forest before meeting her eyes. "I am only to be seen by you, Alijah." He placed his hand on hers.

She quickly grabbed his hand. "Will I see you again? Can you come back?" She had a hint of fear in her voice.

"Seek me here in the forest. Stay in the cover of nightfall so none bear witness to your search. Be safe, child, and may the Father shine his glory upon you." Mavet pointed to the path. "The sun rises. You must go."

"I'll be back tonight," she whispered, and then she released his arm. She slid her bag on her shoulder and snuck down the path to the dormitory's back door. Before she turned the knob, she looked back over her shoulder and raised her hand to say good-bye.

Mavet returned her glance and bowed his head. He turned his back, and in an instant, he was gone. Alijah scurried into the building and into her room, latching the door behind her.

> *"For I know the plans I have for you,"* declares the Lord, *"plans to prosper you and not to harm you, plans to give you hope and a future. Then you will call on me and come and pray to me, and I will listen to you...and will bring you back from captivity."*
>
> —*Jeremiah 29:11–14*

CHAPTER 11

Alijah's mind was busy all night. Every time she did fall asleep, she had a recurring dream that replayed in her head as if she were watching a movie. She dreamt of her parents and the day they disappeared. She kept telling herself it was just a dream, but every time, it seemed to become more and more real. It felt like her dreams were taunting her, forcing her to relive that day.

She could smell the sweet fragrance of her mother's perfume. Alijah wasn't sure why, but her eyes focused on Annabel's hands. In her dreams, she could not move her head no matter how desperately she wanted to study her mom's face. Her gaze stayed steadily on the hands, whose fingernails grew just slightly past the tips of the dainty fingers. The nails never grew long because Annabel constantly bit them, but they were evenly filed and displayed the same pastel pink polish she had used for years. Her hands were nicely manicured but were beginning to show their age.

"Mom, please let me help you fold that laundry."

"No, honey, I've got it. You're visiting today, and you don't need to help with anything." Her soothing voice was like music to Alijah's ears. The rapture had been so long ago, and Alijah was missing the comfort of her sweet voice.

She heard her father emit an unmistakable smoker's cough from behind. He had smoked cigars for years, and they had taken their toll on his lungs. Annabel only allowed him to smoke outside the house, so it never smelled bad. Jonathan was a stout man with broad shoulders and a significantly receding hairline. He had refused to buy a hairpiece and said that if God wanted him to have a thicker head of hair, he would have issued him a scalp that held on to it better.

"Daddy, when are you going to quit smoking?" Alijah was always trying to get him to quit. As often as she could, she rambled off statistics and handed him countless brochures that illustrated diseased lungs and cancer treatments to scare him. Nothing ever worked. He reminded her that everyone dies at some point in time and always told her, laughing, "When it's my time, I'm going out with a big old Cuban cigar between my lips." He said it was his one true vice.

Alijah stood up and attempted to grab a towel from the table when her father spoke softly in her ear from behind, "AJ?" He liked to call her that. "AJ, turn and look at me."

Released from the trance, Alijah turned and focused on his face. She was relieved to finally be able to see someone's face. Jonathan's neat gray hair was trimmed short to draw attention away from the thinning spots. He had thick eyebrows that pointed slightly upward past the midpoint of his eyes. His nose was slightly crooked due to a break he had received during a fight back in his high school years. His lips were thin and smooth and revealed white teeth that had a slight separation in the front middle.

"What is it, Daddy?"

He placed his hands on her cheeks and leaned forward. "My sweet baby girl, it breaks my heart to know what you must face. As much as Momma and I want to help you, we just can't. Judgment is coming, and all will have to answer for their choices. It will seem like there's nothing left to believe in, but I promise you, it only seems that way. Whatever you do, do not—do you understand—do not believe the false prophet or the Antichrist. They will deceive you. Remember, you cannot in any way take the mark, even if it is to save your life. You can't even pretend to take one. Do not deny the Lord Jesus under any circumstances. There is one who will help you. Follow him, learn from him." Tears filled his eyes. "My sweet little girl, I'm so sorry I can't be there to take care of you. But know that I love you, AJ. Momma and I love you more than any words could ever say."

Alijah reached for his hands but couldn't grasp them. "No, Daddy, not you too. Oh please, don't go! Dad, Daddy, I can't do this alone!" she cried out, swinging her arms forward. She tried to take hold of him, but it was like trying to grasp smoke.

As he faded away, he spoke his final words, "Ask the Lord for forgiveness and you will never be alone again."

Daylight stung her eyes. The cold loneliness of the morning poured through the small window above the table in her dorm room. Alijah lay in bed and pondered the dream. "Why does it have to be so real? Why do I have to relive the rapture? Am I not being punished enough?" She could still smell her mother's perfume and was deeply troubled by the inability to see her face this time. She was afraid of forgetting all the people she loved.

She dragged herself from the bed, just as she did every morning and then stretched to try to loosen her stiff body. She used to joke around with her mom, saying that all she really needed was someone to oil her joints. Mornings were particularly bad for her, but she did the only thing she could—suck it up.

With her stomach growling, she made her way to the tiny refrigerator. Excitement rose when she remembered she had the food Doc and his wife had given her. Beef stew wasn't the ideal breakfast food, but she couldn't resist old-fashioned protein and vegetables. Her first instinct was to heat up everything and gorge until she was ready to explode, but she knew tomorrow, she would be looking for more.

"I'd better spread this out. I'll just have a little this morning and save the rest." While she heated up a small serving, she glanced out the window.

The only window in her dorm room was about two feet by two feet. It didn't let in much light, but having even a little sun stream through it felt good. The best part of all was the view of the path that led to the woods. She loved looking back there because that path led her to the freedom she was no longer accustomed to having in everyday life. The only friends she had left were the ones from her dorm and the people in the settlement.

Alijah gazed out the window and watched the trees sway in the gentle breeze. While enjoying her view, she noticed a large shadow fly over the dorm. It triggered her memory, and she wondered, *Last night...was last night real? Did that really happen?*

She ate her breakfast and thought about the angel, trying her best to rationalize what she thought had happened. She found herself in the same old thought pattern she used to have, and she reasoned that none of it could have been real. "Wait a minute," she said out loud, and she quickly looked down to examine her foot. She had fallen asleep in the same socks from the night before, and sure enough, one was covered in dry blood and was stuck to her skin.

When she took off the sock, she found black-and-blue marks down her foot, around her ankle, and up to her calf. She examined her leg closely but did not see any signs of broken skin or swelling. "I don't understand. What happened?" she rambled to herself as she surveyed the remainder of her body for damages. She had a long gash that ran from the front of her bicep to the back of her arm. Her pajama shirt and bedsheets both showed signs of continuous bleeding throughout the night.

For a few minutes, Alijah contemplated why her ankle was healed but not her arm. She replayed the events of the evening again until it triggered the memory. "The angel touched my ankle but not my arm. Oh, Lord, thank you for sending me your angel!"

* * * * *

"Brother, what weighs on your mind?" A deep, bold voice interrupted from behind.

There was no need for Mavet to turn his head; he knew the sound of his brother's voice. "A blessed day to you, Ra'av. Come, my brother, and sit with me, please."

Ra'av looked like his brothers with pale grayish skin, white hair, and mighty but nearly translucent wings that had hues of charcoal gray and midnight blue gracefully woven together. His armor was black and had an image of a scale engraved on it. He walked forward slowly, examining the small table Mavet was sitting beside. Mavet was resting his hands close to one another, and his fingers were overlapping. Ra'av observed his posture. He sat across from Mavet and asked, "Why are you uneasy this day?"

Mavet lowered his head and placed his hands flat on the table. "Do you ever wonder what it would have been like to be born mortal?"

His brother leaned forward to place his elbows on the table. "Why do you question your existence? Is this because of the mortal woman you watch?"

"She is a gentle and good soul. Her light grows stronger each day."

"Do you feel envious of her?"

Mavet searched for the right words to say. He thought back to the first night they met. He remembered the beating of her heart and how it echoed through the forest like a pounding drum. He remembered the fear in her eyes while she hid in the brush from the man who was trying to harm her. Mavet could still feel her warm hand on his cheek. Raising his head, he replied, "No, brother, it is curiosity I feel rather than envy."

Ra'av leaned back with his hands on his lap. "I am only as I was created, nothing more and nothing less. I have no desire to be more than what I am. We have a glorious purpose and love, dear brother. We have eternal love both for our Creator and from our Creator. We have love and receive love from our brothers and sisters. It is all any creature could ever hope for. To desire more would mean we have fallen prey to the weakness that torments the humans. I fear this girl is clouding your judgment."

Mavet looked down again and shook his head from side to side. "No, you misunderstand. She has only provoked a thought."

The angel leaned in closer. "No, it is you who misunderstands. The Lord granted your wish to guide the human. He forgave your trespass into the human realm, but you must take care not to transgress again. Lord Jesus and our Creator have given you a glorious opportunity to guide a soul to salvation, but you must take care not to lose yourself in this journey."

Mavet responded, "My feelings for this human are clouded. I know we are not capable of feeling love in the same capacity as they are. However, I have felt her touch. I have heard the rush of her heartbeat, and her light consumes me, Ra'av. I am confused because for the first time in my existence, I feel...fear."

The angel in black armor reached out and touched his brother's shoulder. "You have felt the soul of a human. They are powerful and bold yet fragile and weak. The exhilaration of a human's touch has always been a lure for our kind. They are loved by the almighty Creator in a way that differs from his love for us. That love has intrigued our kind since our creation."

"Ra'av, what of—"

"Search deeply. What do you feel? Jealousy, longing for a mate, or is it the fear of a father yearning for the safety and salvation of his child? You must be certain, for if you are mistaken in your desires, you may mislead her and inadvertently sacrifice her soul. She will be the one who suffers an eternity for your mistake, so move cautiously."

Mavet answered, "I fear for her safety in the cursed world. I fear for her soul."

> *If we claim to be without sin, we deceive ourselves and the truth is not in us. If we confess our sins, he is faithful and just and will forgive us our sins and purify us from all unrighteousness. If we claim we have not sinned, we make him out to be a liar and his word is not in us.*
>
> —1 John 1:8–10

Chapter 12

It was about six thirty in the morning when Alijah was awoken by screams. She sprang up from the bed, slid off the edge, and fell to the floor on her knees. "Darn it all!" she protested loudly. "I'm not going to have any blasted knee caps left by the time this is all done!" She struggled to disregard the pain and scrambled to get to the door. She peered through the solitary peephole that was placed oddly below eye level in the middle of the door. The dorms were relatively safe to live in, but with the ever-decreasing amount of food available, people were desperate. Lately, crime between residents in the dorms had increased significantly. People were getting hungrier and hungrier as time went on. With no jobs, people without the mark had no choice but to rely on the food program Emil created.

He wanted everyone to pledge allegiance to him, but to force people to do so, he had to skillfully squeeze them into a hard place while still appearing benevolent to the rest of the world. The perfect solution was to keep the so-called nonbelievers from being able to care for themselves, forcing them to turn to the "kindness" of the government.

The sovereign overseer created an assistance program for food in which people who weren't a registered part of the unified community were given ration cards that were filled once a week. The food items allowed were two types of canned meats and various canned vegetables. No drinks of any kind and certainly no fresh foods were offered. The only drink that unregistered residents were allowed was tap water. A couple times a week, people were attacked when bringing home their rations. The thieves targeted larger families for their extra food.

Alijah looked through the peephole to see two men run down the hall. She figured it was another food robbery and wanted to stay quiet. Since she was alone, she could be an easy target.

A faint tap on the door startled her. "Alijah," a whisper crept through the doorjamb. "Alijah, it's Chante. Are ya in there, hon?"

Alijah opened the door to pull her in and then quickly shut and barricaded the door. "Are you okay, Chante? Did they hurt you?"

"They didn't see me. But I was scared, girl! I'm okay, but I think they've all lost their darn fool minds."

"That's for sure. It happened faster than I expected it to. I mean, I know people are hungry, but we're all on the same team here."

"Yeah, but if the food situation doesn't change, they're gonna start eating each other!"

"Emil has it planned out good, I tell ya. Hey, where's Michel? Is he okay?"

The friends had taken a seat at Alijah's table. In the middle of the conversation, Chante noticed the gash on Alijah's arm. "He's fine. He's at his brother's dorm in Oak Harbor. They're going to be closing that dorm down soon and forcing everyone to transfer to Everett. I guess trying to squeeze us a little more. Now what happened to ya, girl?" Chante pulled Alijah's sleeve up and saw the long gash in her arm. "We've got to get this cleaned up. You can't afford an infection."

Dragging Alijah along with her to the counter, Chante pulled out a handkerchief from her pocket and started heating up some water. "Let's boil some water and get that cleaned up. Do ya have any bandages?"

Alijah bent down, pulled back a small piece of the Formica cabinet, and took out a bag that had a few emergency supplies in it.

"Baby, what happened to ya? Y'all just bruised up and beaten." Chante's eyes widened. "Oh no! Did ya get attacked? Did someone hurt ya? Alijah, tell me what happened."

"I was taking a walk last night. Some guy came after me but didn't get me. I took a beating from the trees, though." Alijah tried to force out a little laugh.

"Last night? Why were ya out at night? Girl, ya know if they catch ya, they'll hurt ya. Was he a soldier?"

"No. I...I don't know who he was, but he wasn't a soldier. He looked pretty well fed, and he was drinking what looked like a beer. I know I shouldn't have been out, but I needed to do something."

Chante pulled the small pot off the single burner. While they waited for the water to cool a little, she scolded Alijah. "That was foolish, pure foolishness. You're a lovely girl, and don't think for one second that those nasty, creepy, soul-sellin' perverts wouldn't hurt ya and then take ya off to prison. We would never see you again. Promise me you won't do it again. Promise me."

The fighting in the hall sounded like it had ended. They heard three doors slam shut and figured everyone had taken their battered, hungry selves home. Alijah turned to Chante and touched her shoulder.

"I love you two for caring about me. You both have looked out for me since we moved into this place. I can't tell you why I go out at night. There's too much at stake. It's really important though that you don't tell anyone. Please, can I trust you?"

Chante looked into Alijah's eyes and made a promise. "Of course ya can trust me, Michel and I both. We would never do anything that would hurt ya. You're our people now, our family, hon"—she leaned in close—"but you're messin' with fire, baby. You've got to know that."

"Chante, what if there was something you could do to help others like us? What if you could make a difference? Wouldn't you want to try? I've been given a chance, and I think Christ wants me to take action. I think, I really think, I need to keep going."

"What are ya doin'? What's this chance?"

* * * * *

The ride to the clinic was especially beautiful, and the forest was particularly serene that day. Alijah rode in tandem with Robert as usual. She had developed basic riding skills, but if the horse ever got out of her control, she wouldn't know what to do.

She glanced at the back of Robert's head. He was a kind man who tried to make life as comfortable as he could for everyone at the compound. Because he and his family were the founders, the growing population looked to him for answers. He never thought of himself as a born leader, but he was the glue that bound the camp together. He had been catapulted into a role he had never anticipated.

"Alijah, Doc and the Mrs. did some talkin' to me about ya." His cowboy accent was strong.

She tried to keep things lighthearted by forcing out a laugh. "Oh no, bad things?"

"Bad things? Are ya jokin'? Baby girl, we all love you." He returned a chuckle. "When ya comin' to live at the compound?"

"God bless you all for caring about me so much, but like I told Doc, I just don't know when I can come."

"You're welcome there, ya know? Don't ya know that? Me, my kin, and the Hardens, we all want you to come. I reckon it would be good for us to have someone like you at the compound. You'd be a real asset."

"Robert, I would love to. I want so much to be out of that craziness, but—"

He stopped the horse and shifted his weight to his right. He turned around enough to catch a glimpse of Alijah. "You're starvin' to death out there. Everyone sees how sick you've gotten. You're nearly nothin' but skin and bones. Baby girl, if you're going for the starved look, you've done overshot it by a mile! We know what's been happenin' out there. Food's going away for those who aren't citizens, and word is, Emil is going to be cuttin' back even more. He wants the last of the Christian believers to take that mark. This should be your home." He slowly turned around and gave his horse a tap to get her moving again.

"There's a couple that has stuck by me since the first night at the dorms. They've kept me safe and have loved me as if I were their own flesh and blood. There are a couple of others too. They've taught me about the Lord. I understand so much more now because of them. I can't just walk away. They're family, Robert."

"If ya say they're good people—preacher types—why didn't they get raptured? Tell me more about them. What's their story, anyway? Why were they left behind?"

"Well, I guess they wouldn't mind me sharing a little. After all, they did share their story with our dorm congregation. Michel and Chante always encourage honesty about our past sins and future hopes."

"I reckon it's good medicine for the soul."

Alijah started by explaining how the three of them met and how Michel and Chante had been a source of inspiration to her. She explained how both of them came from agnostic families. Their parents had thought some type of creator might exist but had never been willing to embrace a monotheistic religion or any religion that people had fought over for centuries.

Michel met Chante in a class during their second year of college. He was the first to seek out Christ. One day, he felt moved to attend a church service, where he spent an hour speaking to a deacon. After that day, he became a devout member of the church. He changed his major in college to religious studies and began teaching adult Sunday-school classes. After many months of tough debates, Chante followed Michel into a life of faith.

They married the following year and remained faithful to each other and the church. During the first twelve years of their marriage, their service to the church became a duty. They both taught what the Bible said but forgot to learn it for themselves. They never truly accepted the Lord or grew in their faith. For years, they only went through the motions.

Shortly after their twelfth wedding anniversary, Chante found out she was pregnant, but the pregnancy was unwelcomed. Chante sat down with Michel to explain what was going on.

"Michel, please listen to me carefully. I love ya so much. You are my past, my present, and my future."

"What is it, baby? You know you can talk to me about anything."

"I failed you. I failed us, but please know that I love you more than anything."

Michel listened intently. He had been quiet while she talked, but he finally realized what she was trying to tell him. "Did you...did you have an affair?"

Chante hung her head low and whimpered, "I'm so sorry. I'm so, so sorry." She reached for him, but Michel pulled away. "Michel, there's something else." She watched Michel freeze in place.

"You did more than just have an affair? How many other ways have you betrayed me?"

Chante blurted out, "I'm pregnant, and I'm not sure—"

"So we've been trying to conceive for the last nine years, and you're telling me now that you're pregnant, and you don't know who the father is?"

They both stood up. Every time Chante tried pulling Michel near, she met resistance. He rejected every plea for forgiveness by pushing her away.

"Forgive you? You cheated on me! I have been faithful to you since day one. Never once, not even in our most feverish arguments, have I ever cheated on you."

Chante's weeping turned into inaudible sobbing. She continued to grab Michel's arms, pushing him to his limit. "Please, please forgive me."

"Forgive you? How do you forgive a whore? A lying whore who just broke up our marriage!" In anger, he reached back and then smacked Chante across her face. The instant he did, he felt pure disgust in himself and cowered backward. "I'm sorry I hit you," he said, running out of the house.

Michel disappeared. For over a week, he neither called home nor answered Chante's calls. He didn't show up for the Sunday-school class he had been teaching. He was nowhere to be found. Chante was filled with worry and regret. She truly loved her husband, but they had grown apart. At that moment in time, she had no idea how to mend their broken lives.

Two weeks later, Michel reappeared. The two sat at their dining room table and finally opened the lines of communication. He admitted that during those two weeks, he had gone to various bars out of town and faltered. It was his turn to beg for forgiveness.

"I have so much to be ashamed of. You fell because I became distant. I focused on all of the wrong things and abandoned you emotionally. I hate myself for calling you that terrible name. I degraded you and struck the woman I love. If I could go back in time, I would never have hit you, and I would have never called you names. But I can't change how reckless and foolish it was to run into the arms of other women. Getting even with you for cheating by cheating was ignorant. Can you ever forgive me?" He reached for her hand.

She grabbed his hand and brought it to her cheek. Her tears slowly dropped onto his fingers. "I will only forgive you if you forgive me. We've come apart at the seams. Will you help me put us back together?"

He popped out of his chair and embraced her. Michel assured her that he did not care if the child was his or not. As far as he was concerned, he was becoming a father. However, just two weeks later, she had a miscarriage. The couple was devastated and came to terms with not having a baby by traditional means. Later, the couple adopted a teenage girl whose mother had surrendered her at just three years old.

Their young daughter quickly fell in love with the couple. She became a member of the church and believed with all her heart that Jesus was her Savior. She always told her friends that the Lord had sent her Chante and Michel.

When the rapture came, their young daughter was taken, but they were left behind. It was then they had to deal with their lack of faith. Like many people left behind, the couple cycled through feelings of anger, resentment, and fear of the unknown during the first months that followed the rapture. They only had two short years with their new daughter, and while they were happy she was spared God's wrath, they felt bitterness for only having such a short time with her.

By the time they were forced out of their home, they acknowledged their faults and became truly faithful.

The night they met Alijah, they felt drawn to her. Even though she was nearly their age, Chante felt almost like her mother and wanted nothing more than to nurture and support her. Michel was drawn to her to feed her spiritual growth. They had found their purpose and intended to follow through. As the three grew in their relationship, they became a family who cared for and protected one another. Alijah came out from the loving wings of her teachers and grew in her faith as her relationship with Mavet grew. But she was careful never to displace the couple from their ministry.

As Alijah concluded telling Robert their story, she explained how important the couple was to her and how great the Lord's purpose was for them. Robert slid off the horse and put his arms out to help Alijah down. "If they're like kin and you know you can trust them, then you get them to come with ya. Same thing with the others, bring them too." Robert gave her big hug. "Please, girl, move before it's too late."

Alijah stood up on her tiptoes and gave him a soft kiss on his cheek. "You trust me that much? To let strangers into the compound just because I said they were okay?"

"I trust ya, Alijah, and I know you wouldn't do anything to jeopardize us. They could do some teachin' to all of us about God. I reckon it would be good. But remember, if they seem to be the least bit resistant, you run away, and get your narrow behind here fast." Robert patted her on the shoulder and kissed her on the forehead. "Now, go on. Doc is waitin' for ya."

> *For since the creation of the world God's invisible qualities—his eternal power and divine nature—have been clearly seen, being understood from what has been made, so that people are without excuse. For although they knew God, they neither glorified him as God nor gave thanks to him.... Although they claimed to be wise, they became fools and exchanged the glory of the immortal God for images made to look like a mortal human being.*
>
> —*Romans 1:20–23*

CHAPTER 13

"Mavet?"

"Yes, Alijah."

"There's something I just don't understand. Well, there are many things I don't understand. Why would God allow such terrible things to happen? I mean, can't he see that he has given us so many reasons to doubt? People from all over the world believe they're right in their own beliefs. Some react with such violence against others of different faiths. Many of the conflicts, if you will, are done in the name of God. What about the dinosaurs? How do we believe the Scriptures when they don't explain so many of these things? The earth is much older than what is implied in these writings. Doesn't he see why there is so much reason to doubt?"

Mavet sat down beside her. "Those are difficult questions, and they are not for a creature such as I to answer. I am an angel. The

Creator himself would be best suited for the explanation—that is, if he felt inclined to do so. I, however, will do my best to address your query. God Almighty is the creator of all that is and was. The heavens encompass more than any human can see or comprehend. He created many children, all separated by time and space. Before I continue, let me speak of the Holy Scriptures you refer to.

"Moses himself, by the command of the Creator, authored the first books of the Scriptures. Within the text, he wrote the laws of El Shaddai as well as an account of his extraordinary journey. Tell me, if the Father stood before you today and asked the same of you, would you write of foreign lands you have never seen? Would you remember the mysterious creatures that lurk in the depths of the ocean? Would you write of the beasts that roam the desert lands far away or the elusive creatures that reside on top of the mountains that reach forth to the heavens? What of the mighty birds that spread their wings and soar?"

She mumbled as she looked at the ground. "I guess not."

"Let us continue. Would you deem it fair to say that language varies throughout the people of your world just as it differed throughout the ages?" He paused and waited for her to answer.

"Absolutely. Both dialect and terminology have changed significantly throughout the history of the world. Here in the United States alone, the English language has changed dramatically since the time of the first English settlers."

"The Holy Scriptures speak of dragons, beasts, and giants, do they not? The Word of the almighty God was written long ago in the verbiage the humans of that era knew. Throughout time and the sins of mankind, the text that your people have upheld differs somewhat from the visions of the prophets. The message, the Word of God itself, is infallible. The laws of El Shaddai have often been sinfully manipulated to meet the desires of the flesh. Some change the text to impose their own standards. They misuse the text and cause separation between Elohim and his people."

"The Creator loves all humans. However, he asks for your faith—faith in him and his Son." He paused when she looked at him with furrowed brows, and her head tilted to one side. "The sons and daughters of perdition debase the oracle of God and use it as reason to harm his children."

Alijah contemplated everything the angel said. "I never thought about that. I just watched over the years as people rewrote it and simplified it. I suppose it is good for people to be able to understand the Word of God, but at the same time, if we've changed things...," she stopped for a moment to consider her next point. "Look at science and what researchers have uncovered from years of study."

"Such as?" Mavet listened without interrupting.

"Well, God gave humans the ability to reason, right? So we did that, and we've found the reasons for the creation of earth. We have created the reason for our existence. We've found remains of different types of ancient man that carbon-date back to way before the Bible was ever written. Look what we as thinking, logical, and free-willed beings have been able to accomplish and create in this world."

Mavet became lost in his thoughts for a moment as he considered the question. "Is it not arrogant for human beings to believe that the Creator's time is that of their own?"

Alijah sat quietly.

"He has given humanity many chances, but they have chosen to forsake him for pride and idolatry. You speak of your creation and the wonders that mankind has created. Your kind has built monuments to themselves. They worship fame and fortune. They twist the words of the Creator to deify themselves."

"When you are presented with the query of who the Creator is versus who the created is, remember the words of El Shaddai as spoken in the account of Job. You are familiar with them—who is this that obscures my plans with words without knowledge? Where were you when I laid the earth's foundation? Tell me if you understand. Who marked off its dimensions? Surely, you know! Who shut up the sea behind doors when it burst forth from the womb, when I made the clouds its garment and wrapped it in thick darkness, when I fixed limits for it and set its doors and bars in place, when I said, 'This far you may come and no farther; here is where your proud waves halt'? Have you ever given orders to the morning or shown the dawn its place?"

He continued while Alijah sat in silence. "Can you loosen Orion's belt? Can you bring forth the constellations in their seasons or lead out the bear with its cubs? Do you know the laws of the heavens? Can you set up God's dominion over the earth? Can you raise your voice to the clouds and cover yourself with a flood of water? Do you send the lightning bolts on their way?"

Alijah remained speechless, unsure how to respond. Mavet continued and asked her to rethink her previous statement. "To those who sin and place blame on Elohim, he has said this, 'Would you discredit my justice? Would you condemn me to justify yourself?'"

She hung her head. "I can't explain how deeply ashamed I am."

He touched her shoulder and spoke softly, "I meant to cause you no shame. I only wished to offer a remembrance of the good words he spoke."

Alijah admitted, "I don't know why we do the things we do."

"It is easier to disbelieve than it is to believe. To have faith in what one cannot see takes a strength that many of your kind lack. Since the rise of the false prophet, faith has become an unobtainable goal for much of the human race."

Alijah frowned with confusion. "False prophet? Isn't Emil the Antichrist?"

"No. The final Antichrist has not yet risen."

"What do you mean? He claims to be the Lord Jesus, and he's trying to force everyone to take the mark of the beast. How can he not be the true Antichrist?"

Mavet removed a leaf that had floated gracefully onto Alijah's shoulder. "Throughout humanity's history there have been several false prophets as well as many Antichrists. They attempted to bring about the end of your people, but the time was not optimal. Think of those who have committed the greatest atrocities in your world's history."

She paused for a moment to ponder whom he was referring to. "There were several world leaders who were warmongers. They attempted world domination and were also considered by many as Antichrists."

Mavet concluded, "However, the one which the Apostle John wrote of was the final anti-Messiah. The one you call Emil is the false prophet who will bring about the final Antichrist." He sighed. "The people of your world have created a new Sodom and Gomorrah, filled with debauchery, corruption, and godlessness. They have forsaken the Creator for a false prophet whose truths are as deceitful as his wonders."

> *Finally, be strong in the Lord and in his mighty power. Put on the full armor of God, so that you can take your stand against the devil's schemes.*
>
> —*Ephesians 6:10–11*

Chapter 14

It was getting worse out there; even walking down the street was dangerous. Noncitizens used to worry strictly about the roaming patrols looking to snatch them up and push them to take the mark, but by this point, the neighborhoods around the dormitories had become filled with poverty, hunger, and, consequently, danger. Those who refused to take the mark were suffering from the effects of malnutrition. They were at their wits' end.

No one could truly blame them for being frantic enough to lash out at others. Alijah reflected on whether she would behave the same way if she didn't have Doc and his wife to help. Though the couple offered anything extra they had, Alijah's body still felt the pain of hunger, and without clean water, her body suffered. She had lost a good deal of muscle mass and had become very weak. The little bits of food Doc was able to share helped, but they never seemed to be enough.

Summer was in full force. The temperatures were rising to ninety-eight degrees, and without many clouds in the sky, not much held back the scorching rays of the sun. The blacktop smoldered under the unforgiving heat. Homeless people fought over whatever shade they could find between the buildings.

Alijah made a point of never leaving the dorm without praying for strength and a blessing of protection. When traveling to pick up her biweekly rations, she always stayed to the main roads, hoping to blend in with the crowd. So far, she had been able to get home without being jumped and robbed.

The long ration lines were particularly dangerous. Fights within the lines were common. Alijah looked down the line she had joined and saw many battered and bruised people sitting on the ground, exhausted from the wait and the heat.

She leaned forward to a man in front of her and discreetly questioned, "Fights again?"

The unshaven man towering at least a foot over Alijah looked back and did a quick visual sweep of her. "Yeah," he whispered, "it got kind of rough up there. Some guys attacked a family when they tried to cut in the line. They held their own, but the husband took quite a beating. You alone?" The man's voice was deep with a hint of an English accent. His eyes were emerald green and almond shaped. His nose came to a bit of a point and was crooked as if it had been recently broken.

Hesitantly, Alijah admitted she was alone at the moment but knew how to handle herself if necessary, which was a bit of lie. She had only been in physical fights with two people in her entire life—the man in the woods and Mrs. Franco. Her recently acquired fighting skills were nothing impressive, but he didn't need know that.

"I'm Tony." He offered up his right hand for shaking. "I realize this is because we don't want the mark, but I just don't understand why we have to be such animals to each other." He inched forward as the line started moving.

Alijah followed close and reached out to shake his hand in return. "Alijah. Are you alone?"

Tony's eyes shifted down to reveal a sadness that reached into his soul. "Yeah. I'm alone." He turned away from her to hide his face.

"Tony, did you...have you lost love ones too? Did God take them, or did they take Emil's mark?"

Noise broke out behind them. The two looked to catch a glimpse of two men wandering down the line. They were citizens who took pleasure in taunting the hungry people. "Look at all of you. You're like dogs beggin' for food." One of the men barked and then laughed. "Don't you people have any shame?" He continued dishing out tasteless insults as he made his way down the line, pinching the women.

He stopped in front of Alijah. "Well, aren't you a pretty little thing," he said, reaching out for her. He touched her head and caressed her hair. "You know you don't have to live like this. You can come home with me." He licked his smirking lips.

Tony grabbed Alijah, pulled her close, and wrapped his arm around her. He sharply threatened, "Don't touch my wife, little man!" and smacked the creep's hand.

The offender put both hands in the air. "Sorry, man. Just wanted to be friendly to the little lady." He laughed in Alijah's direction and wandered into the crowd.

Alijah looked up at Tony and wrapped her arms around his neck. "Thank you."

"Sure thing, love." He backed away a few steps. "Alijah, why don't you stay close for a bit."

The two continued to talk to pass the time. During the course of the conversation, Alijah discovered that Tony lived in the same dormitory, one floor above her. He explained he was one of the last people on his block to be evicted and witnessed the brutality of the soldiers.

On their way home, Alijah snooped through the bag of goods. "A few rolls of bathroom tissue, five cans of meat substitute, three cans of creamed corn, two mini bottles of shampoo and conditioner, and a bar of soap to be used for the bathroom and dishes. How are we to live like this? The rations just get smaller as each month passes by."

"They call it soap, but I am sure it's gravel. It certainly feels like it when I try to shave my beard." Tony laughed. "I finally gave up shaving a couple of months ago because I was spending more time trying to stop the bleeding from the gravel soap and dull shaver. And I must say, they have quite the nerve calling that canned slop food!"

She couldn't help but laugh. "Can-o-crud is what I call it!"

Tony unexpectedly blurted out, "It was my wife and baby girl."

Alijah paused to let the change of subject sink in. "How long have they been gone?" she asked in a gentle voice.

"Since the beginning. She, um, she was always trying to get me to believe. She'd read from the Bible and then try to explain, but I didn't listen. I never understood how she could believe in those stories. I'm from England, you see. I was a chief inspector in London. There were far too many horrors on this earth to ever believe there was a God." The corners of his mouth turned up. "Before we'd go off to sleep, she would kiss my cheek and tell me, 'I will get you into heaven even if I have to pack you in my bag.'"

Alijah stayed quiet.

"I always told her we would talk about it in the morning, but then one day, there was no tomorrow for her. I was watching them from the doorway. Tessa was rocking our baby in her arms and singing a lullaby to her. Then they were gone in a blink of an eye."

Alijah wanted to lighten his heart. "I know we all hurt for the loss, but, Tony, they're safe in heaven. They're with the Lord, safe and happy."

He nodded his head. "Yes, but I want them here with me. Anyway, my sister-in-law was left behind too, but those animals shot her in the back as she walked home one night. Now I'm left alone, and there's no one left for me. I believe in God, but I believe he hates me. If he didn't, he wouldn't have stolen my sister-in-law too and left me to die in this world alone."

She quickly replied, "Tony, he doesn't hate you. You can't judge God for what men do. Free will has always been both a blessing and a curse. Our world is where it is because humanity put it there, not God. We were left behind because we chose not to believe in him."

Tony didn't respond.

"My mom and dad are gone too. They were all I had in the world, and they were taken in the rapture. My mom disappeared while I was talking to her. My dad was cooking dinner. They were there one moment and gone the next. I'm alone too, and sometimes, the pain is far too much to endure. I can't tell you how many nights I go to bed, asking God to let me die, but the answer is always no."

They walked the remainder of the way, exchanging no words. Alijah understood her pain was different from Tony's; after all, she wasn't married. But she knew the anguish of losing everyone she loved. Time made no difference. The pain never seemed to dull no matter how many days passed.

"Alijah?"

"Yes?"

"How do you do it? You've been alone since it all began. I had my sister-in-law with me for some time after the rapture, so at least I wasn't completely alone. She's been gone for six months, and I already can't bear it. At night, I have these dreams of my wife, and they are always the same."

They stopped a few steps from the dorm walkway. She stood close to him and tried to whisper. "I doubted before, but I have seen things that I can't explain. I've experienced something that is so unbelievable, so incredible, that there is nothing in the world that will ever sway my belief again. God is real, and we have to hold on until he returns. No matter how hard things get—and believe me, it's only beginning—we cannot take the mark, Tony. Do you understand? Do not take that mark. Christ will return."

Tony developed a look of fear on his face. "That's what Tessa told me, that I needed to learn about Christ. I don't know where to begin. I've heard of a prayer group in the building. Do you know about them? I'm going tonight. Have you been?"

Alijah was careful. "Really?"

"Yeah, there's a couple I met in the stairwell two weeks ago. The leaders, Michel and Chante. They told me to come by, and I think I'm going to try. It can't hurt, right? I need to do something because I'm losing my mind."

"They're good people, Tony. Please don't betray their trust. They will help you, but never—"

"I have no people or things worth an ounce in my life. No matter how bad it gets, I'm not taking that mark, and I'm sure as hell not about to betray the closest thing I have to a friend. I swear it, Alijah."

She nodded and started toward the stairwell. When they arrived, she reached out her hand to touch his. "Tony, there are a lot like us. We're all hungry, lonely, and frightened. The only thing we can do is hold on to one another, stand strong, and survive until Christ returns for us. I fully expect to see you tonight." She smiled.

Tony dropped his bag and squeezed Alijah tightly as he cried. She dropped her bag on the floor and threw her arms around him. She whispered, "If you open your heart and be faithful to the Lord, you will see your family again. I promise, you will see them again."

The hug seemed to go on forever. When Tony finally released Alijah, he looked down and apologized. "I haven't touched another human being in months. I'm sorry, I should've asked. I'm...I'm..."

"Anytime, Tony. Now I'll see you tonight, okay?"

"Okay."

Alijah picked up her things and continued down to her room.

> *Then Jesus declared, "I am the bread of life. Whoever comes to me will never go hungry, and he who believes in me will never be thirsty... All those the Father gives me will come to me, and whoever comes to me I will never drive away. For I have come down from heaven not to do my will but to do the will of him who sent me."*
>
> *—John 6:35–38*

Chapter 15

"Alijah, I have something for you." Mavet reached his arms behind his waist to untie something.

She was still astonished by the angel. The two had always met together after nightfall, so until this meeting, she had not had the opportunity to fully view the eyes that once reminded her of an endless dark void. In the daylight, his eyes were an amazing deep blue, and looking into them was like gazing into a telescope. There, locked away in his eyes, was the universe, where celestial bodies moved in a perfectly choreographed dance.

She couldn't refrain from commenting, "Your eyes, I swear I can see the cosmos in them."

He answered like a teacher whose student responded correctly, "Angels are a reflection of all the Creator has designed."

Mavet continued on with what he was doing while Alijah watched with curiosity. She studied every movement of his hands as he slowly unwound a blue sash that was wrapped around his body several times. His strong hands moved slowly and purposefully.

Anxiously, she asked the angel, "You have something for me?"

After he removed the sash, he lifted it up between his hands and cupped it. He knelt on both knees and recited words that were foreign to Alijah. She sat only a few steps away from him, still watching his motions. Even though she didn't understand a word of what he said, she knew he was offering some type of a prayer.

A blinding light beamed down from the sky. It was far too painful for Alijah to look at, but Mavet looked up at the heavens without so much as a blink. He stretched out his arms to the sky, stopped speaking, and waited in the light until it faded.

While still on his knees, he brought the sash back to his chest and ducked his head down in a deliberate motion. He extended his arms toward Alijah and asked her to step forward. "Come, young one, and give me your hands."

She advanced cautiously and knelt in front of him. "What was the language you spoke?"

His mouth widened in a smile, and he carefully placed his hands around hers. "The language of Elohim."

"Is it the same language written on your armor?"

"It is." He slowly wound the dark-blue sash around her hands, encircling each one with the unfamiliar silky material. After each hand was wrapped twice, he folded the remainder of the sash in short strips over the palms of her hands. He finished by hovering his hands over hers.

"What is this for, Mavet?" She stared into his dark eyes.

"It is only a symbol, nothing more. To others of my kind, it will demonstrate your devotion to the Creator."

"How will I know it's time?"

"There will be no question in your mind."

Her brow tightened. "But what about the others? Will all the new believers suffer the judgments?"

"The Father knows their hearts. If they are true believers, then they will bear his mark."

"What does the mark look like?"

"It is the true name of Yahweh."

She couldn't hold back an impish smile. "So what's his name?"

"It is for no human to speak." Mavet tilted his head to the left and displayed a curious frown. He studied her face as she stared down at the sash with a look of bewilderment.

"I don't have the seal. Look at me, Mavet. He hasn't forgiven me!" she spoke like a frightened little child.

"Neither the mark of El Shaddai nor the true mark of the beast is visible to any human's eyes."

Alijah's tone of voice changed, revealing her growing anxiety. "What do you mean? The mark of the beast, the numbering—it's on everyone who follows him. The tattoo is a six, and when it's scanned, the microchip adds the other two. You can clearly make out three sixes. They're tattooed on his people everywhere. And doesn't the mark of God come later?"

Mavet turned his head down and briefly shook his head. "Why are humans so quick to believe only what they see?"

Tears welled up in Alijah's eyes before she could stop them. "I'm sorry, Mavet. This is all new to me, and I'm trying. I really am." She covered her face with her hands.

He pulled her hands away from her face enough to meet her eyes. "My years greatly outnumber yours. Even though it develops swiftly with each sunrise, your soul is that of a budding sapling. I easily overlook the fact that your understanding has yet to reach full maturity. Forgive me. I spoke carelessly. My intent was not to cause you sorrow. Please let me explain. The false prophet spoke the truth when he told your kind that the mark was only a symbol. He uses it to confuse those whose faith is weak. Mortals will believe that as long as they have not taken the mark, they will be spared. They fail to see the truth of the darkness. It festers like a disease that rots the very soul of the lost. As for the mark of God, he marks his children as he wishes."

"But I thought we'd have to take the mark to become damned."

"No, during the cleansing, those who refuse to believe the truth will fall. The moment the lost forsake the Lord God, their souls will be marked. Equally, those who bring evil upon the children of El Shaddai will be marked. Those who commit no evil but barter with the false prophet or Antichrist for safe passage will receive both the mark upon their souls as well as the physical mark upon their bodies."

"Barter?"

"One cannot wear the mark of the beast yet trust the Creator for safety. Acquiescing to the mark, false or not, will damn a mortal to hell."

Alijah focused her eyes on something distant, pondering what Mavet said. "I had no idea. I thought maybe if we had a fake mark, we'd be okay."

"Not at all. You cannot deny the Creator or Christ." Mavet stood and took her hand. "Come, night approaches."

"The symbol of the unified community has the earth with three snakes over it. I understand the three sixes, but why the symbol of the snake?"

He didn't answer right away. "Remember, the great deceiver came in the form of a snake in the garden of Eden. The trio of snakes you speak of is not, as you say, biblical. In the mind of the false prophet, however, it may represent him, the Antichrist, and the beast."

She walked close beside him, mulling over another question that plagued her mind. "Life is so hard, Mavet. Except for these times we have together, I feel so alone. Why does it always seem that Jesus is so far from us?"

"Alijah, he is always with you," his tender voice assured her. "If he is not walking beside you, it is because the Lord has walked ahead and anticipates your coming. Remember, young one, that he has faith in you, faith that you will triumph."

* * * * *

Startled, Alijah sat straight up in bed. "It has begun," fell from her mouth. The darkness of the night was as silent as a deep void of nothingness. No noise came from the hallway. Usually, she could hear something outside, either from the hall or from the soldiers. She felt the hair on her arms and neck stand at attention, and chills ran up her spine.

"It has begun," she whispered to herself. "Where did that come from?" She saw no light coming through her window and felt a fearful compulsion to approach the small opening.

Springing onto her feet, she ran to the window and looked at the sky. There was nothing—no moon, no stars, and no hint of a cloud or any light coming from the streetlamps that lined the walkway directly behind the dormitory.

In the darkness of the night, a single light shined down from deep in the sky. Even at a distance, it was incredibly large. But as quickly as it appeared in the sky, it quickly disappeared over the dormitory. Alijah couldn't tell how far it went or what it was, but she desperately wanted to know more. She opened her window as far she could and put her ear to the screen, hoping she would hear something, anything that would hint at what the light was. But she heard no sound at all. She couldn't understand why there were no stars in a clear night sky and no hint of a moon.

One last time, she leaned forward, touching her cheek to the screen. From the still of the night air, she felt her name whispered on her cheek. The voice elicited feelings of exhilaration. She knew the voice; it was unmistakable.

"Mavet, Mavet, is that you? Where are you?" she whispered back.

The only reply was, "It has begun."

"Mavet!" she whispered loudly but feared a soldier hearing her. "Mavet, what has begun?"

She waited by the window for close to an hour, hoping to hear his voice again, but nothing came. She played his voice over and over again in her head as if she had recorded him on an old cassette tape. She tried to rationalize what he could have meant. Every time she thought about it, her mind returned to the same conclusion. The first seal had been broken.

"Oh my! Chante, Michel! I've got to tell them." Alijah jumped up and swung open her door. Her sore bare feet carried her down the darkened hall. She banged on the door and called their names, pleading for them to open to her.

Michel's fearful face peeked out from the dark room, and he pulled Alijah in quickly. He looked her over thoroughly while Chante ran to their side and rapidly fired off her concern. "What's wrong, honey, what's wrong? Did someone hurt you? What is it?"

"It started! I heard him. It was the angel. It started! It started!"

The couple, still in their underclothes, brought her further into their room and led her to sit on the edge of their bed. They flanked her sides closely, trying to calm her down. "Now, sweetie, start from the beginning. What has started? What angel?" Chante asked in a calmer tone.

"There's an angel. He saved me, and I heard him tonight. It started."

"Alijah, you're losing us again. Just go slow, hon." Michel pulled a large chunk of Alijah's hair back behind her ear.

Chante took her hand. "Take it slow."

Alijah turned to Chante. "Do you remember when I was attacked in the woods?"

Michel was stunned. "What?" He swung himself forward onto his knees in front of Alijah.

"Okay, I've been helping out at this clinic for a while now, and one night, I was walking home alone. I have to go through the woods to get home, and it's always late at night. But I was chased, and there he was! He is an angel."

Chante looked at her with complete confusion. "The man chasin' ya was an angel?"

"No, no, no, Chante. The creature who saved me was an angel. His skin was a strange whitish-gray color, his eyes where as blue as the deep sea, and he shined like a lantern in the cover of night. He wore armor that had words, but they were in a language that no one on this earth speaks, and his voice, his voice was gentle and kind. You should have seen his wings. They were massive. I can't even begin to describe how incredible this creature was. It was his voice tonight. It was his voice through the window!"

"Okay, what did the voice say to you?"

"Listen to me! Tonight, I woke up repeating it. I went to my window, and there were no stars or moon, but I saw a single white light coming from high in the sky slowly making its way to earth. Then I heard his voice, the voice of the angel, saying that it had begun. I think it's the first seal. I think the first seal has been broken."

Alijah looked at Chante's bewildered face. Michel touched the two women's knees as he stood up to look out the window. He slowly opened it, hoping to see or hear anything that could possibly disprove Alijah's suspicions.

He seemed to be frozen in place. "Michel, what is it? What do you see?" Chante questioned in a frenzied voice.

He could only muster a raspy whisper. "There's nothing, nothing at all out there. Not a single sound."

"It's started. The first seal has been opened, or it's going to be opened tonight. I know it."

Michel returned to them and took Alijah's and Chante's hands tightly. Chante asked Alijah to explain again about the angel. She did her best to explain everything again without revealing too much about Mavet. "He asked me not to reveal him. I have to do what he said. He's been helping me understand. Guys, he told me the final judgments were coming."

Michel released her hand and reached for her cheek. "We believe you. Is there anything else he told you? Think real hard, sweetheart. What can we expect?"

Alijah lowered her head and sighed. "I've told you more than I should already. All I can say is he told me those who take allegiance with the false messiah will suffer in ways they've never imagined. The angel told me our faith would be tested time and again until we are taken from this world."

The three sat together quietly for a few minutes, reflecting on Alijah's words, when they heard a mighty voice thunder the words, "Come see," from the sky.

The three held tightly to one another and made their way downstairs. As they stepped out on the sidewalk, they joined a growing crowd. Almost everyone from the dorm stood there, as well as a few nearby soldiers. They all silently watched the night sky. The moon eventually appeared, but it seemed to crawl out from the blackness. However, it wasn't bright at all; it appeared to have been cloaked behind a thin cloth.

And then it happened. The moon turned crimson red. Alijah spoke out loud, looking into the crowd. The words just slid out of her mouth without a thought. "The first seal has been broken, and God has released the first angel, the one known to us as the...," she stopped midsentence when she realized she was the one speaking.

The residents and stunned soldiers circled around her and looked to her for answers. A frightened soldier pushed forward through the crowd and asked in a shaky voice, "Who did he release?"

Alijah looked around her, astounded by the number of people now circling her. Many people were standing on the lawn in nothing more than bare feet and pajamas. The soldiers had dropped their weapons to their sides or secured them in their holsters. They looked at her with fear in their eyes.

She took a deep breath and spoke to the crowd. "It's like what's described in the Bible." She nervously stuttered, "I—I—you just—"

Michel touched her arm and gently reassured her. "It's all right, hon, just talk from your heart. The Holy Spirit will help you find the words."

"Please, what's coming?" a voice from the crowd cried out.

Alijah cleared her mind and prayed for help. Calmness overcame her, and words poured from her mouth in a voice that was not her own. "The One who is and will always be conveyed a revelation to the Apostle John. The warning was passed down through the generations, but his children did not heed it. The Lamb broke the seal and has released the first judgment."

Chante's voice trembled as she whispered, "Alijah?"

"The great I Am has kept his covenant with the world. The mighty horseman has ridden out and taken his place." Alijah froze, completely stunned by what came out of her mouth.

The soldier interrupted, "What do you mean by the Lamb?"

Michel touched Alijah's arm and encouraged her to answer. "Um, the Lamb of God. It means the Son of God. Christ broke the first seal and commanded the first horseman to come."

A man in the crowd spoke up, "Wait a minute, that can't be. The Bible states that the moon won't turn to blood until much further into the judgments. I don't think you know what you're talking about."

Alijah turned to the man, replying, "I think we need to focus on the big picture instead of worrying about chronology. Those things I just said, they didn't come from me. I feel it. I know with every bit of me that the first horseman has come."

Another man implored, "If you're right, what's gonna happen to us? Will they hurt us? Should we hide from it?"

"No, I mean yes. I mean, we need to stay out of the way, but you need to make the choice. Do you believe in God, and do you accept his Son as your Savior? Look, as the judgments are poured on the world, there's going to be some serious chaos. But if we are faithful to God, his angels won't hurt us."

A woman called out, "How do you know that?"

The crowd closed in on Alijah. She did her best to reassure them. "Well, those who have offered their souls to God should already bear his mark. It's by this mark we will be safe from his heavenly soldiers." People around her quickly searched themselves and their loved ones for any sign of a mark.

"No, no, you can't see it, but the angels will be able to, and that's how they'll know not to harm us. They won't harm God's children."

The soldier lifted his hand and looked at Alijah. With terror in his eyes, he reached for her. "I believe now. Can I be saved too?"

Tears fell down her cheeks as she touched his hand. She bit her lip and looked into his eyes. "You've chosen the beast."

The soldier fell to the ground, crying out for forgiveness. The crowd surrounded him, reaching their hands to touch him and one another. People bent to their knees while Michel offered a prayer asking for strength for what was to come and for forgiveness for the lost souls who had begun to seek God. But the prayer was interrupted by an explosion that echoed down the street. Everyone turned to see two soldiers on the ground with their guns lying at their sides. They had shot themselves in the head.

Alijah looked at the soldier in her arms. "What's your name?"

He could barely speak but mumbled, "Alex. Alex Rodriguez."

"Alex, there's no escaping, but there's hope. Pray for redemption, and maybe he'll hear and forgive you. But if you do what they did, there will be no hope. Pray with all of your heart, and remember God knows what's in there. You can't deceive him."

Alex heard sirens from down the street and urged everyone to go back into the dorms. He made a promise to Alijah that he wouldn't mention anything about her or the others.

Chante and Michel walked Alijah back to her room. "Lock up, sweetie. We'll hold a prayer session tomorrow for everyone."

"You can't tell anyone about the angel or the medical thing, please! I told you two because I trust you. Please, please, don't betray that trust."

Michel and Chante hugged her tightly. "We would never betray you. No one but us will know about that, but we need to band together with our brothers and sisters to prepare for what will come."

Alijah spent the remainder of the early-morning hours sitting up in bed. She left the window open, hoping to hear Mavet's voice, but he didn't come.

> *Enemies disguise themselves with their lips, but in their hearts they harbor deceit. Though their speech is charming, do not believe them... Their malice may be concealed by deception, but their wickedness will be exposed.*
>
> —*Proverbs 26:24–26*

CHAPTER 16

Weeks had passed since the first blood moon. Everyone waited in fear for the first horseman to show himself. Alijah was exhausted by the questions and worries of the other residents. She continually reminded everyone to keep growing in their faith instead of focusing on the judgments.

But Alijah knew. The last time she had spoken to Mavet, the angel assured Alijah the first horseman had already begun abetting the false prophet, and God's people should not look for him. He assured her the first rider would not be seen like his brothers would.

Alijah took the angel's words to heart and continued to encourage the residents at each prayer service, but every night was a new challenge.

"Tony, where are you going? It's getting close to curfew," Alijah expressed in a worried tone.

"I know, I don't want to go, but I promised a mate of mine that I would drop by after the service. I've learned so much over the last few weeks, and I want to do my part in sharing the gospel. He's never had faith and has so many questions. I thought I could help him, and maybe, just maybe, we can start church services over there at the Ninth Street dorms. Spread the word, ya know. What do you think?"

Tony had only been to about a dozen of their small-scale church services and had been to even less prayer sessions, so she was uncomfortable with him evangelizing alone. "That's nice, Tony, but remember, we are still learning. Why don't you wait until tomorrow, and we can get Chante or Michel to go with you? I'll go too."

"I know, I'm not claiming to be a preacher, but I'm just sharing the passages Chante and Michel have been teaching us. It will be okay, I promise."

"Spreading the Word of God is a great thing to do. But forgive me, Tony, I really wish you would wait until morning."

"It will be fine, love. I'm only repeating what I've learned."

"Be careful out there. You know how dangerous the city is at night. Take care, okay? I'll see you tomorrow." Alijah reached over to Tony for a hug.

He reciprocated by squeezing her and whispering, "Thank you for caring. It's nice to know someone still cares." Smiling, he added, "I'll be careful. I promise. I'm going to take as many alleyways as I can to get there."

Chante, Michel, and a few others in the small congregation exchanged hugs and prayed for blessings on the days to come before they went their separate ways. Tony headed out the building.

A great deal of hate crimes against noncitizens were occurring, and being out when you were not supposed to just increased your chances of becoming a victim. Tony's tall muscular frame gave him a little advantage in a physical fight. Of course, he knew his strength would mean very little if a gun came into play. And always brewing in the back of his mind was the thought that his physical prowess was only a false sense of security. The truth was, Tony, like most other noncitizens, was suffering from the effects of borderline malnutrition. He had already lost some of his muscle mass and had limited energy reserves.

He ducked back down a deserted alleyway and tucked his body behind a large dumpster to avoid being detected by the oncoming soldiers. He was unable to make out how many were there, but he knew the group was definitely more than he could handle alone. He remained crouched as he made his way further down the alley. When it was clear, he turned the corner to the right and continued to make his way swiftly but silently between buildings, taking care to stay hidden in the shadows.

"There it is," he whispered to himself. He gazed between the two final buildings that would lead him to the back of the dormitory. The only thing standing between him and safety was a four-lane street and a single alley that was partially lit. "Come on now, you can do this," he repeated, trying to convince himself. He stayed low and peeked around the buildings to be sure the street was clear. He continued to stay low and bolted across the street, running as fast as he could in a bent position. "See, no problem at all. No one saw me, no incident, no cursed soldiers."

He set his sights on the alleyway and began the short journey to the Ninth Street dormitory. Halfway through the alley, the lights brightened unusually high. Each bulb made an odd buzzing sound as it began to dull one by one until the glow was all gone. The dim moon hid behind buildings and was unable to contribute much visibility to the darkened alleyway. A rush of cold air came from the ground and went over Tony's feet and up his body. Then just as fast as the cold air came, it was gone. The only thing that remained was an eerie, dead calm.

The ground shuddered under Tony's feet, knocking him down. Then the ground instantaneously cracked open and dropped away just inches from his feet. The resulting hole was deep and void of any light. Tony panicked and scuttled backward with the palms of his hands and the heels of his feet until his back hit the wall. With his eyes wide as quarters, he watched in horror.

A low flame-like glow began to seep out. From out of the seemingly bottomless pit came a shadow. It was small at first, only minimally disturbing the light, but it steadily became larger as it came closer to the surface. When the smoky shadow finally finished its ascent, Tony wanted to run, but fear had filled his body and fused his joints and muscles, making him unable to flee for safety. There were no sounds from people or soldiers on patrol; there was nothing but the haunting sound of silence. His body stiffened, and his heart raced until he thought it would explode. The foul stench of sulfur seeped out of the bowels of the earth. Then he saw it—the first glimpse of what was to come.

A single paw came out of the pit, reached into the air, and then came down onto the ledge of the pavement. From its paw protruded five long talons, which dug into the blacktop as the creature pulled itself up with its second paw. As it arose from the pit, fiery light dripped from its body like water to the ground. The creature emitted a ghastly sound as it breathed in deeply, as if it was sampling fresh air for the first time in centuries. When it was completely exposed, it crawled toward Tony and stopped just two feet away from his body.

There, standing before Tony, was a frightening creature with the head of a lion, the body of an ox, the talons of an eagle, and four wings. It glowed as red as a blazing fire, and its eyes were unlike any other earthly creature's eyes. They smoldered like white smoke with a black ring around the pupils. The creature's fur was short, only about two inches long. Each of its four muscular legs looked lean and strong enough to catch the fastest prey on earth. Its long teeth were sharp as blades, and its canine teeth dipped slightly past its bottom lip. The beast spoke in a strange metallic voice in a language Tony had never heard yet somehow understood.

"Human creature filled with confusion and pain, I have come to set you free."

"Stay away from me!"

"Why do you fear? Am I not all that your kind imagines? Is it not written in your Scriptures that a cherub such as I sits at the foot of the Lord?"

"No, isn't it four creatures that…you…you can't be an ang—"

"The apostle was incorrect." It snickered. "I am an angel of the true ruler of all."

"You're a demon!"

"I frighten you? Perhaps this form shall please you more." Dark smoke surrounded the creature as it changed slowly. Once the smoke dissipated, Tony saw the figure of an angel whose beautiful face showed signs of suffering and pain. The angel's once white garment was ragged and dirty. He wore no sash or armor of any kind. Tony looked down to find the creature's feet were bare and filthy. The mysterious angel knelt down to be closer to Tony. He extended his hand to offer a small golden key.

Tony was unable to speak. He muttered only a few words under his breath.

"Here, child, take from me the key to freedom—freedom from the shackles that confine you. For as long as you live, you will never feel hunger. You will find prosperity in a new world that you will help create and shape." The key lay flat on his palm and awaited removal. "All I require in return is a simple promise of loyalty, a gift for a gift. How will you answer?"

"What…what are you?" Tony could barely mumble.

"I am a servant of the one true king of this world. Together, we shall usher in a new, glorious day, the day when mankind will stand and denounce in one voice the creature that dares to calls himself the Creator. He is the beast who discarded his people to die in agony.

Together, you and I shall enter a new garden of Eden. Come, accept my gift."

Still frozen, Tony tried to gather all of his strength. "No, God is the only true God and Savior of this world. You are wrong. He hasn't abandoned us. He will come back. Stay away from me!"

The angel scooted a bit closer, causing Tony to cringe and pull his head back as close to the wall as possible. "It is you who are wrong, earth dweller. He watches your kind suffer in anguish for his pleasure. He plays with your lives as if you were nothing more than a marionette dangling on a string. He sacrificed your mate and baby girl for his own amusement. They do not sit beside him. It is all a lie. Will you accept my gift?"

"How did you...how do you know about them? My wife, my little girl?" Tears rolled down his cheeks.

"I have observed you." The angel shook his head side to side slowly before he met Tony's eyes again. "It is all a lie. Do you accept my gift?"

"They don't sit beside God in heaven?"

"All is a lie. Do you accept my gift?"

"It's you who lies, isn't it? Get away from me! I believe in God!"

The angel moved a little closer. "He laughs at you. You are nothing more than a pawn in his game," his voice uttered in a monotone and condescending voice. "Poor, poor human creatures. Born into a world they do not understand, forever loving a God who does not show even the feeblest compassion for his children. The one you call Lucifer was exiled by that cruel creature, and for what crime, you ask? It was for the crime of compassion." The angel's voice became soft and tender. "It was the exiled one who saw it. He saw the things the one you call God was doing to the humans he was supposed to love. It was he who pleaded for your kind. The fallen one told him the games he played were cruel. He gives you freedom and the promise of eternal life yet lets you suffer. Why?" His voice grew loud again.

"For nothing more than his own putrid pleasure. The angel who was cast out of heaven will set you free. Help us usher in a new day, and you will be eternally rewarded. Do you accept my gift?"

Tony looked down at the ground and muttered to himself, "No, don't you do it. This thing is lying." The hunger pains in his stomach were a cruel reminder that he hadn't eaten in two days because the rations ran out early. He raised his eyes and tried to fight the urge, but the question slid out. "I won't be hungry anymore?"

"For as long as you live. Do you accept my gift?"

Before Tony knew what he was doing, his hand was above the angel's hand, and he was on the verge of taking the key. "You said a gift for a gift. What did you mean?"

"For as long as you live, no more hunger, no more sorrow, no more lone-li-ness." The angel taunted him as he pronounced each syllable. "All I require is a simple gift for a gift."

The thought of no more suffering and no more hunger overwhelmed him. "What do you want?" He grabbed the key.

The angel stood and leaned in toward Tony before scowling and drawling, "Only...your...soul."

Tony looked up and threw the key to the ground. "Oh God, *no*! I didn't mean it! Please forgive me!"

The angel lunged forward.

> *Repent and be baptized, every one of you, in the name of Jesus Christ for the forgiveness of your sins. And you will receive the gift of the Holy Spirit.*
>
> —Acts 2:38

Chapter 17

Deep in the woods behind Alijah's dormitory was a quiet stream. The water traveled from high on the northern peak, followed the southwest side of the mountain, and weaved around its formations down the slope. Like the trees that made up the forest, the stream had many branches that moved the life-giving substance throughout the woodland. In many areas of the forest, the stream pooled inside rocky formations that had risen from the forest floor.

Alijah had a favorite spot along the main stream. It was small pool that was only about waist deep. Because it was at least a two-hour hike through the deepest parts of the forest, very few people knew of it and even less traveled to it. It had been a usual meeting spot for Mavet and Alijah, but they had not met for over a week to have their usual spiritual and philosophical discussions.

As he often did, the angel waited patiently by the familiar pool of water. He looked in the water and reflected on his purpose and what was to come. Mavet desired to know the future that awaited Alijah and what suffering she would have to endure, but he did not dare ask. He knew that she would be persecuted for her renewed belief, and it would be soon. Mavet knew his love for her was that of a father protecting his child, but his attachment to Alijah was strong.

"Mavet, what do you see in the water?" Mil'chamah questioned from behind.

"Greetings, brother. What do I see? I see the beauty of a world that has been torn by her inhabitants," Mavet said as his brother came close enough to cast a reflection on the water.

"We must look peculiar to their eyes. What does your human see when she sees you?"

Mavet sat alongside the stream, looking at his brother. "She is a child of El Shaddai, brother. I have been blessed only with the task of guiding her home." He stared back at the water rippling slowly across the smaller rocks. "She tells me I am beautiful to her eyes. She inquires as to how she appears to me. I have attempted to explain to her that beauty is found only within the soul of the creature. I do not believe she fully understands that I am incapable of seeing her as she sees me."

Mil'chamah knelt beside Mavet and reached his hand down into the water. He then reached up toward the sun and watched the droplets of water trickle from his thin, long fingers. "Her kind has never understood. They believe beauty dwells in the physical vessel, not in what lies beneath."

"Her heart is fragile, and I worry I bring it harm by not reciprocating a similar sentiment. I do not understand their needs."

Mil'chamah let out an unexpected, hardy laugh. "Only El Shaddai and Jesus themselves understand the human condition. You should be pleased, though. Alijah has grown to be a strong believer. With your guidance, her soul has flourished exponentially. The Holy Spirit now emits through her a mighty glow that draws others to the Messiah. You could have offered no greater gift, brother, no greater kindness. Are you to speak with her today?"

Mavet glanced down the path. "I had hoped so. However, since the Lamb opened the first seal, Alijah has been surrounded by others. Now that Kovesh has arrived, the mortals are more afraid than ever. It is now that I see the Father purpose for her. Her soul has become a beacon, a light which calls the lost children to safety."

Mil'chamah laughed. "A beacon indeed. The souls of the believers are growing brighter by the day. Their lights almost reach heaven once again."

Mavet slowly waved his hand through the water and watched the tiny ripples drift across the pond. "Many will still suffer."

"I cannot comprehend why they disbelieved so."

"She questioned me regarding what the humans call mysteries. Many of her kind disbelieved because of the leviathans that inhabited the earth long ago, and some disbelieved over curious depictions drawn in caves. Some believe they evolved from the beasts in the wild. It is staggering the number of reasons they have created to dispel belief in El Shaddai."

"That is the source of their disbelief? Were not the leviathans written in their Scriptures? Caves? Their ancestors lived in caves before mortals developed their civilizations. And evolving from beasts? How odd," Mil'chamah replied.

"Remember, brother, it is not for us to judge. I weep for them and never will understand how they allow the smallest of details to deter their belief."

"Someone comes." Mil'chamah stood up and touched Mavet's arm. "We must retreat behind the trees."

A smile rose to Mavet's face when he realized who it was. Followed by a crowd, Alijah made her way through the thick brush that covered the forest floor between the giant trees. He watched her come forward and organize the crowd of people around the pond.

"Look, brother, a soul that has become a beacon of El Shaddai. She brings others for baptism," he said quietly.

"How grand a thing to see," Mil'chamah whispered.

* * * * *

"What do you mean?" Alijah's voice rose sharply.

A gentle smile creased Michel's face and eyes. "They're here because of you, Alijah. They trust you. The people want you to baptize them."

Her hands quivered. "I'm sorry for snapping, but no, I can't. I'm not worthy of that. You have to do it."

Michel placed his once-muscular arm around her shoulder and whispered, "I can lead a prayer group. I can teach them what the Bible says, but it's you they trust. You inspire them. Over the past month, your words have given them hope. You've given us all hope. It's okay, hon. You can do it. Chante and I will be right by your side the entire time."

Chante lifted her hands and shouted into the crowd, "All right, everyone, listen up. I need your attention over here."

While Chante and Michel talked to the crowd, Alijah sensed she was being watched. She glanced quickly around to see Mavet in the distance.

With everyone focused on the couple, Alijah snuck through the trees. When she got to him, she couldn't control herself and jumped up to throw her arms around him. "Mavet! I was worried I wouldn't see you again!"

He tenderly returned her hug. His warm touch always made her feel much better. Alijah felt safe when he was around—safe and hopeful for the future.

"We will not be able to see each other after the fourth seal is broken." He released her and carefully placed her back on the ground. "It is good to find you well. I see you have been sharing all you have learned. You bring others to his light, and I am most pleased with your accomplishments."

Alijah quickly looked back to be sure she wasn't followed. "Look at them. It's nearly half of the people from the dormitory! We had a prayer session last night, and we couldn't fit everyone in the room, so they were standing in the hallway. Isn't that wonderful?"

"Glorious indeed."

She laid her hand on his chest plate and looked up at him. She exhaled deeply and then said, "They've come to be baptized today. But for some crazy reason, they want me to do it. Me! I don't know why they chose me. I mean, Mavet, I've never been baptized myself. I'm not worthy of the honor."

"Why do you deem yourself unworthy?" he questioned with a look of confusion.

"Why? Are you joking? I was left behind because I wasn't worthy!"

Mavet looked down and shook his head. "Do you forget our discussions so quickly? In El Shaddai's eyes, all his children are worthy of his love. Only when you fall from grace and forsake his love are you unworthy. You, however, are a dear child of El Shaddai who has given your heart and soul to Christ. He loves and blesses you. Therefore, you are, as you say, worthy."

Before she could respond to Mavet, she realized they weren't alone. Alijah turned her head and took notice of the large angel standing beside them. His stature was grand, much like Mavet. He was tall with broad shoulders. His eyes were dark blue, but instead of the universe, she could see red flames burning within his eyes. His skin appeared smooth and pale. His facial features were perfectly formed, and his jaw was slightly squared. He wore armor as red as the fire burning within his eyes. The angel carried a sharp-looking long sword.

Similar to the light that emanated from Mavet, the second angel was bright to her eyes. Although he looked fearsome, she did not feel any reason to be frightened in his presence. Her mouth hung open as she took in a quick deep breath.

"Do not fear, Alijah. He is my brother and will cause you no harm," Mavet reassured her.

When she realized her mouth was still hanging open, she quickly retracted her jaw and tried to recover. She shifted her weight to subtly scoot closer toward Mavet and moved her hand to his forearm. "Hi." She cautiously extended her hand to offer a handshake. "Forgive me for staring. If I may ask, what is your name?"

"It is for no human to speak the true names of my brothers," Mavet explained. "He is the second rider."

"War! You are war, or, um..." She realized she had blurted that out with odd excitement. "Rather, you will bring about war." The right side of her lip lifted slightly in embarrassment. "I'm sorry. I'm not excited about what's coming. It's the excitement of meeting you." She let out a nervous chuckle and looked down.

Mil'chamah took her hand and finally spoke, "I do as I am created." His voice was deep and powerful. "Feel no shame in your offering of kindness. Nor feel shame in doing the bidding of El Shaddai, little one. I wonder"—he tilted his head to the side—"would you allow me to lend you aid? I will baptize you so you may go forth with a reborn soul to baptize others in his name."

Mavet laid his hand gently on her shoulder. "Go with my brother, Alijah."

She heard Chante call out her name and question where she had gone. The angel prompted Alijah to walk forward. As the two emerged from between the trees, Chante waved her left hand in the air and encouraged Alijah to hurry. "Come on, sweetie! Everyone is waiting."

Alijah was filled with exhilaration by the very thought of touching a powerful angel of God. Even the little bit of anxiety she had felt about explaining him to the crowd had subsided. She watched Chante and the group carefully as the two approached. Chante's bright smile faded and was replaced by a look of bewilderment. "Sweetie, who's your friend?"

Nervously, Alijah looked to the left, searching for a suggestion from the angel. Instead of seeing the intimidatingly large horseman, somehow he had given the illusion of being a young Egyptian-looking man with black hair and brown eyes. He was approximately five foot four, just a few inches shorter than Alijah and was rather stocky. He returned Alijah's baffled gaze with a smile before he responded to Chante. "You may call me Uriel. I am here to baptize Alijah."

To Alijah's disbelief, the group of people stood in silence as she and the man approached. Michel had planned for months on being the one to perform her baptism, but neither Chante or Michel questioned the appearance of the strange man from the woods or why he would be the one to baptize Alijah.

Uriel walked near the couple and stopped at about arm's length from them. From an untraceable source or direction, a warm and gentle breeze brushed past all of them. The breeze rustled the leaves of the foliage and made a soft whispering sound. The sun illuminated the beauty of nature all around them, and the pool of water glistened under the bright light, awaiting the beginning of the baptisms.

The angel reached out his hand and briefly touched the couple's foreheads. They watched him in silence as he laid his hand on Michel's shoulder. "Believe not the deceiver, for eternally blessed are the those who have found their way home."

Michel moved to follow the man, but he then stepped back and held tightly to Chante. They observed Alijah and Uriel entering the water.

The comforting warm water reminded Alijah of the angel's soothing touch. She watched the other believers kneel to the grassy floor and begin to pray. Uriel, holding Alijah's hand, called out to Chante and Michel and asked them to stand in the water beside him.

Alijah could still see Mavet through the trees. Her imagination went wild as she tried to visualize all the things he could be thinking about her. Since the first night they had met, she worried the angel felt he had wasted his time with her. As she watched him, she saw that familiar sweet smile he had offered her before. A part of her wondered if he was proud of her actions and spiritual growth over the last several months.

The horseman wrapped his arm around her shoulder. Alijah imagined what it would have been like if Mavet were the one holding her, but those thoughts faded when the angel in disguise pulled her backward toward the sparkling water. He recited a beautiful prayer that seemed to fill the air. Alijah listened to every word, feeling each one in her heart and hoping that God heard her. Her view of Mavet between the trees faded when the water slowly consumed her body and face. Even though her baptizer was an angel destined to help bring about the end of life as she knew it, Alijah felt no fear in his arms. When he pulled her up from the water, she felt an unbelievable and indescribable sense of relief and joy.

After she arose from the water, the angel completed the prayer in a language she had only heard Mavet speak. While she didn't understand what the prayer was, it evoked a feeling of splendor. Uriel took both of Alijah's hands and squeezed them. "Be blessed throughout your days here on earth. Face your trials, knowing the light of the Father shines upon you. You are now my sister in the kingdom of El Shaddai. Go forth and share the ritual of baptism with all who are willing." He smiled at Alijah and touched her forehead.

Chante, Michel, and Alijah stayed behind in the water while they watched the man walk toward the trees. Before entering the thick woods, he turned to smile and nod at the trio.

Alijah peered into the trees to look for any sign of Mavet. He was close behind his brother, and he met Alijah's eyes and lifted his hand to signal good-bye before disappearing from sight. As always, she was grieved by their separation and wished no one had been around so they could sit and talk. She whispered softly to the angel, "I miss you, Mavet."

Another warm gust caressed her cheek. On the wind was the sound of his temperate voice whispering, "Tomorrow." After she watched him slip away into the woods, her heart raced in excitement with the knowledge that she was born again. She reverted her attention to the large group that was waiting for her direction. Public speaking was never her strong suit, so she knew talking to them would be a challenge.

She breathed deeply and improvised the best she could. "Today we take the next step in our journey as believers in Christ and in our mighty God. The symbol of baptism represents the death of our selfish, sin-filled lives and the rebirth of our dedication and love for our glorious God, who has given us one last chance to get it right. When you enter the water, do so only if it's in your heart. Declare to God that you believe without doubt that Christ is your Savior, and offer your promise to never again put anyone or anything before him. When you come up, we will all celebrate a new life in his light!"

Alijah began with Chante and Michel, and one by one, each person arose from his or her knees and entered the water. She offered a short prayer, making it slightly different for each person. Much to Michel's surprise, the baptism prayers came naturally to Alijah, and by the end of the afternoon, everyone who attended had been baptized.

The small clearing in the dense forest became a place for celebration. Alijah watched the group in amazement. Even though they were standing around, drenched from head to toe, they were all smiling and laughing. No one in the group had truly laughed for about a year.

The large group embraced one another like they had known each other all of their lives. Tears of joy flowed. Just hours before, they had entered the clearing only as acquaintances, but that day, they left as a close-knit, strong family of believers. Although many knew there would be more sorrow to come, they found peace in the promise of an eternal life of joy with their God.

In the midst of the celebration, silence rapidly fell. Everyone jumped to their feet and watched as someone emerged from the other side of the woods. Without thinking, Alijah, Chante, and Michel ran in front of the group. They knew that if someone was there to hurt them, there would be little they could do, but the trio was ready to defend their family of believers.

A frightfully armed soldier in his uniform appeared from out of the wooded area. Alijah held her breath while she waited for the soldier to come closer. Soon enough, she realized who it was. "Alex?"

He walked toward Alijah. When he noticed who she was, he dropped his rifle and pistol on the lush forest floor. His eyes were bloodshot, and he appeared to have been up all night. His right hand was wrapped in some kind of cream-colored cloth. She grew more concerned when he stumbled toward her and then dropped unexpectedly to his knees.

"It won't come off!" he cried out as he reached his hand toward Alijah. "I tried, but it just came back. It won't go away!" Alex continued to speak, but he cried with enough intensity that his words were virtually incomprehensible.

The trio knelt beside him, and Alijah began to unravel the cloth from his hand. The old rag unveiled a horrible sight. Part of his skin was peeled back and caused Alijah to feel sick to her stomach. The top of his hand was horribly burned.

"Oh, dear Lord, Alex! What have you done?"

Chante folded her body down and vomited. Michel rubbed Chante's back and then leaned forward. "Oh wow. I'm not a doctor, but I'm pretty sure that's got to be a third-degree burn. Most of his skin is gone."

While Alex struggled to regain control of his emotions, Alijah surveyed him for further injuries. He was in desperate need of medical treatment, but she didn't have access to supplies without exposing the clinic. Her attention shifted when she noticed something else. "Michel. Oh my gosh, Michel. I would not have believed this if someone had just told me. Look!"

Michel leaned in. "What is it?"

"The tattoo, it's...it's on his other hand. How can that be?"

Michel wrapped his arm around Chante and shook his head. "He promised his soul by accepting the mark. The beast isn't going to give it up that easily."

Alex took a deep breath. "I thought if I put my hand in the fire I could burn the numbers off, but a few minutes later, they just appeared on my other hand. How is that possible?" He threw himself against Alijah.

She did her best to comfort him, rocking him back and forth and rubbing his back. "You have to understand, Alex, I don't think you can just remove it. It's a part of you now."

"I'll cut it off!" he shouted.

In unison, Alijah, Chante, and Michel screamed out, "No!"

"Listen to me," Alijah commanded. She pushed back on his shoulders and took hold of his face. "I don't know if you can be forgiven. I don't know any more than anyone else. We are all still here for our choices. But with all of my heart, I don't believe that lopping off a hand is going to solve your problem. I mean, look at what happened, Alex. You tried to burn the tattoo off your hand, and it just went to the other one. Look, I believe firmly that if we can find redemption by praying, giving ourselves to God, and believing in him alone with all of our hearts and souls, there just may be a chance. Even if it's a small one, maybe there is a chance for you to be forgiven. Now get up!" Alijah struggled to get them both to their feet.

She took him by the hand and led him to the water with everyone in tow. They joined arms in prayer, and then Alijah lowered Alex backward into the water. When she lifted him up, the entire group sang out in praise and held the circle for several minutes. Michel and Chante hugged Alex tightly before they exited the water.

He struggled to offer a smile as each person in the group gave him a warm hug before they walked away. By the end of the evening, all the attendees had trickled back into the forest, heading for the dorm. Alex followed the group back home, full of questions for Michel and Alijah and trying to learn all he could.

"I don't know if this will help me, but I am going to do everything you've told me. I mean, if there's the smallest of chances… right?"

Alijah offered him a smile. "That's right, Alex."

"Here, I want you to have this." Michel offered Alex a small Bible. "You have been entrusted with our secret, Alex, and we offer you the Word of God. Now hide it, and learn everything you can in secret. Find truth and a virtuous purpose in God. We will all pray for you."

Alex looked at Alijah. "I'm sorry if I scared y'all. I didn't mean to. But you can trust me. I won't repeat anything I've seen here and definitely won't reveal anything about you guys. But do you think, maybe, can I come see you again?"

They stood at the forest's edge behind their dorm. Chante and Michel looked at Alijah for direction.

"Alex, do you realize how dangerous this is for us?"

"I would never betray you. Please, I just need your help, your guidance. I've been a staunch atheist all of my life, so I don't understand the Bible or even know where to begin."

Alijah looked at him and then replied with deep hesitation, "You begin by praying as we did. Then open the first book in that Bible and read it, and believe every word it says because it's true. Come by in a couple days. You know where I live." She lowered her voice. "Please, please don't betray us." She touched his elbow. "Now go take care of that hand before it gets infected."

Alex hugged her. "Thank you! I swear you can trust me. I won't disappoint you."

> *Dear children, let us not love with words or speech but with actions and in truth. This is how we know that we belong to the truth and how we set our hearts at rest in his presence: if our hearts condemn us, we know that God is greater than our hearts.*
>
> —1 John 3:18–20

Chapter 18

Bang! Bang! Bang! Alijah pounded on Tony's door.

"*Buongiorno*, Alijah. He's not there," said a lilting voice to her left. She hopped back in surprise.

"Excuse me, momma, it's me."

"Alessio!" Alijah breathed a sigh of relief. "You startled me!" Alessio was a sweet man in his fifties who had immigrated to the United States less than ten years before, right around the time Emil rose to power. He was born and raised in Florence, Italy, and still spoke with a heavy accent. His English was fairly good, but he often forgot to finish his words, and his speech included a rhythmic flair that made Alijah smile.

He was always the first to make light of his short stature and receding hairline. Disheveled thick eyebrows arched over his big green eyes. He had a thick and slightly crooked nose. Like many others, he had lost a significant amount of weight since all the troubles began.

"I was just checking on Tony. I haven't seen him in several days, and he's not only missed the last couple services, but he missed the baptism. Have you seen him? Do you know if he's okay?"

Alessio shook his head rapidly. His accented voice was permeated with concern and sympathy. "I don't know. He's been gone for days, I think. The last time I seen him was a few services back. I'm worried. It's no like him to skip services."

"Tony, where are you?" She turned quickly toward Alessio. "Wait a minute! That night Tony was going to meet a friend in the Ninth Street dorm. We all learned so much from Chante's and Michel's teachings that he wanted to share it." Her voice deepened, and she spoke her words more slowly. "What if he got hurt on the way there? What if...oh no! What if he was captured by soldiers or robbed and is hurt and hiding in some abandoned alley or building?"

Alessio hugged her tightly. "He is *un uomo intelligente*. He'd take good care going out after curfew. But perhaps, we should retrace some of his steps. Come, we look."

"Alessio, I don't understand Italian."

He laughed nervously and struggled for words. "Sorry. I forget my English sometimes. I just mean he is a smart man, *sì*. He would take care going out."

It was midafternoon, so the two had adequate time to do some searching. They quickly plotted out a probable path, hoping they could retrace some of his steps. They knew, however, the likelihood of finding Tony on the street was minimal, but they had to try.

"We must be careful, Alijah. Those soldiers will get curious if they see us moving through the back alleys."

"I agree. Alessio, do you have any idea of whom he knows over there? I mean, if we could find his friend, then maybe he'll know where Tony is. Perhaps Tony stayed over with him, especially if he was injured. He could be there recuperating."

Alessio stopped for a moment and stared off into the sky. "*Un momento*, I think his name was Spencer, and if I remember, Antonio say he lived on second floor. Sì, I think so."

"Well, that's a start, I guess. Hopefully, there aren't many Spencers on the second floor." She smiled. "You want to give it a try?"

Alessio smiled and offered her his right arm. "Come, come, we go there now."

They departed on their search and watched for any signs of Tony. The street was surprisingly full of soldiers, citizens, and unregistered people alike. Alessio and Alijah walked at a steady pace to keep from drawing any attention. Soldiers on street corners occasionally stopped people to check for the mark.

As they exited an alley, the two stopped abruptly and focused on a homeless man who was sitting on a curb across the street. The old man gazed back as if he were examining them. Alijah released Alessio's forearm and walked toward the man. Alessio followed closely behind her.

The man on the curb was excessively skinny and looked like he hadn't eaten in a month. He was filthy and bruised. His clothes were frayed and raggedy, and his bare feet displayed many scars. Alijah could only imagine the wounds were from walking barefoot throughout the streets for far too long. In his right hand, the man held up a dirty piece of cardboard. On it were the words "Transgress, defy the beast. Repent! The Messiah comes."

Alijah and Alessio bent down to talk to him. The man's brown eyes were sullen and puffy, set in a face that showed a lifetime of suffering. The gentleman was a painful reminder of how things were yet to become much worse.

Alijah asked him, "When was the last time you ate?" The man smiled but didn't answer.

"If you come back here later tonight, I will bring some food for you, okay? I don't have much, but I'll fix up something for you.

Okay?" The man ducked his head down as if he were saying thank you and then turned his gaze to Alessio.

Alessio touched the homeless man's ankle. "Here, I have more shoes at home. Take mine." Alessio plopped to the curb, quickly removed his black striped flip-flops, and then placed them on the man's feet. "Ah! Perfect, they fit, sì." As Alessio pulled his hand away, the man reached out and grabbed it.

He spoke in a soft voice, "I thank you for your gift, friend. Blessed be those who bear the marking of El Shaddai."

"What do you mean we bear the marking?" Alijah inquired.

He responded, "Alessio, your actions suit your name, defender of mankind. And you, Alijah, the beacon who shines as bright as a star."

Alessio looked on with uncertainty and reached his arm out to wrap it around Alijah's shoulder. "How do you know us?"

Alijah turned to Alessio and said, "By El Shaddai, he means God." She turned back to the unfamiliar man. "We bear his mark? How do you know that? Are you an angel?"

"The final Antichrist has been chosen. Be warned. He will betray you."

Alijah hurried through the questions that invaded her mind. "What? What do you mean? Who is the final Antichrist, and why would he betray me? Do I know him? And who am I going to guide?"

"Your soul is strong, and your light will lead others to Christ. For that is the reason those cast out from heaven fear you. Beware of the one chosen. His will is no longer his own. He will betray you." The man turned his head to Alessio. "You will be tested. You both will."

Alessio stammered, "Will we suffer?"

The man touched him sympathetically. "Child, tribulation has begun. Those left behind will all suffer in some manner. It is the consequence of your choice, but take heart. Christ has heard your prayers and bears witness to your deeds. El Shaddai has forgiven you, and in time, you shall sit by the side of Christ in the kingdom of heaven. Always remember."

Alijah reached out and took the man's hand to ask him for more information, but when she touched him, a familiar peace fell upon her. As she looked into his eyes, she called out his name. "Mavet?"

The man smiled and put both hands on her cheeks. "I cannot intervene. I will keep watch, but it is your trial. You will be tested. Hold on to your faith with all of your might." He released her, swept his hand down Alessio's arm, and then was gone without warning.

"What? Where did he go?" Alessio questioned. "Could he have been an angel?"

"What did he mean about the final Antichrist?" Alijah frowned as she searched her memory.

Alessio became agitated and rambled on, barraging her with questions. The more he talked, the thicker his accent and the choppier his English became. "*Mia cara*, you call him Mavet. Who is he? Do you know him? Have you seen him before? How does he know you? Alijah, momma, tell me, who is he? Tell me!"

Alijah grabbed his hand and pulled him to his feet. "Come on, we have to get out of here before those soldiers come. Are you going to be okay without shoes?"

"Sì, momma, let's go, but you have much explaining to do."

The path was void of any soldiers, so the two hurried the remainder of the way. Alessio winced from the pain of running barefoot on the rough street.

In the Ninth Street dorm lobby, the duo stopped to catch their breath. "Oh, Alessio, your feet! We've got to get something for you, even if it's my socks."

"I'm fine, no worry. Let us focus on finding his friend."

An older woman walked past them before she stopped to look at them. "Hello there. I've never seen you two before. Are you new to the building?"

Alijah tried her best to disguise her nervousness. "Um, no, well, yes. I'm looking for a friend of mine. Do you happen to know what apartment Spencer lives in? He said he lived on the second floor." Alessio stood close, also trying to remain calm.

"Spencer...Spencer who, sweetheart?" the woman questioned in an irritated tone.

Alijah's anxiety soared as she scrambled for an answer. As hard as she tried, she couldn't come up with a logical reply, but Alessio chimed in. "We only met him twice. He told us he was staying here at the Ninth Street dormitory. He told my daughter here the room number, but unfortunately, she's forgotten."

The woman smiled. "Oh, an Italian. I love Italy. Curious though, your accent is pretty heavy, but your daughter doesn't have one at all. How long have you two been in the United States?"

"Oh, sì, I've been here a few years, but my daughter was only born in Italy. She came here with her madre many years ago. Do you speak Italiano?"

"Really? How odd. Where in Italy are you from?"

"Firenze."

"Oh yes, it is so beautiful there!"

"Sì, I agree. So tell me, do you know this Spencer?"

The woman examined them carefully. "Yes, I do, but you might want to stay clear of that one. I heard he killed his girlfriend. Granted, it was many years back, and I suppose he did serve time in prison, but he only leaves the dorms now for his rations."

"Even so, we hoped to talk to him. What room is he in?" Alijah said with a smile.

The woman's narrowed eyes continued to scan them, but she released her pursed lips to say, "Well then, he is in room two zero eight. Tell him Mrs. Winston sends her regards."

"We certainly will. *Grazie*."

The woman looked them up and down one last time before she went on her way. Alijah and Alessio turned and made their way upstairs.

"What a nosy old broad!" Alijah complained under her breath. "Daughter? Do you realize we're only about fifteen years apart?" She giggled.

Her companion shook his head. "Sì, but you look like you are in your twenties, and I would be proud to have you as my daughter." He returned a smile. "I was wondering when she was going to ask me what size undergarments I wear! What I found most interesting though is that she never once took notice of my bare feet." They both held back their laughter.

> *Guard my life, for I am faithful to you; save your servant who trusts in you. You are my God; have mercy on me, Lord, for I call to you all day long.... You, Lord, are forgiving and good, abounding in love to all who call to you.*
>
> —Psalm 86:2–5

Chapter 19

A tall man cracked open the door. "Who the hell are you?" he muttered in a heavy Southern accent.

Alessio squeezed Alijah's arm and made ready to push her out of the way if the man became aggressive. "I'm looking for a Spencer."

The man was obviously agitated. "I'll tell ya what, you tell me who the heck you are, and what y'all are doin' here, and I'll think about not breakin' my foot off in your butt, boy." He opened the door a little more and stepped forward.

The two shuffled around, Alijah stepping back and Alessio stepping in front of her. "We are looking for no trouble." He raised his voice, and his English got choppier.

Alijah took a deep breath and told the man their names. "Our friend said he was coming here to meet Spencer. All we know is that he lives on the second floor. A lady downstairs said that he lived here in this room. Are you Spencer? If not, do you know who he is?"

The man looked surprised. "Alijah? You're Alijah? Get in here quick. I'm Spencer. Come in quick!" He pushed open the door and surveyed the hallway. He pulled Alessio in by the arm. "Come on, these people here are nosy, and they talk—talk way too much."

The two hurried through the door but stood close to it, keeping their backs to the wall. "Be prepared to run," Alessio whispered into her ear. She kept her hands clamped around his forearm.

Spencer turned to them and smiled while he extended his hand in an inviting handshake. "Sorry if I scared the two of ya. It's just, Tony never made it here. Somethin' weird happened that night, and I've been lookin' for ya. I even went over to your dorm, but he wasn't there. I tried lookin' for ya but didn't know where you were. I asked around, but either no one knew you, or they just weren't giving you up. Have ya seen him?"

Alijah stepped toward Spencer and shook his hand. "No, we haven't seen him in over a week. He told Alessio and me that he was planning on coming here. I asked him not to go, but he said he needed to. Do you know of anywhere he may have gone?"

Spencer covered his face with both hands. "It's my fault," he muttered to himself while he appeared to fight back tears. "He came here 'cause of me. He's been teachin' me everything he's been learnin' from that preachin' couple at your place. If he's hurt, it's 'cause of me."

"I'm Alessio." He reached forward to shake Spencer's hand. "Let's think on this, sì?"

After drying his eyes, Spencer reached out. "I'm sorry for bawlin' already, but over the last week I've been imaginin' the worse, and now that y'all are here, I'm afraid I'm right." He adjusted his shirt and continued, "Alessio, you're exactly as Tony described. Ya know he loves playin' cards with ya? He's been trying to convince me to head on over to his place to join a game. Well, come on and sit, I ain't gonna bite. I'd offer some food but, well, ya know. Come on and sit."

Alijah sat close to Alessio and instinctively held his arm again as he started talking. "Spencer, a minute ago, you said something weird happened that night. Can you explain?" Alessio sat back, breaking free of Alijah's grip before he wrapped his arm around her.

Spencer took a deep breath and rolled his eyes toward the ceiling before he focused on his guests. "I don't reckon you're gonna believe this."

Alessio let out a hardy laugh. "After what we encountered today, try us."

Spencer shifted his weight forward to rest his elbows on his knees. At about six foot two, he was taller than Alessio. Spencer was a lanky man who had a significant amount of scruff on his chin. His long arms showed evidence of once being excessively hairy but now sported uneven patches where hair had fallen away.

Dark circles that surrounded his light-blue eyes were like shadows on his dry, patchy skin and sunken-in cheeks. "Ya know, that night he was comin', well it was getting late, so I was watching out my window to look for him. I, um, I was watchin' with binoculars 'cause he comes down the same route every time. At first, I thought he just changed his mind, but then I saw something. I saw..." He cupped his hands over his face.

He was clearly struggling for the right words to explain what he witnessed. Alijah pushed herself forward and knelt in front of him. She could see the deep sadness in his eyes, so she stroked the top of his hands tenderly to offer comfort. "Spencer, please tell us what you saw. Maybe it will be some kind of clue that could help us find him."

"Ya know, he was comin' here to teach me about God. Look, I ain't gonna lie to ya. Fourteen years ago, I was battlin' anger issues. In the middle of a fight with my girlfriend, I...I got angry and shoved her, and she...she tripped backwards and went over our balcony and down four stories. She died in the hospital a few days later. See, Tony knew me since he and his wife moved here to the States and knew I was havin' trouble with it all. After that rapture thing, he began to believe in God and tried hard to convince me that it was all real." He paused for a moment and looked back and forth between Alijah and Alessio. "I always thought Christians—hell, I thought everyone who believed—were nothin' but a bunch of hypocritical, Bible-thumpin', brainless sheep that hid behind an idea to justify their feelings of superiority. Told him religion was nothin' more than a crutch. Truth was, it was way easier to make fun of religious types than it was to believe there was someone...up there."

"Spencer—" Alijah tried to interrupt.

He let out a puffing sound. "I asked him why, if there was one, anyone could love and worship him if he hated his so-called children 'cause they didn't believe. Not only did he hate us for not believin', but also, he caused others to hate us for believin' what we believe in."

"Spencer, God doesn't hate us for not believing in him. He wants all of his children to come back to him, so much so that he allowed his Son to be sacrificed. I know it's been popular to criticize Christians for sharing his Word, but it is what he commissioned us to do. And I know there were those who called themselves faithful and did exactly the opposite of his commandments, but that wasn't God's doing. Hate is actually the absolute opposite of who God and Christ are."

Spencer smiled and squeezed Alijah's hand. "I'm tryin'. I'm tryin' hard to understand. It's hard, ya know. I caused the death of someone I loved. How could he forgive that?"

"Look, Spencer, God doesn't arbitrarily forgive things, but if you are truly repentant and faithful, then there are many things he will forgive. It's not like you can kill a bunch of people out of malice and say, 'Oops, I'm sorry. Forgive me.' You have to own up to what you've done, seek forgiveness with everything that's in you, and then sin no more. Christ made that possible with his sacrifice."

Alessio nodded his head. "Sì, I believe it too."

"Tony told me I've got to keep prayin' and beggin' for forgiveness. He said I'll know I've got forgiveness when I get it."

Alijah chimed in. "Spencer, I'm no theologian, pastor, preacher, or anyone special, so what I say to you is just what I hope and pray for. I believe God is forgiving, and he loves us all even though we sin like there's no tomorrow." She snorted when she tried to force out a chuckle. "I think people say a lot of these things because it justifies what they want to believe or not believe. Let's face it, accepting responsibility for the way we sin is a very bitter pill to swallow. What better way is there to take the heat off ourselves than by blaming God for all the wrongs in our life? Look at all the wars that happened throughout history. How many of those were done in the name of God? All the time I spent thinking what a joke religion and its followers were was time I should have been asking God for the wisdom to help people see that he isn't to blame for the wars, pain, and suffering. No, it's our brokenness, we are the cause."

Spencer nodded. "I heard it. That day, I heard a voice call, and I heard those trumpet thingies. I believe it was the rapture." His voice softened and quivered as he continued. "I listened to all these people who spent their lives provin' there's no god of any kind. They say that the Bible and all those religious-type books were made-up stories—folklore, ya know—and their teachin' only encouraged the ideas of hatin' one another 'cause they weren't the right religion, right nationality, or even the right colors. Did ya ever notice the inconsistencies?"

Alijah moved her feet and shifted from kneeling to sitting cross-legged. "Yep, but we all need to remember that the human race throughout history has spoiled almost everything we've touched. You say inconsistent, but the Bible is the constant, it's us that are the inconsistencies. Really, we have an incessant need to over-rationalize and nitpick things until there's nothing left. She reminisced for a moment before glancing at both Alessio and Spencer. "You know, what made having faith even harder was that so many fanatics preached about God but spewed nothing but hate toward others. They called themselves God-fearing men and women but encouraged violence and hatred toward others because, again, they weren't the right skin color, race, nationality, or sex. Can you blame nonbelievers for thinking we're all a bunch of nuts?" She shook her head. "But that's in the past now, and what matters is that we find faith and help all of our brothers and sisters who wish to find Christ. That is why Tony came here for you. He wanted desperately to help you find your way to God."

Alessio shook his head in agreement. "We need to help each other, even if it puts us at risk. Antonio knew this."

Alijah reached for his shoulder. "God forgives. He loves us all. Christ died for us so we could be saved—all of us."

"Have you heard the rumors of what's happenin' to those who don't take the mark? What them sorry sons of pigs are doin' to people nowadays? Emil finds us unholy. That's a joke in itself. I heard they're roundin' us up like cattle goin' to a slaughterhouse. Once they go into those prisons, they don't come out. That's why I hide in here. Tony came here to give me a chance at redemption. He knew it was risky but came here anyway."

Teardrops fell slowly as he struggled to spit out the words. Alessio knelt beside Alijah and offered his hand, speaking to Spencer. "We are in this together. We all made the mistake of thinking the human race was the be-all and end-all of everything. We lived for today, never thinking about tomorrow. We only thought of how to help ourselves and never cared who we crushed to get it. We are paying our dues now, but Christ will come for us. Sì! It is up to us to accept him and learn to have faith, even when it seems there's nothing left to have faith in. Antonio is a good man, and we should try to find him."

"I saw someone in the alley. I wasn't sure if it was Tony or not, but I saw the strangest thing. The alley lights were bright as day and then quickly went dark. After that, the two buildings shook like they were doin' the shimmy during some earthquake, but nothin' else moved."

"An earthquake?" Alijah asked with disbelief.

"I'm tellin' ya the truth!"

"I believe you. I do believe you. What else happened?"

"It gets weirder." Spencer looked up and let out a deep sigh. "Okay, here it goes. A red glowin' light came up from the ground. It was like a fissure or somethin', and then a light came from it and kept glowin', and somethin' crawled out of it. I couldn't see it too well, but it looked like some type of animal, almost like a lion or tiger. But bigger. Much bigger. It wasn't normal. It had a lot of heads or somethin'."

"Were you watching through your binoculars still?"

"Sure was. I could only make out a li'l bit of the person, but it looked like he or she was sittin' on the ground against the trashcan. I couldn't make out the face, but I imagine something like that comin' out of the ground is going to scare the holy—you know what—clear out of them."

Alessio pushed for more answers. "Sì, sì, sì. What else?"

"Listen, all I know is it was quiet down there, and then all of a sudden, I saw that thing lunge forward after whoever was down there. It crawled down the same dang fissure or hole or whatever it came out of, and then it was gone. And...and so was the person. The lights in the alley came back on, and it was empty. Do you understand? Empty! Just some trash cans, and to make it sound even screwier, the hole was gone too. I stayed up 'til three thirty that mornin', and nothin' else came through there. The next day, I went down to the alley. Everything was normal, includin' the concrete and asphalt. I turned to leave, and I saw this." Spencer walked over and fetched something from underneath his mattress. "Here."

Alessio and Alijah stood up and reached out to take the article from Spencer. Alijah held it up and trembled. "Oh no. Alessio, this is Tony's jacket. He put it on after he hugged me."

"Are you sure?" Alessio asked, looking through the pockets of the jacket.

"It's his," Spencer confirmed. "Look at the tag inside. His wife, Tessa, well, Tony was always leaving his jackets behind, and she enjoyed teasin' him, so she wrote his name on the tag in her favorite color, pink."

Alessio dropped the sleeve of the jacket and turned away. Alijah began to cry. "Oh, Tony. What's happened to you?" Spencer wrapped his arms around her, and they both cried.

"Ya see, he's in trouble, and it's my fault."

"No, it's not your fault." Alessio's accent thickened again as he laid a hand on Spencer's shoulder. "He's a believer and felt he needed to share what he had learned. He thought—no, he thinks—it's his purpose. We have to find him, Alijah. We have to find Antonio."

Alijah stepped away, and a cold chill slithered down her spine. She looked back over her shoulder and repeated the words Mavet had spoken, "'The final Antichrist has been chosen.' Alessio, it's Tony. He will be the betrayer." The three stood in silence.

> *Dear friends, do not be surprised at the fiery ordeal that has come on you to test you...But rejoice inasmuch as you participate in the sufferings of Christ, so that you may be overjoyed when his glory is revealed.*
>
> —1 Peter 4:12–13

Chapter 20

Alessio sat across from Alijah as they shared a plate of canned vegetables. Both of them sat with their shoulders drooped and their chins low.

Alessio wiped the corner of his eyes with the back of his hand and spoke slowly. "I've asked everyone I know. We've looked everywhere, and no one knows what happened to Antonio. Mia cara, I think he is lost to us."

"I'm afraid you might be right." Her words were barely more than a whisper. "It's been eight weeks, and he hasn't been back, even for his rations card."

The two said nothing to each other for several minutes, and Alijah thought back over the last two months since Tony had disappeared. She also had not seen or heard from Mavet in nearly two weeks. She had searched for him and called his name in the woods repeatedly, and she wondered if he was forbidden to return to her now that the first seal had been broken.

Since the blood moon had appeared in the night sky, the moon and stars seemed to give off very little light. Alijah feared going to the clinic in such dim moonlight, especially not knowing where Mavet had gone. She knew Doc must have been in desperate need of help, and she guessed the off-the-grid community was worried by her disappearance.

"Alijah, you still no explain why you called the man on the street Mavet. How do you know him? How did he know my name? Was he an angel? And why did he call me protector and you chosen one? What is this?"

She put her fork down and moved to the chair beside Alessio. "I met someone, someone incredible. He has been teaching me, helping me understand what is to come, and how to seek forgiveness for my choices. He helped me find my path to Christ. Alessio, he is a real angel. He is my friend, and I care for him so much." She looked down, trying to fight her emotions. "But I'm worried because he hasn't been back, and he's not responding when I call out his name."

"An angel?" His eyes opened wide. "Christ, he comes then?"

Alijah closed her eyes and knew she should not say much more, but her separation from Mavet was weighing heavy on her heart. "I can't tell you much more, but just know he is a soldier of God and an incredible gift to me."

Alessio sat still beside her, opening his mouth only to say, "Mavet?"

"Please don't ask me more. I can't expose him any more than I already have. Christ gave him the chance to help me. I'll never understand why he allowed it, but I have been sharing with others everything Mavet has taught me."

Alessio grabbed her hand. "I know why you were chosen, mia cara. Look how people flock to your side. They see the same thing I do, your love for life, people and how the Holy Spirit shines brilliantly in you. So explain no more. What a glorious thing indeed! Sì, sì." With a big smile and his head bobbing up and down, he added, "Christ, he is coming back for us!"

She returned his smile and offered her hand. "Here, I have something I want to share with you." She stood up, headed to the little refrigerator, and then pulled out a small blue container and a brown paper bag.

When he saw what was in it, he exclaimed, "Aye, momma! Where did you get this?"

After heating it, she shared with him the main course—a chunk of chicken breast and some vegetables. She even offered a few strawberries for dessert.

"How did you like it?"

"It was wonderful! I have not had chicken in over a year. And fruit—glorious strawberries, so fresh." He popped out of his seat and gave Alijah kisses on both cheeks. "Grazie, grazie!"

"I gave Chante and Michel some too. My doctor friend and his wife are so sweet. Once in a while, they send food with me, fresh stuff too. Doc insists I eat better. He said I'm too skinny."

"Send them my love for this!" Alessio picked up the plates and started cleaning. "But we need to talk, Alijah. If the angel was telling the truth about the final Antichrist, then you should be leaving this dormitory. It's getting dangerous. Now we need to worry about the other man, for we don't know if the soldier will tell." He reached forward and rubbed her arm. "You know I love you as if you were my own *bambina*, but you need to leave here. Will the doctor take you in?"

"I won't leave if you, Chante, Michel, and Spencer don't come." She put down the old dishtowel and leaned back on the counter. "I've been speaking with the leader at the camp, and he has agreed to take up to thirty more people. That's all they can support right now, but he's making arrangements with other groups to make room for more. Let's face it, those judgments are coming, and no believer will be safe. I'm going to stay here until I can get the last of the people in this dorm out."

"Why don't you, Chante, and Michel leave first? I will wait here and help the others go."

"No, I need to do this, Alessio. They trust me. I just can't run off without them."

A faint whisper crept through the door. "Alijah. Alijah, are you there? It's me, Tiffany, from one fifty-two. Open up."

They exchanged a bewildered glance, wondering why Tiffany would be at the door. Alijah opened the door and offered the woman a warm welcome, but Tiffany pushed through and shut the door behind her.

The fifty-seven-year-old woman stood at about five feet five inches. Like so many others, she showed the unmistakable signs of malnutrition. Up until about fourteen months before then, Tiffany was morbidly obese and weighed over four hundred pounds. She had lost almost three hundred pounds over a year, but because of the rapid weight loss, she had been left with uncomfortable, loose skin that she always hid with oversized clothes. She had been married for twenty-two years. Alijah never met her husband, he was murdered during the mass evictions. He had died trying to protect Tiffany when she was being pistol-whipped by an angry, brutal soldier. He had loved her long brown hair, but since his death, she had kept it short and shaped to her face, which was showing accelerated signs of aging. Her hazel eyes were sullen, and her pallid complexion differed greatly from her once-glowing skin. She never fully recovered after the murder of her husband and always told Alijah there was no need for beauty because there was nothing beautiful in the world anymore.

She entered the room, panicked. Her eyes darted between Alessio and Alijah, and she grabbed Alijah's arm tightly. "Soldiers! Soldiers are here, and they're looking for you two and Chante and Michel. Tim from the down the hall is warning Chante, but you two have to get out of here!"

"What?" Alessio stepped forward.

"Now! They're downstairs. We're trying to slow them down, but they are pushing their way up. Go down the backstairs quickly!"

"But...but...my parents' things, this is all I have of them. I can't lose everything!"

Alessio started to push her to the door. "We come for your things later."

"Alijah, please. I will gather what I can after they leave and save it for you, but please go."

"Under the bed is a box. Grab that and my parents' pictures. You get out of here so they don't catch you. Alessio, come on!"

Tiffany hugged them tightly and whispered, "God be with you." She scurried out the door. Before Alijah and Alessio had a chance to follow her out, two soldiers swung open the door.

"Run! Alijah, run!" Alessio shouted as he hurled his body against the soldiers and knocked them to the floor.

"Alessio!" she cried out.

"*Andare*! Go!"

"I'm sorry," she whimpered as she bolted for the door, but as she tried to run past the soldier, another one reached out for her right ankle and caused her to trip. She shrieked and kicked his hand to escape his grip.

Alessio broke one hand free long enough to grab the soldier by his hair. He pounded his head on the cheap linoleum floor just hard enough to stun him. "Let go!" Alessio bellowed.

Alijah broke free and tried to grab her friend, but he pushed her away. "I will find you! Go!" She passed the hallway lights that protruded into the walkway. They flew past her head as she sprinted down the hall. But just steps from the stairwell, she collided with a soldier who was significantly bigger than she was. They both collapsed on the floor.

He quickly flipped her around and pinned her to the floor. "You! Yeah, it's your turn now." As he grumbled the words, a baseball bat came down square across his shoulder blades.

"Get off her, you miserable barbarian!" Eiji shoved the soldier off Alijah. Eiji was a thirty-eight-year-old immigrant from Japan. He had been in the United States for twelve years and married his wife, Alicia, shortly after the rapture.

"Go, Alijah. Go quickly." He lifted her up to her feet.

"Come with me. He'll kill you when he wakes up!"

Eiji held her hands tightly. "Don't worry about us. I'll cover this up. God be with you." He pushed her toward the stairwell.

Alijah looked back and saw Eiji and Alicia standing together. "God be with you," she repeated.

Alicia blew her a kiss through the air. "We love you, but you have to run. Run into the woods, honey. You can lose them there. Go."

The echo down the stairwell sounded like a herd of charging buffalo. Alijah, filled with panic, swung open the back door and darted into the courtyard. The noise alerted a nearby group of soldiers, who quickly pursued her.

"Oh please, Lord, help me," she called between gulps of air. She scrambled to zigzag between the large trees and prickly brush in an effort to lose the soldiers. Her wide eyes scanned quickly and planned each stride so she could avoid tripping over a root, as she had done before. But she pushed through the forest so fast that the low-lying branches painfully dug into her face and arms.

Out of nowhere a heavy weight fell onto her shoulders and forced her to the ground. It knocked the wind out of her, and all at once, her face was shoved into the damp dirt, and her right arm was pulled behind her back. It suddenly occurred to her that she had been caught.

She fought as hard as she could, but the soldier overpowered her. Her hands were secured behind her back by metal handcuffs before two soldiers lifted her by her forearms. Pain throbbed in her shoulders, and she could feel the cold dirt and warm blood on her face. The soldiers said little to her as they guided her through the woods and back out to the clearing.

She watched while more soldiers pushed the residents back toward the dormitory building. Other believers stood at their windows and cried for her, but the unyielding soldiers yanked on her arms and forced her forward. One man from the crowd leapt out and tried to help her, but a soldier tripped him and then clubbed him in the temple with the butt of his gun.

A heavyset man waited for her by a large black SUV with the logo UCTO imprinted on the door. This soldier belonged to the Unified Community Taskforce Office, which was the head of security for Sovereign Overseer Emil himself. Alijah knew this was no ordinary arrest.

"Captain Davidson, we have her, sir."

The portly man called to her, "Alijah Rossi?"

Alijah stood in silence and simply stared at the captain.

"Nothing to say? Help her, boys."

She looked over to her left just in time to see the butt of a rifle come through the air and land in her ribcage. Pain seared through her abdomen. Gasps came from the crowd, and a resident cried out, "Let her go, you animals!"

Sarcasm dripped from the captain. "Insolent little girls will not be tolerated. Answer my question before I have my soldiers encourage you some more. Now, are you Alijah Rossi?"

She tried to fight the tears back but felt as if she were being stabbed in her side. Standing up as straight as she could, she mumbled, "Yeah."

The captain ambled toward her. He was a clean-shaven Caucasian man with a crew cut. His face sported a hooked nose and eyes that were farther apart than normal. Judging by the jewelry on his body and the fact that he was quite overweight, Alijah assumed he had been a part of Emil's team for some time.

"For such a little thing, you sure have been a lot of trouble. Our good Sovereign Overseer Emil has taken a special interest in you. He would like to meet you personally. So after you, please." He pointed to the SUV.

The angry crowd demanded that she be released. Some people lunged forward to fight for her, but their efforts were in vain. Those who tried to fight were coldly beaten.

As the soldiers tried to get her into the SUV, Alijah did not give in without a fight. With her wrists locked behind her back, she used her feet by throwing them high in the air and propping them on the frame of the door.

"Look, lady, this can get a whole lot uglier. You are going to see Overseer Emil conscious or unconscious. It's all up to you."

"Go to hell! Oh wait, you don't need my invitation. Y'all have a one-way ticket to the center of hell specifically reserved for betrayers of Christ!" She pushed back as hard as she could in order to knock them off their feet. She kicked with everything she had, but in the end, another soldier grabbed her feet and forced her into the SUV.

On the way to the capitol building, Alijah tried to plead with the soldiers. She begged them to release her. She recited Bible verses and urged them to repent for their wicked ways before it was too late. But no one was interested in what she had to say.

The soldier in the front passenger seat looked back with what looked like pity in his eyes. "You should stop talking about that. You know people die very badly, spouting that stuff. Just forget about your faith for a minute, and think about what's goin' to happen to you if you don't learn to conform."

"Set me free, please."

The soldier to her right leaned in close to her ear. "We're all prisoners. No one will ever be free again. You've got to accept it."

The soldiers looked forward at the road and refused to speak to her again for the remainder of the ride.

> *Listen to my prayer, O God, do not ignore my plea; hear me and answer me. My thoughts trouble me and I am distraught because of what my enemy is saying, because of the threats of wicked; for they bring down suffering on me and assail me in their anger.*
>
> —*Psalm 55:1–3*

Chapter 21

Alijah was brought into a large room with double doors and no windows. Elaborate, expensive-looking paintings in gold frames adorned the bright-white walls. The centerpiece of the room was an extravagant, large ivory-and-glass desk, sparsely decorated and situated near the middle of the back wall. Two black leather sofas were positioned near the desk. In the very center of the room stood a single black post with a sculpture of a ram's head on it. Dread consumed Alijah when she noticed that behind a half wall was a large metal cage.

A single desk chair faced the wall. A tall dark-skinned man was speaking to whoever was in the chair. As he came forward to greet Alijah, she did not recognize him. He had handsome facial features, hair cropped short and plastered to his head, and a single diamond earring. He was a trim man who looked fit and muscular. He wore a blue three-piece suit, and a small nametag identified him as Mr. Stevenson.

The gentleman looked Alijah up and down before he spoke, "Welcome, Miss Rossi, to the capitol building. I am Mr. Stevenson, the first assistant to our glorious Sovereign Overseer Emil. He is happy to have you as our guest today."

Her eyebrows rose, and she scoffed at the man. "Guest? Really? Why don't you try a little truth before the lies? I'm a prisoner of your glorious Sovereign Overseer Emil."

A quiet laugh came from behind the chair. Mr. Stevenson replied, "Oh, miss, prisoner is such a harsh—"

"Oh, but *prisoner* is the proper word for it when your band of flying monkeys chases me out of my home, tackles me, handcuffs me, rifle-butts me in the ribs, and then stuffs me into the backseat of an SUV for a five-hour drive. *Guest* is not the word I would choose to describe this!"

The man in the chair commanded someone to unbind her hands. Mr. Stevenson looked at a soldier, who quickly removed the handcuffs from Alijah.

"I know that you are a highly educated forty-five-year-old woman. I suggest you exercise proper etiquette before you speak to our great overseer. He is not as lenient with disobedience as I am." With disdain in his voice, he commanded the soldiers to take her to her room.

Mr. Stevenson turned and walked away while the soldiers led Alijah to the cell behind the half wall. They slammed the door shut, and all Alijah could do was stand by the door and pray.

From behind her, a voice rang out. "Alijah?"

She recognized the voice and swiftly spun around to see him. "Alessio? Chante? Oh no!" Alijah ran to them. Alessio was leaning across Chante's lap and was covered in cuts and bruises from where he had apparently been severely beaten. Chante's head hung low, and she looked as if she had been beaten as well.

Alijah threw herself onto Chante and Alessio. "Yeow! Not so tight."

"I'm sorry." Alijah backed off and touched them both on the cheeks. "This is my fault. They were looking for me."

"I was no good protector, and it is I who should be sorry." He touched her face. "No..., they hurt you?"

Chante didn't speak; instead, she lowered her head and helped Alessio sit up. He reached his arms out and hugged them both. "So this is the suffering the angel warned us about."

Alijah sniffled. "I guess so. Wait! Where's Michel? He got away." Her voice perked up, and she smiled for a moment.

Alessio looked at Chante and stroked the back of her head. "No, Alijah, those cowards shot him in the back when he tried to push Chante out of the way. We don't believe..."

Alijah didn't know what to say, but she was consumed with guilt. She reached her arms out to Chante and squeezed her tight. As the night slipped away, the three of them wept for the loss of Michel.

The next morning, the soldiers tossed some bread into the cell. About a half hour later, they delivered a small platter with three warm bottles of water, three hard-boiled eggs, and apples. "That should be an improvement from what your kind normally eats," a nasty soldier said with a snicker.

Another soldier slid a bar of soap and three towels into the cell. "Clean yourself up, girl. The overseer would like to talk to you."

There was no privacy in the cell. The toilet and sink were completely exposed, so every time one of the three friends needed to use the toilet or take a sponge bath at the sink, the other two stood in front and held up towels. The morning passed quickly as they huddled in the corner and waited to see what their futures held.

They looked out from the cell. The trio could do nothing but watch as a multitude of men and women in suits rushed in and out of the room. Everyone spoke in low voices that made it nearly impossible for the prisoners to overhear.

"Did you hear that?" Chante leaned in close to her friends. "They were talking about camera crews. Are they going to televise whatever he plans to do with us?"

"Remember what's in the Bible. They can't force us to take the mark. We've got to give ourselves willingly," Alessio whispered. "Whatever you do, don't you say you accept the mark."

The double doors were opened all the way, and two large television cameras mounted on black pedestals were wheeled into the room. Shortly after the cameras arrived in the room, a crew of six impeccably dressed people unraveled wires and set up the broadcasting equipment. Alijah caught a glimpse of one of the cameras. The crew was from the worldwide broadcasting station UCNN, also known as the Unified Community News Network.

"Emil's broadcasting network. They spin everything to be sure all news leaves Emil in a positive light," Chante said as she studied the interviewer who prepared for the broadcast.

Alessio placed his hand on the back of their necks and pulled them in close. "Sì, they also filmed the massacre at the messianic Jewish temple last year. They cut up the film and added new footage to make it look like Emil peacefully dispersed the protesters himself with gentle words instead of automatic machine guns. They murdered everyone in the temple."

Chante swung her head from side to side. "It was a blood bath."

"Okay, it's official. I am afraid, I mean really, really afraid," Alijah whispered.

Alessio breathed deeply, narrowed his eyes, and quietly agreed. "Sì, we need to pray."

The three held tight to one another and began their prayer. They struggled for words as the fear rose higher. "Dear Lord in heaven, our Father, our strength, please be with us now. If today we fall, we beg with all of our souls. We beg of you to take us home. We beseech you, please be with us now." They repeated the short prayer again and again.

One of the soldiers walked up to the cell and glared in for a moment before he spoke, "All right, girl, time to see the overseer."

Instinctively, Alessio grabbed Alijah and pulled her down behind him before he literally sat on top of her. He knew in the end he could not protect her against the heavily armed soldiers, but he was compelled to try.

The soldier stepped forward and pointed his rifle directly at Alessio's chest. In panic, Alijah screamed out, "No! I'll come, I'll come!" She snapped her arms and legs forward and wrapped them around Alessio as if she could've stopped a bullet. "No, please no! I'll come willingly."

Alessio struggled with his English, and his breathing became rapid. "No, you not go with them!" He tried to keep her pinned down.

"She doesn't have a choice. Get up." The soldier stepped forward and slammed the butt of his rifle into Alessio's forehead. The two women screamed as they watched his eyes roll back into his head. Chante instinctively jumped on top of Alessio and covered his head with her chest while Alijah pulled herself to her feet. The soldier grabbed her by the hair and dragged her out of the cell.

Chante cradled Alessio. There was nothing she could do but watch the cell doors slam shut and cry out for Alijah. The soldier turned around with a smirk on his face as he dragged Alijah by the hair into the center of the room.

> *So do not fear, for I am with you; do not be dismayed,*
> *for I am your God. I will strengthen you and help you;*
> *I will uphold you with my righteous right hand.*
>
> —*Isaiah 41:10*

CHAPTER 22

Alijah struggled to get to her feet, but the soldier had a handful of her hair. Her scalp felt as if it were on fire as he continued to drag her. Every time she got to her feet, the rubber soles of her old, worn-out tennis shoes caught on the marble tiles and caused her to stumble back to her knees. Instinctively, she reached down toward the floor with one hand, hoping to relieve some of the pull on her scalp.

She locked her other hand around the soldier's wrist and tried to fight back, but she couldn't gain any leverage. He dragged her all the way into the center of the room, where the single post, about forty-eight inches in length, stood waiting. Mr. Stevenson watched.

A mild voice carried throughout the room. "Now that is no way to treat a woman. Mr. Stevenson, I expect better."

"Yes, my lord." Mr. Stevenson reached down in a hurry to break the soldier's hold on Alijah's hair.

The soldier quickly released Alijah. With trembling in his voice, he responded, "Please forgive my deed, my lord. I meant no disrespect to your glory."

"Do not speak," the voice ordered.

The two men carefully helped Alijah to her feet and held her arms to steady her. They secured one of her wrists in a metal handcuff and attached the other cuff to a long chain. The chain was then threaded through the ring on the ram's head that was mounted on the post. At the other end of the chain was a short but stocky man with overly tanned skin and light-blonde hair. He kept the chain securely wrapped around his right hand.

"She is ready for you, my king," Mr. Stevenson said to the man at the desk.

Alijah's eyes focused on the handcuffs while she calculated the odds of breaking free. She had no idea what was about to happen to her, which frightened her beyond description. She could hear Chante and Alessio as they yelled out to her from behind the half wall.

"Be strong, baby, be strong!"

An eerie voice made its way to her ears. "Hello, my child. Are you in pain?" Alijah looked up and focused on the man who spoke. "I am your sovereign overseer, my child. I have brought you here simply to save you. To save your...beautiful...soul." Emil reached out his hand to touch her face.

When she looked at him, she saw the face of a man who was exceedingly handsome. His pitch-black hair was cut in a businessman's style that was neat, tailored, and clean. His eyes were as blue as the sea after a storm. His facial features were properly structured and placed, which left him with a flawlessly symmetric face. His six-foot-five frame was strong. He was a man whom many women would hope to have as a companion. But Alijah knew he was nothing but pure evil from the deepest levels of hell.

When his hand touched Alijah's cheek, she jumped backward, pulling on the chain as hard as she could. She caught the soldier holding the chain off guard, which caused him to drop it. She tried to run, but he caught the chain and jerked her back. The metal cuff dug into her skin and caused it to bleed. Her reaction had been sudden because what she felt in Emil's touch was an evil unlike anything she had ever imagined.

Mr. Stevenson and the soldier lifted her up and forced her forward. The soldier who had been holding the chain secured it to a hook on the floor by the fireplace. Emil looked on in silence.

"Now look at that. You have cut yourself." He looked over at another assistant and demanded, "Tell Pamela to tend to her wrist." Focusing his attention back on Alijah, he asked, "Now, why did you do that? How can you fear me? Am I not handsome to your eyes?" One corner of his mouth upturned in a smirk.

"I know what you are."

In his normal dramatics, Emil raised his hand and slowly waved it through the air. "I am here to help the human race rise above the chaos that has consumed it since your creation."

"You are the false prophet who will stand with the Antichrist. God is coming back, and you will be punished."

"Silence, cockroach!" the soldier behind Alijah shouted.

"No need for name-calling," Emil said sensitively. "Both of you. Alijah, you have much confusion. It is I who have come to save you."

"No, you haven't."

"It is not polite to accuse others of lying."

"You're a demon."

He snickered. "Do I look evil to your eyes? Do I appear to be a monster?"

"You aren't what you seem."

Emil leaned in closely. He stopped only about fifteen inches from her face. "Neither are you, little one. Neither are you."

"Second Corinthians eleven says that Satan himself masquerades as an angel of light. It is not surprising then if his servants also masquerade as servants of righteousness."

He placed his hand on his chest. "Those accusations are hurtful. Besides, you boast of your Lord, but did he not fail the world? He is the cause of all of this. Don't you know this?"

"Everyone blames God, but it's not his doing. He is my Shepherd, and he alone is my Savior. He is coming back and will reveal you to everyone."

"You really want to know, don't you? Well, look closely and see." Emil's facial features became almost translucent. Beneath the surface, Alijah could see a being that appeared to have been, at one time, a beautiful angel of God. She imagined this creature had been cast out from grace into the depths of hell long ago. Being banished from God's light and enduring centuries of suffering had created a tortured, frightening creature. His eyes appeared lifeless. Part of his face was charred and cracked and appeared malformed, as if the bones underneath had been broken many times and then healed out of place, creating a sharp, boney facial landscape.

His smug smile revealed his hatred of God. Alijah's peripheral vision caught a glimpse of shadowy wings that were singed and twisted. He lifted his partially burnt hands to grasp her shoulders. A feeling of nausea overcame her as she caught the foul stench of his breath as he whispered, "You all belong to the one whom I call father. Will you live on as a child of Lucifer and sit beside him as he rules for eternity, or will you die a horrific death today and spend eternity burning in the depths of hell?" He kissed her cheek.

She shivered and cried out to anyone in the room who would listen, "Didn't you see that? Didn't any of you, people, see that? He's a demon! He's evil!"

Emil moved several steps back to stand near Mr. Stevenson. "They see the truth. I am the only one who can stop them from burning in the fires of hell. Which, my child, is where you will be going."

"Christ has forgiven me. Therefore, I am saved and have no reason to fear death, demon."

"We will see. Bring my brother to me," Emil commanded. A hidden door opened from the wall behind Emil's desk, and a man emerged.

Alijah feared the worst. She couldn't escape the feeling that she was going to be tortured. She had no idea if she'd ever have the strength to fight it. Her mind ran wild with what might happen to her. She knew the only way the mark meant something was if she volunteered to take it. In her heart, she knew she would not be persuaded easily, but she questioned how much torture she could handle before she broke down. She remained on her knees, filled with trepidation about what was coming.

"Alijah? Alijah, open your eyes. It's me, Tony. Talk to me."

She opened her eyes quickly. "Tony? What are you doing here? We've been looking everywhere for you." Tony was looking wonderful, and it was clear he had been eating normally again. His face had filled out. He was clean-shaven, and he was wearing new clothes. "No, Tony, you gave in?"

He knelt to the floor in a nonthreatening posture. Eye to eye with Alijah, he said, "We were wrong, all wrong. Don't you see it? The God we've been praying to is the deceiver. He is the lie. Religion and all of those so-called Scriptures were lies meant to distract us from the true ruler of the—"

"What have they done to you? God is real, and he is coming. Please remember."

"No, love, we had it backward. Do you really think that a god would not know his teachings would be corrupted if left in the hands of humans? A true god would know that we couldn't be trusted." A wide smile broke across his face, and a small chuckle escaped from his lips. "The real god would hide his true identity until he was ready to come for us. Think about all the inconsistencies in the Scriptures, all the things that were not explained, and the only thing that religious leaders could say is we have to take it on faith. How convenient! Haven't you ever wondered why that is? Why would a god who claims to love us let his people suffer and die?" He leaned in closer. "Why would he let your baby sister be eaten alive by cancer? The pain, Alijah, she died in so much pain. And why would he give up on millions of his children whose only crime was losing their way? Why, Alijah, why?"

"We created the diseases that have ravished the human race. We corrupted ourselves. We were the ones who took God's words and twisted them into whatever suited our desires. We created the corrupt system. Please, Tony, remember. If it wasn't the rapture, then where did the millions of believers go? Why did only they disappear and not others?"

With a deep sigh, he replied, "Oh, Alijah, you are so wrong. No real god would abandon us in our hour of need."

"He has not abandoned us. God is the King, the one true Father of all of us. His Son is my Savior, and he will come back for me."

"Why do you insist on believing that rubbish? The true redeemer is coming, and he will only take you if you have rejected everything but him. The only way to do that, the only chance at an afterlife, is through our Grand Overseer Emil. There is no other way."

"God is the King of kings. His Son, Jesus Christ, is my Savior who is coming back for me."

Tony's voice began to show signs of agitation. "Focus, Alijah!" He placed both hands on her cheeks. "We are both so alone here." Sweetly, he whispered, "Stay with me. Take the mark. Stay with me, and we will stand together at the right hand of the real savior of this world. Wouldn't you like that?"

"God is the K—"

"Please. I don't want to be alone. Stay with me. For as long as we live, we won't be hungry again. For as long as we live, we will not suffer. The only thing you have to do is accept it, and I will free you right now. Your friends, I will release them too. I will give you everything you could ever want in this world. Look, here is the key." He reached out his hand to show her the same key he had been offered before he was taken. "Put your hand on it, and take it. It is the key to your freedom, their freedom, and our life together. It's my gift to you, and all you need to do is take it." He kissed her on the lips and whispered again into her ear, "Stay with me, and we will share a love unlike anything you could ever imagine. All you have to do is take the key."

Her chin trembled. "Why did you give in, Tony?"

"Take the key, love. It's your freedom. It's their freedom." He pointed to the cell.

Tears welled in her eyes, and her voice cracked. "God is the King of kings. His Son, Jesus Christ, is my Savior and—" Suddenly, she felt pain rush through her left cheek. She looked up to see Tony place his hand back into his pocket. His face was twisted and voice was filled with disgust and rage.

"If it wants the Creator so badly, then let's send it to meet him. Kill it."

"No, no, we wouldn't want to make her a martyr now, would we?" Emil snickered. "Didn't I tell you she would be stronger than that? We will continue the way I had intended in the first place. Bring the crew in now, and stand her up. Willing or not, she will belong to the true ruler of this place."

The soldiers quickly pulled her up to her feet and straightened out her clothes. Mr. Stevenson let out a snicker. "One should look her best before appearing on national television."

The camera crew consisted of five men and one female interviewer. The interviewer, Sally Tackett, was well known by the public. She had been the sole interviewer for Emil since the beginning of his second US presidential term. Anywhere that Emil wished to be seen, she was there.

Her interviews were always biased and had progressively gotten worse over time. They were nothing more than rehearsed plays acted out on a global stage. Any information she reported always showed Emil in nothing less than a radiant light. Alijah knew that whatever was going to happen that day, it would be spun into a tale of Emil's wondrous graciousness.

Alijah closed her eyes tightly and prayed without words. She wondered if Chante and Alessio had heard what was going on and wondered what they must have been thinking. Her mind was filled with dread as she played out the thoughts of what Emil and his minions might do to her and the other two. She knew she could do nothing to protect them. She focused on her breathing and tried to calm herself.

A wave of peace overcame her, and when she finally gained the courage to open her eyes, she was amazed. Beside Emil was an angel who looked much like Mavet. He had a crown on his head, and strands of his long white hair gently slid down his soft wings. He held a white bow and shield in his hands. His armor was white and had the language of God seared into the metal. Even though the angel stood beside Emil, he watched Alijah.

The angel offered a somber smile and dipped his head to her. Alijah reached her left hand out to him. "Please, help me! Save us."

Emil silently turned his head and searched for whom she was speaking to. The angel still did not speak.

"Please stop them. I beg of you, take us from here. Can't you see we're God's children?"

Emil barked at the crew to begin recording. "You will belong to my father, girl!"

The flames in the fireplace began to roar. A soldier in a pressed uniform took a fireplace poker from the mantel and stoked the fire. Sally checked her makeup and positioned herself to begin the interview. The camera crew performed their last-minute tasks and announced they were ready.

> *I consider my life worth nothing to me; my only aim is to finish the race and complete the task the Lord Jesus has given me—the task of testifying to the good news of God's grace.*
>
> *—Acts 20:24*

CHAPTER 23

Emil, with Tony beside him once again, stood in front of the large black camera and began another one of his long speeches. "Good afternoon, my children. I hope this day finds all of you well and happy." He displayed an enormous fake smile. "Beside me today is my brother, Tony, who has recently joined my staff to help. I have blessed you all with peace and serenity. All who know me have a good life of wealth and happiness. Across our globe, all who have the citizenry card and implant enjoy a plethora of food and exciting services to keep you healthy and contented. In fact, no one who knows me wants for anything at all."

Emil shook his head at the camera to illustrate his disbelief. "Yet there are those who still foolishly resist. As you know, a great many still await their false gods. They foolishly resist health, wealth, and serenity in the name of some invisible, unprovable version of a god. Some of them believe in it so wholeheartedly that they seek to dismantle our fine community and sabotage us." He frowned like a child and raised the pitch of his voice. "They wish to sabotage me! Until now, I have been forgiving enough to allow you who refuse me to live in wonderfully crafted apartments for free. You are given free food and electricity as well as many other needed services. I do everything I can to support you while you take the time to decide whom you would believe in." His voice dropped low again as it filled with sarcasm. "Am I so bad? Have I not proven to you that my intentions are altruistic and genuine? Have I forced you to pledge your allegiance to me?"

Emil lowered his head, and Tony sympathetically touched his shoulder to comfort him. Sally spoke her lines and asked a series of irrelevant questions clearly designed to make Emil look wonderful as usual. Her questions were short and rather unintelligent, such as how these events made him feel and why he so generously provided for everyone, including those who sought to destroy him.

Emil once again took control of the discussion. "Today, my fine people, is a glorious day. Today, I have before me one of my lost children who has chosen to give herself freely. Miss Alijah Rossi was faithless, angry, lost, alone, and hungry. She spewed lie after lie about me and has convinced her faithful companions to break every law they could. She held illegal baptisms to her false gods and prayer sessions in unauthorized sanctuaries, and she has convinced hundreds of people to follow her bogus religion."

The camera panned over to Alijah but quickly focused in on Emil once again. She took the opportunity to yell out in an effort to dispel Emil's lies, but one of the soldiers quickly taped her mouth shut. "Pay no mind to her ramblings, my people. What she says now is only her fear overtaking her. You've seen her body; she has fallen into a deep depression and starves herself. She withers away as punishment for the death of her family, of her little baby sister. Miss Rossi comes to me broken and afraid, but today, yes, my children, today she will be reborn into a world of light instead of the world of shadows she has been living in."

The soldier ripped the tape off her mouth, stinging her skin as the tape held on to the fine hairs on her face. When Alijah realized the camera was focused on her, she shouted, "He's evil! Christ is the Lord!" The camera panned back quickly. Mr. Stevenson raised his right arm and smacked her across the face.

"Listen to her not, for she has come to us with an evil addiction, an addiction that she will be cleansed of. Today, she will take the mark to show her allegiance to me, but because she is still filled with doubt and fear, we shall help her accept it. Miss Rossi will need to undergo a baptism by fire to completely purge her sins. What she screams out today is only her fears being released. Let us prepare her." Emil motioned the soldiers to gather the tools.

Cries from behind the wall rang throughout the room. "You're gonna burn her? Help her! Someone stop them!" Chante screamed.

Alijah continued her protest and recited different passages from the Bible. She repeated each passage louder than the last.

"Alijah, you waste your breath. All of your words will be edited out," Mr. Stevenson said happily.

The angel in white armor finally spoke, "Believe not the false prophet, for he cannot take what you do not offer."

Alijah turned her head in his direction. "Please! Help me!"

"The light of God shines upon you, young one."

At that moment, the soldier pulled the chain tight and forced Alijah's palm to lie across the ring, while another soldier pulled a branding iron from the fire. He walked toward Alijah.

Her eyes grew wide. "Oh God, no! No! No!"

Alessio bellowed from behind the half wall, "*Mostri*! Monsters!" The metal bars on the cell rattled as he repeatedly threw his body against the door in vain.

"Savages! Alijah, don't accept it, baby! Don't take the mark!" Chante yelled.

Alijah threw her head back and shouted to the heavens, "Please, don't leave me!"

Emil could not see the angel, but he could feel his presence. Infuriated, he growled, "She is mine." He took the branding iron from the hands of the soldier and pressed it hard against Alijah's hand. The most horrific pain traveled deep into her bones as the glowing iron seared its mark deep into her hand. The heat penetrated each capillary, each vein, and coiled itself like a serpent around the little bones throughout her hand and wrist. He left it against her skin while he laughed out loud to the heavens. "You can't have her!"

The blistering sound of her flesh burning was muted by her screams of anguish. Her shrieks filled the room and traveled throughout the building until the air in her lungs was completely diminished. Instinctively, she breathed in a deep gulp of air. The awful noises in her lungs rattled thunderously as her tears flowed like thick raindrops from the sky.

The smell of her scorched flesh filled the nostrils of everyone in the room. Alessio dropped to his knees and sobbed loudly. Chante leaned across his back and prayed out loud between her own cries. The two could not see where she was burnt or how bad it was, but the stench permeating the air made clear to them what had happened. Soldiers and news crew alike turned their heads from the horrendous scene. Sally stood behind one of the cameras and violently vomited.

Emil lifted the iron from her hand after leaving it on for what felt like several minutes. A part of her skin was stuck to the iron, which caused it to tear. Both Tony and Emil where quite pleased with their work and looked at the cameras again. Emil continued his long-winded speech and commanded everyone to rejoice because another soul had been saved. Once the cameras were turned off, Emil demanded that Sally come to him.

The newscaster had composed herself, but her bloodshot eyes gave her away; he knew she had been crying. He grabbed her chin and pulled her close. "Stop your blubbering, woman, or you will find the same fate." Tony reiterated Emil's comments to the camera crew and soldiers.

Alijah wept when she saw the mark of beast on her hand. She called out no between her coughs as she struggled for air. The angel came closer and knelt beside her.

"Child of El Shaddai, look at me."

She struggled to focus her vision on the angel, but her mind was filled with horrifying thoughts of damnation. She could barely speak because her voice was failing her. "Make it go away," she pleaded.

He kept his hands by his side. "It is not my place to intervene."

"Please, help...," her last words trailed off until she became completely inaudible.

He tenderly lifted her chin. "The Father has not forsaken you, child. Remember, it is only the flesh that has failed and not the soul. Seek sanctuary in your forest, for I bring the first of the judgments."

"No! She is mine!" Emil bellowed as he charged forward. His words echoed throughout the large room. "You cannot have her!" Emil became ferocious and lashed out. He threw furniture around the room and shouted out in a language no one understood. Tony watched in anger and huffed like a raging bull being challenged by a matador's red cape. The angel stayed beside Alijah and smiled.

Tony lifted his right arm and shook his fist. "Out, all of you, out!"

The room cleared quickly, and only Tony and Mr. Stevenson remained with Emil. Mr. Stevenson removed the handcuffs and helped Alijah to her feet. The angel moved back beside Emil.

"Angel!" Emil spoke as if he were vomiting each word. "Your kind is not welcome here. It is my father's time to reign. Leave this place. I command it!" His face twisted as he lost all control, briefly revealing his true identity.

Mr. Stevenson's eyes grew large as he watched Emil. He was startled by the revelation that overcame him. This was the first time he had seen Emil in his true form. "She's right. It's all real."

Tony stormed over and kicked a stray chair out of the way. It suddenly dawned on Mr. Stevenson that he had been overheard, but it was too late. Tony reached back and punched him in the temple, hard enough to knock the large muscular man to the floor. "Do not look upon him, you putrid parasite. You are the lowest among the servants of the true ruler of this world and will never be worthy of looking upon his soldiers." Tony immediately ordered him to take Alijah back to her cell and then focused his attention on calming Emil.

Mr. Stevenson walked her back and opened the cell door. He told Alijah, "It's going to get worse, a lot worse. Think of them." He pointed toward Alessio and Chante. "I know what he intends to do to your friends, and believe me, what you suffered today, he means to do much worse to them. We are all damned. It's just time to accept it."

"She belongs to God, not the beast," Chante said.

Mr. Stevenson helped her into the cell and right into the arms of Alessio. "Don't be stupid. Do you really think you can win? There's no way out of here. There's no way out of any of this."

Alessio and Chante took hold of Alijah's arms. Chante stood still and stared at Mr. Stevenson. "Because we believe in God and our Lord Jesus Christ, because we have unwavering faith in their grace and goodness, we have already won. It is you who needs saving."

Frightened, Alessio's Italian accent grew strong, and he fought to enunciate. "*Signore*, please. Go aways. Leave the door open and walk aways."

Mr. Stevenson looked down and turned his head as he pulled the cell door until he heard the click of the lock. The man looked back at Alijah with great sadness deep in his eyes and then walked away with his head hung low.

Alijah wrapped her hand with the bottom of her shirt and then buried her head into Alessio's shoulder. They led her to the back of the cell, where they sat and wrapped the only blanket they had around her. Alessio wrapped his arms around the girls and held them both securely. Chante pressed her head against Alijah's head and began to pray again.

Alessio wept hard and begged her for forgiveness. He grieved aloud for his failure to protect her. "I should have not stayed behind. I should have run with you. If I had, maybe I could have stopped them from—"

"Hon, it's not your fault." Chante put her hand on his arm. "You could not have stopped them from taking her any more than Michel could save me. Except"—she drew in a breath—"we would have lost you too."

Alijah pushed up and tried to settle into a seated position between the other two's tangled legs. Her face showed her anguish. Dark circles surrounded her bloodshot eyes; her skin was pale; and her hair was a tousled mess. Every time she breathed in, a low-pitched wheezing could be heard. Chante wiped away Alijah's tears with her thumbs and then pushed the hair falling on her face back behind her ears.

"There's an angel here," Alijah tried to speak out. "The first horseman."

Alessio looked at Alijah, but no words came out. Tears crept slowly down Chante's cheeks, but she was able to respond. "An angel? If there's one here, why didn't he help you?"

"He said he couldn't intervene. This was my trial, I guess."

"He spoke? What did he say to you?"

A sharp pain in Alijah's head tormented her. She reached up with her left hand to rub the back of her head. "I really need an aspirin."

"Sweetheart, what did the angel say?"

She looked down at her right hand that was still wrapped in her T-shirt. Her voice was raspy. "It hurts so bad. I never imagined anything hurting so bad."

Chante touched Alijah's chin and lifted her head to meet her eyes. "Baby, I know, I know it hurts. I can't even imagine what you are going through—"

"He laughed as he marked me."

Alessio spoke up, "Alijah, remember, you must remember. No one can force you to take the mark. If they do, it means nothing."

Chante rubbed Alijah's shoulder. "That's right, baby. He's right. You are not damned."

Alijah whispered, "That's what he said."

"The angel? Did the angel tell you that? And what else did he say?"

Alijah stared at the floor and whispered, "It hurts so bad."

Chante rubbed her cheeks. "Please focus, sweetheart. What did he say?"

Alijah managed to get a deep breath of air and sniffled. She tried to recall the angel's words. "He said that the beast couldn't take what isn't offered to him. He said God hasn't forsaken me." She stared off into the distance and became lost in thought again.

"Alijah? Alijah, is that all he said to you?"

She looked back at Chante with worried eyes. "Alessio, Chante, the angel...you guys, the angel said we have to get out of here. He said we have to seek safety in the forest because he's here to bring the first judgment. We have to find a way out because it's going to get a lot worse."

"All right, ladies, we need to figure a way out, no?"

Alessio unraveled Alijah's hand from her shirt. The skin was charred and flaky. Bright-red lines encased the emblem of the new world; the mark would be completed once the microchip was inserted. Around the destroyed skin were patches of white with small amounts of oozing blood puddled up from where a layer of skin had peeled back. Chante shuddered and turned away.

Alessio breathed in heavily. "Mostri!" He hesitated and turned his eyes away. "We have to get you to a doctor. This is bad, very bad."

Startled, the three turned toward the front of the cell. A soldier, the same one who had dragged Alijah by her hair, stood at the door. "Poor little lost lambs. Your shepherd came and went, leaving you all behind. Now the little lambs better follow their new shepherd before they go to the slaughter." He snickered before he rattled the door and walked off.

"I would like to call him something foul right now."

"I as well, Chante. I as well," Alessio agreed. "Now what can we do about the hand?"

He rinsed off Alijah's wound with the bottled water he still had. Alijah tried to control her screams the best she could, but the pain was excruciating.

Chante held Alijah close. "I don't think we should cover this up with material, hon. Anything we use will stick to it, and I certainly don't want it to be material from one of our old dirty shirts."

A few hours later, the trio fell asleep in the corner, holding tight to one another. From within the darkness of the night, a soft voice called to them. "Alijah, Alijah. Wake up!"

In her drowsy state, Alijah whispered back to the darkness, "Who's there?" She squinted hard to glimpse anything.

"It's Alex."

"Alex?"

Chante and Alessio stood quickly and helped Alijah up. The three stumbled to the cell door. Alex was in full uniform, but it was a uniform that was unfamiliar to them. "Please help us, Alex," Chante pleaded.

"Listen, I don't have much time. The change of the watch is in forty-eight minutes. I'm not supposed to be here since I'm just a foot soldier, but when I found out you'd been captured, I felt it. I knew what I had to do."

Alessio questioned, "How did you know where we were?"

"I didn't. I just knew you were captured. It was all over the TV. They had been announcing your public assimilation for days, but when they tried to air you taking the mark, something happened to the video. It was blank."

Chante blurted out, "What? Do you mean everything they did to her was never televised?"

"Nope." Alex stifled a chuckle. "I hear Emil was furious."

"Do the people think she converted?"

"No, not at all, from what I hear." Alex met Alijah's eyes and hesitated before he continued, "There are others...like you."

She scowled. "Like me?"

"Yeah, like you. They are calling you a beacon. The others too. Beacons to the truth and the light of Christ. They are saying those like you have been chosen by Christ himself to bring all believers together before the worst judgments are poured onto the earth. From what I hear, those like you are scattered across the world. Your strength, faith, and hope are like a light that the followers of Christ have a need to find. Your light calls them together." He paused again when he saw that Alijah was confused and irritated.

"You know how you've helped me, how you've helped everyone in your dormitory, for that matter? Well, the word spread quickly. Exiles from all over Washington are traveling to find you. Alijah, people who never even heard of you know who you are, and they are traveling here to find you."

"That's absurd, Alex. I'm nobody."

"You're wrong. You are a beacon." He looked over his shoulder to be sure no one had walked in. "Rumors have been soaring through the ranks. They say that almost two weeks ago, believers left their dorms in search of you. No one can explain it, but they just knew it was time to find you."

She shook her head. "That can't be right. Think about it, Alex. We were arrested just a few days ago." Chante and Alessio shook their heads in agreement.

Alex looked stunned. "Guys, you all were arrested nearly five weeks ago." They didn't speak but just looked at Alex as if he had lost his mind. "I had no idea who your doctor friend was, either, but I heard something. It was a voice, a voice that was kind and gentle. It told me to go to the forest. I just started walking, and there he was. I knew you were being held for assimilation, but I didn't know you were here at the capitol. Think about it. Why would Emil be so angry over an ordinary deviant? I mean, I'm sorry, that's Emil's description of Christians."

"I'm confused," Alessio admitted with a deep sigh.

"Look, we're running out of time. Your friend Doc is waiting for you. He too knew you were alive and knew that you needed him. I told him I would come for you. I'm gonna get you out of here, and when I do, we have to head straight to the Ark so you're there when the others arrive."

"The Ark?" Chante inquired.

"That's what they're calling that community Doc is in. Now how bad is that burn?"

Alessio wrapped his arms around the girls. "Bad. It's real bad."

"Here." Alex handed a small bundle to Chante. "Doc said you'd need this. Now go ahead, and wrap her hand up, and I'll be back"— he looked down at his watch—"in thirty-seven minutes. Be ready, because we're going to have to move fast."

Alex snuck out the back door. Alessio looked through the white bundle to find a small bottle of burn cream, a sterile bandage, and a wrap. Alijah's friends worked quickly to wrap up her hand and gather whatever supplies they had left. They wrapped the small blanket around Alijah's shoulders, put their shoes on, and pretended to sleep while they waited in the corner.

> *Do not let your hearts be troubled. You believe in God; believe also in me. My Father's house has many rooms... If I go and prepare a place for you, I will come back and take you to be with me that you also may be where I am. You know the way to the place where I am going.*
>
> —*John 14:1–4*

Chapter 24

"Pssst. Let's go."

The three jumped up and headed to the door. "We ready," Alessio whispered back.

"We have to move fast," Alex warned as he unlocked the door. "I had to knock someone out to steal this uniform just to get in here, and then I had to take care of four other soldiers to clear the way. With that many missing soldiers here at the capitol, it's going to draw attention. Come on!"

The group stayed low and hustled through the darkened corridors. On the way through the building, Alex explained that since Alijah entered the capitol building, the lights in the hallways all over the building had been out. Emil demanded that electricians work around the clock to figure out what was wrong.

Chante whispered, "That's a help."

"Or a blessing," Alessio murmured.

They came to the final hallway. "Up ahead is the exit. I took care of the two soldiers who guard it. It's the staff entrance, and at this time of night, there should be no traffic at all. With a blessing from God, no one will have noticed they're missing."

Alessio held tight to Alijah's waist. "It was a long drive to the capitol. How are we going to get back to the woods behind the dorms?"

Alex turned back to him. "There's an official car parked in the back that the news staff uses."

Chante looked at him. "Do you know how to hot-wire a car?"

"Nope. I know how to use a key, though." He faked a smile. "I stole it a few hours ago."

Alessio took Alijah's hand. "Chante, come—take ahold of my belt. Hold tight."

Chante moved behind Alessio and grabbed both his and Alijah's waistbands. "I'm ready."

"Quiet." Alex put his hand out.

An unfamiliar voice from behind the door said, "Where's Richard and Trevor? Aren't they on duty tonight?"

"Yeah, but they're probably patrolling the area. It's about that time," someone with a raspy voice responded.

"Kenny, did you, ah, did you hear about that woman Emil has up in his war room?"

"Do you mean the one both Emil and Tony were hell-bent on finding?"

"That's the one. Did you hear what they did to her?"

Kenny lowered his voice. "He burned her pretty bad, from what I hear. Why, though? Do you have any idea who she is, Sven?"

Sven lowered his voice even more, which made it difficult for Alex and the others to hear. "I hear they think she's some kind of chosen one. She's convinced a whole lot of people that there really is a god. If you ask me though, I think there's a lot more to it all because she actually scares Emil and Tony both."

"How can a woman scare those two? They're animals."

"You remember the four alpha soldiers who were up there to protect Emil's war room? Well, they said he was yelling about an angel. The girl was talking to someone who wasn't there. It freaked Emil out, and he started throwing furniture around and talking in some bizarre language. They said Tony kicked everyone out, but not before a couple of the guys noticed something was wrong with Emil's face. They said it...it...changed, and he wasn't human."

A voice came over the radio. "Delta eleven team, do you copy?"

Kenny responded, "Delta eleven here, over."

"This is command central. An alarm is going off in the southwest entrance. Check it out now, over."

"Copy that command. Delta eleven out."

Before the soldiers' voices trailed off in the distance, Alex could hear one of them add, "Man, what if what she's saying is true? What if that prophecy is true?"

"Sven, if it's true, we're in a lot of trouble."

Alex stuck his ear to the door. "I don't hear them anymore. Do you?"

Alessio shook his head. "I cannot hear them either. Do you think it is safe to go?"

Alex listened for a few more seconds. "I don't hear a thing." He looked back at Alijah. "I have to get you out of here." He stood to his feet and reached for the doorknob.

Alijah broke the momentary silence. "Wait, Alex, what if someone is guarding the door now? They could kill you."

He looked down at the floor. "Alijah, my fate is sealed. I took the mark. My life isn't important anymore. What is essential is that one of God's beacons needs to be put in place to save those who can still be saved." He turned the knob.

"Don't say that—"

He put his index finger over his lips and slowly opened the door, being as quiet as possible. He pushed through the doorway and searched carefully for any signs of life. When he saw the way was clear, he placed the ignition key between his fingers and signaled to the trio. "It's clear. Hurry."

Chante and Alessio each grabbed an arm and got Alijah quickly to her feet. She was dazed, still suffering from shock. The agonizing feeling in her hand had grown to the point that her whole body shook. The pain traveled up past her elbow and shoulder and up into her neck. It took all her strength to muffle her cries, and she did her best to lift each foot until she reached a jogging speed with Alessio.

Chante could hear the low whimpering moans. "Hold on, baby. We're almost there." Alex crouched low and ran ahead to open the car. He continuously checked around them to be sure no one was in sight and then cautiously unlocked and opened each door. He did one final check before he went back to help them get Alijah to the car. "Jesus, I know I haven't bothered to listen to you before, and I know I haven't given you any reason to forgive me, but I'm begging you now, please help me get them out of here. Please help me save them." Alex handed the keys to Chante and asked her to get into the driver's seat. "Be ready to start it, and drive as soon as we're in the car. Keep the headlights off. We can't chance drawing any attention."

"What's going on here?" a voice from behind shouted.

Chante held tight to the driver's side door and the roof of the car. She had only been able to get her right foot into the car. Alex and Alessio stopped in their tracks.

"Alessio, get her to the car." Alex turned toward the voice.

Alessio hesitated, acting as if he were going to stay and help Alex. Alijah's eyes rolled back into her head, and she lost her balance and fell to the pavement. Alessio snapped his head toward her and quickly swept her up into his arms. He made his way to the car, cradling her. He struggled because malnutrition and injuries had made him weak.

Alex looked toward the voice. "I'm moving the prisoners to the detention center."

The soldier walked forward and shouted, "I don't think so. Get over here now."

Alex pointed toward the building. "You don't think so? Tony himself ordered the transfer. You've got a problem with it? Then take it up with him, if you're dumb enough to." He turned around and headed for the car.

"Watch your mouth, boy. I didn't sign off on any transfer orders. As a matter of fact, I know the overseer has a special interest in that little lady. I also know that Tony has plans for her two friends. So you want to try a different one?"

Alex continued to walk until he was right behind Alessio. "All right, all right. I have the orders in the car."

The man continued after them. He demanded, "Girl, get away from that car, and the rest of you had better stop. I'll call this in."

Alex froze in place. Alessio turned back to look while he held Alijah against his chest.

She looked at the strange man. In fear, she spoke out, "I know him. He's that man who arrested me. Captain Davidson." Alessio squeezed her as closely as he could.

"Go. Just go." Alex turned back to the captain. "No, you stay where you are, boy," he said with a snarl. He lifted his handgun and pointed it at Davidson. His hands trembled.

Davidson sneered at Alex. "You worthless piece of Christian trash. Your pathetic kind doesn't have the fight in them to shoot anyone. Now put it down before you hurt yourself."

Alex continued to walk backward with his sight fixed on Davidson. "How confident are you in those calculations? Get her in the car, Alessio."

Alessio froze in place with Alijah still in his arms. "Alex, he's not worth it. You come."

Davidson walked forward slowly, and Alex took another step back. The captain continued forward, gradually closing the distance. "That's a little violent for you, people. You want to know what I think? I think you're bluffin'."

Alijah's hand rested lightly on his shoulder. "Alex..."

Alex kept his focus, but his breathing became labored. "Get her in the car, man!" His sweaty palms hindered him from keeping a steady grip on the gun. He watched as Davidson finally came to a complete stop. "It doesn't have to go down like this. You turn your back, and we'll leave. It's that simple. Emil's evil, and his so-called brother isn't much better, and what's coming is a lot worse. The prophecy is true. Are you going to seal the deal with the beast, or are you going to seek forgiveness?"

Davidson shook his head. "Forgiveness." He chuckled. "Please! I'm a loyal servant of the next ruler of this world. I got nothin' to worry about, unlike you worthless Christians." He slowly moved his right hand behind his waist.

Alex released his hand from the gun and rotated it to reveal his mark before he placed it back on the grip of the gun. "That's where you're wrong. I'm no Christian." He pulled the trigger.

Davidson hit the ground and screamed out in pain. Alex turned and ordered Chante to start the car, and then he spoke to Alessio and Alijah, "I only shot him in the leg, but it should buy us enough time to get out of here."

Davidson spewed his hatred. "You're worse than Christians. You're a betrayer to your own kind, and you're gonna burn for it, boy! Burn!"

Alex turned his head and lifted his gun again, but it was too late. Davidson raised his bloody hand and revealed his gun. He pointed it directly at Alijah and pulled the trigger. The piercing gunshot thundered through the night air, stinging their ears.

"No!" Alex swiftly moved to block the path of the bullet. Alessio gasped, and Chante shrieked. Before Alessio had the chance to react, he was knocked over by the force of Alex's body being thrown into him. Alessio and Alijah collapsed on the pavement, and Alex landed on top of them. Alijah reached her injured hand around to Alex's chest and tried to elicit a response. Davidson laughed and cocked his pistol for another shot.

Chante tried desperately to start the car, but in her state of panic, she flooded it. "God, please help us! My Lord Jesus, save us."

Alessio could only watch as Davidson hobbled toward them. Every muscle in his body suffered from extreme fatigue, and combined with the weight of both Alijah and Alex on top of him, he couldn't move or reach Alex's gun. He watched the large man move slowly in the moonlight. Over his head, Alessio could see the blue four-door sedan waiting. He could almost reach out and touch it.

Davidson stopped and hovered near the three of them. He glared down with evil in his dark brown eyes. "Looks like you lose." He raised his gun and pointed it directly at Alijah's head.

Alessio reached with his free arm, pulled Alijah's head back to his chest, and covered her eyes. "You no look, momma. My girls, I love you both, and I see you in heaven beside our Lord." His voice cracked right before he grimaced and locked his jaw. When the car started, Chante scrambled to reach the passenger door to grab Alessio. The next gunshot broke the silence of the windless night.

> *Seek the Lord while he may be found; call on him while he is near. Let the wicked forsake their ways and the unrighteous their thoughts. Let them turn to the Lord, and he will have mercy on them, and to our God, for he will freely pardon.*
>
> —Isaiah 55:6–7

CHAPTER 25

Everything was still. No words, no sounds. Chante reached over and touched Alessio's head. Tears rapidly flowed from his closed eyes. He continued to hold Alijah's body closely. Chante whimpered, "No, oh please, no." The next shot was fired.

An unfamiliar voice spoke, "Come on, get up." Chante was the first to open her eyes. The voice whispered to her, "You need to get back in the driver's seat, miss. Get ready to go. Other soldiers are coming."

Alessio opened his eyes and saw Mr. Stevenson with a gun in his hand. Near him, Captain Davidson's body was sprawled out on the ground.

Alessio reached back and touched Chante's cheek. He looked down and whispered, "Alijah?" He met her eyes, which gave away her bewilderment. "Are you okay?"

Alijah quickly looked over her shoulder at Mr. Stevenson. "You? Why?"

Mr. Stevenson sighed and knelt down beside Alex. "I, uh, I was watching on the cameras in the security room. When this one here opened the cell door, it triggered a silent alarm. I followed you out." He looked down at Davidson. "I hated that man." He sighed and looked back at Alijah. "I believe it. I believe it all. It's far too late for me, but you, Alijah, you have a purpose."

"Alex!" Alijah called out.

Mr. Stevenson had reached down and was beginning to lift Alex. "He's still breathing, but I don't think he has much time. He was shot in the chest." The sound of barking dogs traveled from around the building. "No time to talk. We've got to get you all out of here."

Chante clambered back into the driver's seat. Mr. Stevenson cradled Alex in his arms while Alessio helped Alijah into the backseat. The pain in her hand and head was intensifying. She struggled to stay conscious, but she knew she had to stay awake to help care for Alex.

"Put him back here," she said.

Mr. Stevenson closed Alessio's door and went over to Alijah. He placed his hands on the lowered window. "Alijah, for what it's worth, I'm sorry." He glanced down at the pavement. "I just wanted you to know that."

"Come with us." She reached out to him.

"No, I'm dead already." The barking grew louder. "You've got to go. Now!"

He stood to meet the approaching soldiers. He reached back and hit the car with his fist before he raised his gun.

Two soldiers emerged from the darkness. "You there, out of the car, now!" Chante put it in gear and pushed down on the gas pedal. Alijah looked back in time to see Mr. Stevenson open fire. She could see the sparks of light each time a bullet exited his and the soldiers' guns. Suddenly, she saw nothing but darkness, and she knew Mr. Stevenson was gone.

Her heart was heavy for him. Even though he was a part of her imprisonment and torture, in the end, he came to their rescue. As they drove away, the building faded into the distance. The road ahead of them was long, and she was panicked about what might follow them. She knew very well if Emil had been that determined to convert her, he certainly wouldn't allow her to escape so easily.

Chante stirred Alijah from her thoughts. "Do you know how to get back to the dorms without using the freeway?"

Alex tried to speak in between coughs but mostly choked on blood. "No, stay on the freeway, the fastest way."

Alijah found a UCNN jacket on the floor and pressed it against his chest. "No one will be looking for this car for a few more days." He drew in a gasp of air. "I swiped it from the network's fleet. Those chumps will be looking for...one of the cars from the capitol's security force." He struggled for air. "Buy us some—"

"Stop talking, sweetheart," Chante interrupted.

Alex was lying with his head in Alijah's lap and his knees up against the window. She laid her blanket across him and tried to keep him warm.

"I'll stay on the freeway then. If we can stay on it, we'll get to the dorms in about four hours." She glanced at Alessio.

Alessio got on his knees in the front seat to reach back to Alex. "Press it down on the wound. Keep the pressure on it. *Si?*" He watched Alex's face.

Alex was pale and shivering more by the minute. "He's losing a lot of blood, Alessio."

"I'm scared." Alex could barely get the words out. "I know I can't survive this—" The coughing became so bad that he couldn't finish his sentence.

Alessio's breathing became rapid and shallow, and he whispered to Chante, "I no think he's gonna make it. He's no looking good." He looked back and asked Chante to lead a quick prayer.

For the moment, Alijah forgot about the excruciating pain in her hand and head. "Stay with us, Alex. We love you. Please hold on. We're not giving up on you, so don't you dare give up on us." She held his hand over her heart and watched him diligently.

* * * * *

Emil had run up the price of gas, making it impossible for anyone other than government workers and the wealthy to own and drive cars. For mile after mile, the long trip home was oddly quiet. The moon and stars were dim, so the night was dark, cold, and lonely. The cars and trucks on the road were only official government vehicles and a few private cars.

The streetlights that the quiet group of friends steadily traveled past did their part in illuminating the way. Chante kept the small network car at a steady pace. She kept close to the speed limit to avoid any chance of standing out. No one spoke for more than half the ride home.

"How is he?" Chante asked quietly.

"He fell asleep. I know he probably shouldn't be sleeping, but his breathing is steady. I don't think he can make it much longer," Alijah whispered. She tried to get comfortable in the white leather seats. The neon-green glow of the dashboard illuminated the darkened interior.

Alessio woke up and quickly looked around. "Sorry, I fell asleep. Is everyone—" He paused and looked back.

"Hanging in there," Alijah reassured him.

He sighed and settled back down into his seat. "Chante, how are you? Do you need a break? I drive?" His rhythmic accent wavered as he searched for words.

"I'm okay, and we're almost there. We've been driving for four hours, so it shouldn't be much longer."

"I'm sorry."

"It's okay, sweetheart." She reached her right hand over to stroke Alessio's cheek. You two have taken the brunt of the beatings. They never got a chance to get to me. You need the rest more than I do."

"Turn off, now!" Alijah shouted.

Chante was stunned for a second. "What?"

She slapped the top of Alessio's seat repeatedly. "Now, now, right there." She pointed at the upcoming exit. "That one."

Chante slowed the car and quickly turned off. "What's wrong, baby? Why did we turn?"

"I don't know, something in my head just said to turn off. We need to look for Jackson Street. I think there's an entrance to the southwest side of the national park at the end of that road."

Alessio interrupted, "But the forest is tremendous. To enter this far off from where we usually go could get us lost. And where are we going to go once we arrive? Are we going to the doctor friend? Do you know where to find him?"

"Yes, we need to find him. I have no idea how to get to him from here, but I know we need to go this way."

After a few miles, Chante brought the car to a stop. She let out a little gasp and pointed at the highway in the distance. "Do you see that?" They looked out the windows and saw in the distance that all cars were stopped, and flashing red-and-white emergency lights pierced the darkness. "It's a road block. Alijah, how did you know?"

"Aye, momma, how could you know that?"

"I don't know. I just did. But we've got to get moving. We don't want anyone to see us just idling on the side of the road." Alijah continued to care for Alex even though she knew her efforts would be in vain. The bleeding had slowed, but the wheezing sound changed and grew worse.

The rale in his chest alarmed them all. A new, dreadful bubbling sound came from him, but his friends were not ready to give up on him. As they drove the final stretch to the entrance of the forest, Alijah continued to pray for his salvation.

When they finally arrived, Chante drove the car as far as she could into the lush green trees. Alessio covered it with as much of the green-and-brown brush and broken limbs as he could find. They hoped to hide the car enough so that it could be days to weeks before anyone would locate it. Close by was an old forest-ranger station that had long been abandoned. The vegetation in the area obviously had not been cared for in several years.

Dawn was breaking. Alessio searched the abandoned station thoroughly for any type of supplies that could help them through the next leg of the journey. The only things he could find were a few tattered, dusty blankets, an old medical kit with nothing more than a few Band-Aids, and a couple of oil lamps.

"Well, it's not much, but it's something. We need to help keep some body heat in." He gathered everything and headed back outside.

Chante and Alijah worked their way through the car. They found three UCNN jackets, a flashlight, one bottle of water, and few candy bars. Alijah let out a nervous giggle. "I think it's been over a year since I've had chocolate."

"I used to love chocolate, and Michel, now, Michel was the chocolate hound. I always had to hide few bars of candy for myself, or he would devour all the chocolate in the house." Chante smiled.

"For many years, I told Mother that I be sure chocolate was a food group," Alessio chimed in.

Alex coughed hard. "It's so cold," he whimpered.

Chante quickly put a jacket on him and wrapped one of the old green blankets around his shoulder. They wrapped Alijah's blanket tightly around his chest, trying to keep some pressure on the wound. The others covered up as much as possible before they began their trek into the lonely woods.

"No, no, Alessio, you wear the jacket," Chante demanded.

He shook his head briskly. "You take it." She tried to protest, but he continued to put it over her shoulders. "You must have it. I be fine. Do not worry about me. The sun is coming up, and I be warm enough." He turned and wrapped the other jacket around Alijah, insisting she keep her hand warm and protected, and he put the dusty blanket around his head and shoulders.

Chante and Alessio placed Alex's arms over their shoulders and picked him up. Alijah joined in by putting her left hand into her pocket and threading Alex's feet between her waist and arm. The group started into the dense forest. They knew it would be tough because of the temperature and their exhaustion. The beatings Alessio had endured left him weak and in pain. Chante had driven all night and had trouble keeping her eyes open. Alijah, still suffering from the trauma she had undergone, struggled to just stay on her feet.

The sun rose in the soundless morning sky. The group walked for an hour before they surrendered to their exhaustion. Huddled together, they leaned against a thick tree and shared small sips of water. Even though the sun was doing its best to warm the damp forest, the temperature was staying in the low forties. The majesty of the forest was breathtaking, but Alijah shook from the cold. Her body fought to hold on to the little bit of heat it had.

A dreadful cough emanated from Alex before blood spattered across Alijah's lap. A second later, his head fell onto her shoulder and slid down her chest. She scrambled to cradle him. "What happened?"

Chante and Alessio cuddled around them to block the blistering cold winds. Chante pulled off her jacket and laid it across his chest. "It's all right, baby. We're not leaving you behind." She leaned toward Alessio and whispered in his ear, "Judging from that noise in his chest, the bullet must've penetrated his lung."

Alex's jaw quivered. "Do you think I'm forgiven"—he looked off between the trees and pointed—"or are you here to take me to hell?"

From between the mighty trees, a figure approached slowly. Panicked, Alessio called out, "Who's there?"

The petite figure stopped beside Chante and knelt. The pale-skinned woman with piercing dark eyes was dressed in a silky white robe and had a blue sash around her waist. She wore silver armor and carried a bow in her hand. Her arrows were mounted securely on her back. "Fear not, disciples, for I mean no harm."

Chante's voice cracked as she asked, "Are you an angel?"

"But you have no wings," Alessio said.

"Our wings are often hidden from your kind. It is unnecessary for most humans to be aware of our presence."

Alijah put her hand on Alessio's shoulder. She recognized the engravings on the armor. "Look at the writing. It's the language of God."

Alex gasped. Alijah pulled her right leg up to support him the best she could and asked the stranger, "Why are you out here? Was it you who called me here?"

The angel slowly blinked and placed her bow on the ground beside Alessio. "You bear the mark of El Shaddai. Only the weak of faith and those who bear the mark of the deceiver need fear the judgments." She looked over at Alijah with interest. "It was not I who drew you here. Messiah himself speaks to the beacons."

The windy forest chilled their bones even though the sun was steadily climbing higher. Alijah cleared the blood from Alex's face. "Please, please. Alex is a good man. He is the reason why I'm alive, the reason why we all are alive. I know he took the mark, but he believes. He was baptized and has begged for forgiveness. Please, is there anything we can do to save him?"

Alessio and Chante both wrapped their arms around Alijah and Alex as they searched the angel's face for an answer.

The angel reached for Alex's hands. "I see before me children of El Shaddai." She turned his hands to show neither hand had the mark.

"It's gone! The burn is gone and so is the mark. Ladies, do you see?" Alessio pointed to Alex's hands and then touched the angel. "He has been forgiven?"

The angel placed Alex's hands on his chest and smiled at him. "You laid your course of your own free will, bound for the gates of hell. However, child, the Father has turned his ear to you once again and has heard your cries for redemption. To him who is all, you have offered your mortal body as recompense for your offenses." She looked up again to address their pleas for help. "It is he who offered his own life in place of yours. It is by his sacrifice you may complete your task."

"Alex, look at your hands! There's no mark, no burns. Alex, you've been forgiven." Alijah tilted his head enough where he could see his hands. "You found your way to Christ, and God has forgiven you."

He looked down at his hands and then turned his eyes to meet Alijah's. "I am?"

The group quietly waited while the angel looked up at the clouds and treetops in silence. She stared up for several moments before returning her gaze. "His mortal days have come to a conclusion. Alex, as you call him, has been called home. It is time to bid him farewell."

Almost hysterical, the group wept for the loss of another friend. They held tight and prayed one more time with Alex. Chante reached out to the angel and hoped to convince her to allow just a little more time. "We've had so little time to have Alex in our lives. Can't we have just a little bit more?"

The angel gently swayed her head from side to side. "I cannot comprehend your reluctance. Is it not your desire for him to sit beside the Creator? Explain yourself."

"Well, yes, we prayed every day for guidance in teaching him. We thought it impossible for him to find salvation. I never believed we would be able to help someone like him. Our hearts are filled with an indescribable joy that our friend has been granted deliverance, but we are deeply, deeply saddened in losing him so soon."

"It is time for celebration, not mourning. He will wait for you in heaven beside Lord Jesus." She ran her fingers along her bow to reflect on something unknown to them. "Your choice of words intrigues me. Impossible? Have you not yet learned that in the Father, everything is possible?"

Alijah wiped the corners of Alex's mouth and said, "But he willingly took the mark."

The angel gazed at them. "The Lord God has never desired the destruction of his people. Even as the end of your time draws near, he leaves the gates of heaven open to all who repent and seek him." She turned to Chante. "What was, still is. It is why the Christ died in your place. His gift to your kind has neither dwindled nor faltered in any manner."

"Amazing." Alessio shook his head. "It felt impossible to save anyone who accepted the mark of the beast."

"The bondage of the mark is eternal. However, Lord Jesus has found favor with this child." The angel paused for a moment. "You must remember that what seems to be an insurmountable task often only feels that way. Understand that the sons and daughters of perdition render themselves sightless with their unwillingness to differentiate lies from the truth. They look to the mountain before them with no desire to seek the meadow that lies beyond. Your love and devotion to the Lamb of God has given you an enormous strength, a strength that has helped you move the very mountain that separated this soul from the light of the Creator. The Lord Jesus has chosen you three to travel the journey together—the teacher, the guardian, and the beacon."

She paused for a moment and reached for Alex. The wind stopped unexpectedly, and an eerie silence fell on the forest. Alijah brought her head down close to Alex's forehead for a tender kiss. She whispered close to his ear, "We wouldn't be alive if it wasn't for you. You're my brother in Christ, and I will always remember you and the beautiful sacrifice you made today." She led a prayer to thank Christ for placing him in their lives and for accepting Alex into heaven.

Chante and Alessio leaned in closely to join the prayer. They offered their love and gratitude for what their friend had done. Alex reached his hands up and offered a semblance of a smile. "My sacrifice? You knew I could betray you with a single word, but you risked everything to help someone like me. You've all taught me so much, and you, Alijah, the beacon—" He forced himself to draw in a breath, though it looked painful. "It was you I followed out of the darkness and into the light of Christ. I love you all so much more than I could ever say." A tear slid down his cheek. "I'm not afraid anymore. For the first time in my life, I'm not afraid." He touched their heads and whispered, "Thank yo—" Before he could finish the word, his arms slid down to his chest as his life crept away.

> *See what great love the Father has lavished on us, that we should be called children of God! And that is what we are! The reason the world does not know us is that it did not know him. Dear friends, now we are children of God, and what we will be has not yet been made known. But we know that when Christ appears, we shall be like him, for we shall see him as he is.*
>
> —1 John 3:1–2

CHAPTER 26

The angel had disappeared into the trees. The trio sat soundlessly for a while before they got up to search for a final resting place for Alex's body. Alijah reflected on what she had seen and heard over the last twenty-four hours. She could no longer speak about the emptiness that tormented them after having lost another dear friend, and she suspected the other two felt the same way.

Pain seized her once again. Her head throbbed from the seemingly never-ending barrage of stressors. "Another friend buried," she whispered to the heavens. To her, the loss of Alex was just another tragedy added to the long list of sacrifices she had already endured. Her emotions were torn for the friends and loved ones who had come and gone over the years. She had lost track of how long it had been since the rapture. She understood all too well why she was left behind, and she had no doubt that the tribulation period of the end-times was to be characterized by sadness, fear, and violence against believers. She didn't question that all believers of God would be persecuted in some manner, but from time to time, she wondered why Christ had chosen her to be one of his beacons.

The three knelt by their friend's body. Chante prayed over him to say the final good-bye, and Alessio put his arms around the two ladies and brought them in close to his body. "You both ready? We have a lengthy journey ahead."

No one spoke, but Alijah violently trembled.

"Are you all right?"

She snapped at him before she could stop it. "All right? Are you kidding? I'm tired, Alessio. The constant pain, the hunger, and that feeling of never being free of this misery just exhausts me so I have nothing left to give. Why won't he let me die, Alessio? I'm ready for my turn to be called home"—her voice grew louder—"and I can't remember what being all right is like!"

Chante bit her lip, but the words came out anyway. "I can't take much more either!"

Alessio gave them both a tight squeeze to calm them. "You know what I tire of? Hmmm? I tire of crying. Do you have any idea what a blow it is to my manliness to constantly be crying?" He tried to lighten the mood by overly rolling his *R* and forcing a laugh. "Our work is not done. It's why our Savior has not called us yet. It's what our brother here gave his life for."

Alijah shook her head quickly and pushed him away. "I want to die too."

His words came out as a roar. "No! Aye, momma, never say that again! We need you. I can't bear to lose you—either of you. Would you let Alex's death be in vain? That Mr. Stevenson, even with the depth of his sins, gave up his life to see us free. Michel! He gave his life for Chante to get away. Would either of you let their gifts be for nothing?"

Chanted sniffled, nestled her face into the curve of Alessio's neck, and pulled Alijah in close. "Jesus chose you to gather his people, and he chose us to help you." She continued with a deep sigh, "No, we can't fail him. Our Lord and Savior never gave up on us, so I'm not giving up on him. We are strong because he is with us. No, Alijah, we will see this through."

"I don't know why he chose any of us, but his reason is not for debate, sì? We will get through this together. I love you both." Alessio pulled Alijah back to him and held her and Chante tighter than he had ever before.

* * * * *

They had walked for hours with no end in sight. None of them actually knew where they were headed, but they stayed on the path Alijah felt was right. The sun crept down as the dark moon bullied its way up into the sky. Because of the angle of the sun and the height of the trees, the forest darkened quickly. The cold had become bitter and harsh, which made it difficult to keep a fast pace. Even the leaves on the trees seemed to shiver in the dropping temperature.

Alessio had been beaten badly before Alijah had been brought to the cell. "I must sit." He took hold of his side and dropped to the floor. His body had been pushed to the limit by the beatings, the malnutrition, and the lack of meaningful sleep. Those combined with the great distance the group had walked exhausted the man. Alijah saw how he had taken up the responsibility of caring for and supporting her and Chante, and she figured he pushed through a lot more pain than he let on. They tried to help him, but they themselves could barely stand.

The trio snuggled up together and wrapped themselves in the blankets. To block some of the wind, they hid behind one of the mammoth trees that dominated the forest. They shivered together while Chante hummed a lovely hymn she said her mother sang to her as a child. The violent wind turned into a soft breeze that caressed the leaves above them. Every time it blew, the leaves rustled soothingly, singing harmony with Chante while the three faded off to sleep.

Alijah dreamt of her life before the tribulation started. Deep in sleep, her mind conjured up visions of a time before her sister had passed. Four months prior to the cancer that took Angela's life, the family took a trip to the mountains. The girls always loved nature hikes, but they never made it far because their short legs tired out, and their parents had to carry them back down the worn paths.

This particular trip was different because the family took a trail they had never traveled. There was to be no talk of cancer, death, or heaven. A big picnic basket held the girls' favorite treats, and the girls' parents came prepared with games and a large blanket for cloud gazing and naps. The day was glorious; the sun was high, and just a few puffy clouds danced in the sky. The smell of fresh grass filled their nostrils with the scent of nature.

When they finally exited the trees, they stepped into a picturesque field that appeared to go on forever. Alijah and Angela ran deep into the field and frolicked in a sea of wildflowers. Tiny periwinkle, purple, and yellow flowers swayed in the breeze among vivid green blades of grass. The parents watched in joy as their little girls held hands and danced through the field. They listened to their babies giggle uncontrollably as little girls often do. For the first time in months, the family was at peace.

"Come on, my little butterflies. It's time for lunch." Jonathan always called them his butterflies. He loved his wife, Annabel, and adored their two little girls. Jonathan was a strong man emotionally and physically, but he had lacked faith in God for the early part of his life. His absence of faith had not come from lack of effort by his parents. He attended Christian schools but quickly grew tired of the idea of an unseen force that expected him to reject worldliness.

By the time he was in high school, rebellion and hormones had overtaken him. He questioned religion and quickly became blinded by all that science claimed. It wasn't until his late twenties when he met and married his beloved Annabel that he changed. His wife challenged him and taught him that she believed in God, not religion. By the time Alijah and then Angela had been born, he had become a born-again Christian who loved Christ and God in every way. He had become quite content with his little family and his life.

The family sat on the cozy blanket and opened the picnic basket. Jonathan filled the girls' paper plates with the food from the basket. "Jonathan, serve yourself next, my love." Annabel had always known where she wanted to go in her life. She had no desire to have a high-profile career or long working hours; her dream was to be a stay-at-home mom and housewife. She always laughed and told people that she didn't want to set the women's rights movement back fifty years; she just loved being a wife and a mommy. She also valued being able to craft and create things to keep her house beautiful.

Annabel just appreciated the beauty of a peaceful life. Jonathan, an engineer who made a comfortable living, had always told her she was free to seek education or a career if she wished more for her life. He encouraged her to even take a few college classes to stimulate her mind, but he did admit he loved having her at home.

The family sat together on the oversized brightly colored blanket and enjoyed their spontaneous Friday afternoon out. After lunch, they sang songs, told stories, and shared little jokes that filled each of their hearts with joy. Before ending their day, all four of them lay across the blanket and imagined what animal each cloud formed.

"Alijah, baby girl, wake up. Are y'all okay?" a voice called down from the sky.

The brilliant sun was glaring down in her eyes, and opening them was painful. She squinted and reached her hand up to guard her eyes. She could feel something in her hand.

"They're comin' to. Alijah, open your eyes," the voice commanded.

"What?" She pushed the light away and focused.

"They're alive. Oh, thank you, dear Jesus, thank you. Alijah, talk to me."

Her mind cleared, and she recognized the figure. "Robert? What are you doing here?"

He pulled her hair back. "Oh baby girl, we've been lookin' for ya! Doc told us that y'all were out here, four of ya." He helped her sit up. "He told me you'd be comin' in from the southwest gate. We've been searchin' for y'all since last night. Are ya hurt?"

"Chante, Alessio," she called out.

"It's okay. They're right here. Y'all are just dazed."

Alessio and Chante slowly came out of their sleep, and their eyes darted back and forth between the people in front of them. "You know them?" Chante asked.

Alijah reached her hand out and touched Robert's shoulder. "Yeah, I know them. This is Robert and some of the guys from the settlement. Guys, these are my friends—I mean, my family—Chante and Alessio."

Robert and the guys tipped their tan cowboy hats toward them in an old cowboy fashion. "Ma'am. Partner." They pulled off the blankets and helped the three friends up. "Alessio? You're Italian, right? The good Doc told us Alijah'd be travelin' with a lady friend, an Italian man, and a soldier, but we seem to be missin' the soldier. Where's he?"

Alijah looked down so her tears didn't show. "He passed away last night."

"I'm sorry to hear that. Was he saved?"

Chante smiled and nodded her head. "He sure was."

In unison, the cowboys called out, "Hallelujah!" They tied up the horses and built a small shelter near a newly crafted fire. They helped the trio huddle under the shelter and warm up with the help of plump winter jackets and clean thick blankets.

"Daniel, heat up some of their food, and Tim, hand me those canteens, will ya?" Robert organized the group and spoke quickly and nervously. "From the looks of it, none of y'all have eaten in some time. That over there is Daniel. He's gonna cook ya some warm food. It's not gonna be a big servin', 'cause Doc said y'all would be in rough shape. Best not give ya too much in one sittin' to keep y'all from gettin' sick. Now, while the food is cookin', who's hurt?"

Chante spoke up first, "I'm okay, but Alijah's hand is very bad, and Alessio was beaten severely."

"He's hurt. I think his ribs are broken on the right side," Alijah chimed in.

"No, no, no. I'm fine." Alessio fussed and tried to shoo Robert away.

Robert ignored him and pushed on Alessio's side. The poor man nearly fell to his knees. The cowboy opened a bag of supplies and tightly wrapped a bandage around Alessio's ribcage. He did his best to cover up the cuts and get Alessio settled before making his way to Alijah.

"Please, my wounds are insignificant." Alessio took Robert's hands in his own and paused. "They burnt her, Robert, her hand. It's very bad. Please care for her," he pleaded.

The men froze in place. Alijah had been traveling to the settlement for over a year and knew everyone there fairly well. The news of her injury caused the cluster of cowboys to gasp.

"Chante and Alessio both worry too much. I'll be fine, guys."

Daniel mumbled, "They did what?"

Robert moved close to Alijah and sat beside her. The fire had grown high enough to warm the immediate area without being large enough to draw attention. The flames revealed the anxiety in his eyes. His voice shook, and in a raspy whisper, he asked, "What did they do to ya, baby girl?"

Alijah sighed and tried to change the subject without success. "It's just a little burn. No biggie. I'll be running around, causing trouble in no time." She let out a nervous giggle and looked down at the bandage. "That's not my blood on the bandage. Unfortunately, it's mostly from Alex."

Chante protested heavily and reminded her that she could end up with a horrible infection. The statement prompted Robert to take her arm by the elbow. Tim knelt beside Robert and shined his small but bright flashlight onto her wrapped hand. Tears welled in his eyes as Robert cautiously unraveled the bandage that had become excessively tattered and soiled over the previous twenty-four hours.

With each pass of the dirtied bandage, Robert's hands shook harder. "Sweet Lord in heaven!"

Anger erupted throughout the group when they finally saw the extent of the damage. The cowboys took turns cursing Emil and his followers. They called to the heavens for retribution, but Robert kept still and quiet. He bit his lip and kept his head low. Alijah reached her left hand to his face to offer him comfort.

He still had a hold on Alijah's arm when he opened his mouth to finally speak, "This is just like ya. You're consolin' me when it should be me consolin' you." He looked up at her. "I'm sorry." It was all he could get out before he wrapped his arms around her. "You're a lot stronger than I could ever be." After a minute, Robert rinsed her hand with distilled water and rewrapped it while he quietly prayed.

The other cowboys finished taking care of Chante and Alessio. Everyone sat under the shelter and shared a warm meal with fresh vegetables. They watched the soft breeze gently caress the flames. For the remainder of the night, the trio slept peacefully while the cowboys stood watch over them.

Come to me, all you who are weary and burdened, and I will give you rest. Take my yoke upon you and learn from me, for I am gentle and humble in heart, and you will find rest for your souls. For my yoke is easy and my burden is light.

—Matthew 11:28–30

Chapter 27

Dawn brought a new day for Alijah and her companions. Robert and the cowboys prepared breakfast and broke down the camp swiftly. Everyone knew they would need to get started early in order to arrive at the community before nightfall. Chante and Alessio were paired with the other cowboys on horses while Alijah rode with Robert.

During the trip, Robert caught the trio up on some of the current happenings in the community. Much had changed since the last time Alijah last visited. The population had already grown by leaps and bounds, and they were anticipating many more. But what transpired after the first group of people arrived was what Robert and the original residents were most astounded by.

"Alijah, do ya remember how I've been pushin' for everyone to be tight-lipped about the community?"

"I'm lucky if I remember to put my pants on in the morning." She smiled and stifled a snicker. "But I know we've all had to be careful with who knows about us. If the wrong person finds out about it, the soldiers could come."

"Yes. I've tried to protect the families livin' there. Well, the night after you were taken, Martha and me had a half-hour conversation in our bedroom with an angel who told us there would be more believers comin', and we needed to help them."

Chante and Alessio nearly fell off the horses doing a double take. "An angel came to you?" Chante questioned excitedly.

"Sure did. Then two days later, he came back and told me to seek out the believers lost in the woods. He said they wouldn't find their way until the beacon returned, so we'd have to help them. We found people from two different dormitories just wanderin'. And they were askin' for you, Alijah."

"Doc and I were pretty scared because we knew we weren't gonna have enough food. We planned out how to ration our stores while thinkin' on how to increase our crops. That night, the whole group sat down and prayed real hard for help in providin' food. After that, Doc and I went into the storehouse to get everyone a little somethin' to put in their stomachs, and there it was. Food—there was food everywhere. The whole storehouse was packed with fruits, vegetables, and bread."

"Praise God! Incredible!" Alessio called out.

"Amen, brother," one of the cowboys responded.

Chante hugged the cowboy she was riding with. "Thank you, Lord."

Robert continued, "The next mornin' we watched as seven cows, multiple chickens, and even four sheep just strolled up to the compound. I don't reckon we'll be havin' meat but once a week for a bit, but I'm grateful to the good Lord above for providin' enough to get us started."

Alijah gave Robert a little squeeze. "It's remarkable. What a blessing. Where are you putting everyone?"

He sighed. "It's tight, and we've got people sleeping everywhere, but the folks who came in brought supplies to help out. They brought blankets, pillows, clothes, dishes—any supplies they could scrounge up and carry. They even brought the cans of the horse pucky Emil's been feedin' y'all."

"We should stop at the dorms so I can grab some things and food I have stashed. I really need to get my parents' pictures and the few keepsakes I have left." Alijah hoped to convince him.

"No, baby girl, we can't go back there. Emil is lookin' for ya—all three of ya. They're gonna be watchin' your room."

"Robert, I need those pictures. They're all I have left of my family."

He smiled in return. "Baby girl, do ya really think we'd leave ya hangin'? Martha and I got your stuff in our room at home. That lovely lady Tiffany, that man Eiji, his wife, and Spencer all went back to the dorms and collected anything they thought might be important to ya."

"Spencer made it too? Oh thank you, Lord! Thank you for that!"

The group rode for hours before they stopped for lunch and a rest. They continued talking softly about everything that had been happening. Alijah listened intently to the cowboys with both excitement and apprehension. She knew this was only the beginning of the trials, and she was concerned about how the settlement would accommodate another big group of believers.

While everyone continued the ride, Alijah nodded off with her head against Robert's shoulder. He kept the pace slow and careful so she wouldn't fall off the horse.

* * * * *

"Baby girl, we're here," Robert's soft voice roused her.

She raised her head to see her surroundings and was relieved to find they had arrived at the compound. Nothing much had changed, including the clinic. While their medical facility was small from the beginning, it was effective nonetheless. Doc and his family worked faithfully to keep the clinic operating at its full potential.

"Alijah! Oh thank you, dear Lord." Doc reached up to scoop her from the horse.

"Oh, Doc, it's so good to see you!" Alijah reached down. "I've missed all of you so much."

Doc's wife Meg jogged up to Alijah and threw her arms around her, nearly knocking Alijah over. "Oh my gosh, you look awful!" A quiet laughter crept across the growing crowd. "You're nothing but skin and bones—bruised up skin and bones at that." She forced a laugh, but her smile faded as she looked Alijah over. "I love you, sweetie, and I can't tell you how happy I am you're back home with us."

Everyone climbed down and stretched from the long ride while the cowboys took care of the horses. A crowd gathered as introductions were made. Doc ushered the trio into the clinic tent to begin triage. While Meg checked Alessio and Chante, Doc focused on Alijah's hand.

"It's bad, Doc. I've never seen a burn like it." Robert explained what Emil did.

After he unwrapped her hand, Doc's mouth dropped open. "Sickening. He's truly a demon straight from hell. I'm sorry, I just can't believe, what was the point of this?" He exhaled deeply. "All right, we need to get to work. Sweetheart, bring me the burn kit, would you?"

Chante and Alessio stood next to Alijah. Meg returned quickly with the supplies and whispered in Doc's ear. As she walked out the door, she turned and smiled at the trio. Doc reached out to Chante to wipe the tears that had fallen down her cheeks. "Why so sad, sweetness? Our Lord and Savior brought you home to us."

Alessio slid his shirt on after his ribs were taped thoroughly and wrapped his arms around Chante from behind. "We're with you, mia cara."

She quickly reached up to return Alessio's hug. "I feel so blessed to be here and surrounded by all of you, but my heart still hurts so much. I miss my Michel." Her eyes glistened with gathering moisture.

Alessio kissed her on the temple. Doc and Alijah reached out to hold her hand. The cowboys moved in closer.

"Our Lord has provided us an extraordinary day, indeed," Doc said.

A voice came from the doorway, "Baby."

Momentarily, she forgot her pain, and Alijah cheered and kicked her legs in exhilaration. The whole gang joined in the cheers. Alessio shouted, "*Gloria a Dio*! Chante! *Guarda chi si vede*! Look!"

Chante's knees buckled, but fortunately, Alessio and Doc caught her before she could drop to the ground.

"Babe," the man's voice shook with joy.

Chante trembled and exhaled, barely uttering, "Oh!" In front of her was her beloved Michel. Alessio and Doc helped her place her arms around his neck. They hugged and kissed as if they hadn't seen each other in years. Applause erupted from everyone who watched.

An overwhelming sense of delight mingled in the crowd. Doc went on to describe how he had been compelled to seek out Michel at the forest's edge, even though they had never met. When they found Michel, he had a single bullet wound in his back. The bullet had gone through his back, around his kidney, and out his abdomen. While his internal organs went unscathed, he had lost a significant amount of blood. Once they returned to the camp, Doc performed a quick surgery to repair his weakened body.

Michel shared his love with Alessio and Alijah. He thanked Alessio for fighting to keep his Chante alive. He expressed his gratefulness to him for being strong for Alijah and protecting them both throughout the night. Alessio was his normal bashful self as he refused to take credit for his deeds, insisting that it was Alijah and Chante who were the strongest.

Like everyone who had witnessed Alijah's wound, Michel was taken aback. "Why? How could anyone do such a thing?"

Alijah was filled with emotion as well. "Michel, we thought we'd never see you again. We were so heartbroken to think we had lost you." She sniffled and squeezed him tight. "Don't you worry about me. Doc's got me covered, right?"

Doc rubbed Michel's shoulder. "Absolutely, but right now, we've got to get that hand treated. How bad is the pain?"

"The burn itself doesn't hurt much anymore. I think it's numb, but my hand hurts something awful. The swelling hasn't gone down since it happened, and it kind of feels like, well, it feels like pins stabbing me all the way up the arm. And it looks like it's going to explode."

He examined her hand carefully. "It's definitely a third-degree burn, but the skin is also torn."

"Emil left the branding iron on for a long time, and when he lifted it, I think my skin went with the iron. Remembering still makes my skin crawl."

"I need to cleanse the wound, Alijah. I've got some pain meds over there. They're not very strong, but they'll take the edge off."

Alijah shook her head. "No, Doc, we don't have many pain meds left. Save them. We may need them later on."

Doc looked into her eyes and reminded her how much pain she was going to have to endure. He could see dirt, as well as other debris, already building up in the wound. He urged her to accept the medicine, but she refused. They had her lie back on the table.

Robert stood beside Doc near a little table that her burnt hand rested on. Alessio came around and sat down by her head, holding her shoulders down, and kissed her forehead. Chante held Alijah's left hand with Michel close by. Doc prepared for the debridement.

Alijah stared at the ceiling and tried to forget what was about to happen. She was excited to be at the compound again. Out of the many times she had been there, she never imagined being so relieved to be away from the city and the chaos. No more ration lines, no more violence in the dorm hallway late at night. In the middle of her thoughts, she realized someone was screaming. She focused her eyes on Alessio, who still hovered above her head. "What was that? Who was screaming?"

Doc's voice beside her said, "Done."

Everyone looked at each other before they looked back at Alijah. She quickly panned the room to find that her friends were shaken up and crying. She focused again on Alessio and repeated her question. He responded with his voice trembling. "Aye, momma." He brushed the tears from her cheeks. "It was you."

"I've done all I can, but as I said, this is a full-thickness burn, and it's consumed a good deal of the top of her hand. I'm thinking we're going to need a skin graft before this wound will close."

"I was screaming?"

Chante kissed her left hand. "You were screaming before you lost consciousness. You were out for a good twenty minutes."

"What do you need, Doc? I'll go into town and get whatever she needs," Robert offered.

"We'd have to break into a hospital to get those kind of supplies." Doc looked back at Alijah. "I'm going to pump you full of antibiotics. Unfortunately, we're going to have to change this wrapping every day to prevent infection. I'm sorry, sweetie." He caressed her cheek. "I hate to cause you more pain, but we can't have you getting an infection. With a severe-enough infection, you could lose your arm." Doc wrapped her hand again and insisted she stay inside the clinic building, where she could be hooked up to an IV and stay under Doc's watchful eye.

> *You will keep in perfect peace those whose minds are steadfast, because they trust in you. Trust in the Lord forever, for the Lord, the Lord himself, is the Rock eternal.*
>
> —Isaiah 26:3–4

CHAPTER 28

Spencer was the first of the dorm residents to arrive at Alijah's bedside. He greeted her with open arms and planted a kiss on her cheek before saying, "I thought I'd never see you again, either of you." He grabbed Alessio by the back of the neck to give him a peck on the cheek as well. He returned to Alijah's side and pulled something out of his pocket. "I thought you might want this."

His large open hand revealed a chain with a locket. Recognizing it immediately, she became weepy. "Mom's locket. I was praying it would be mixed in with the things you guys brought from the dorm." She looked into Spencer's eyes. "How could I ever thank you?"

He shook his head. "I spotted it the night we went back to clear out your dorm room. I caught a glimpse of it around the base of the lamp. It must have popped off during the scuffle when they arrested y'all. I saw the pictures of you and your dad inside, and I figured if there's anything in that room that ya wanted, it would be that locket. We got all the personal stuff we could find, but I thought this—"

Alijah interrupted him and wrapped her arms around his waist to squeeze him tight. She was so appreciative of her friends risking their personal safety to collect the things that were near and dear to her heart. She knew she could never express how deeply grateful she was.

Robert's wife, along with one of the ladies from Alijah's dorm, came forward with a plate of food and fresh water for the weary travelers. Eiji's wife followed behind with clean clothes for Alijah. All the while, the crowd continued to grow. Talk of the beacon's arrival into camp spread like wildfire. Many people came to the clinic to hear more from her. It wasn't long before questions started to arise.

A woman's voice called out, "Alijah, when will Jesus return for us?"

"How much more do we have to endure? How much more do we have to suffer? Doesn't God think we've suffered enough?" a man questioned in desperation.

Another man shouted out, "Yeah, that's right. So when are we gonna get taken too? Is there a second rapture?"

Someone else chimed in, "Wait, how can that be? I always thought there was only one rapture, and it was after Christ returned. I'm sorry if I'm wrong, but I read nothing about beacons in the book of Revelation."

A tall, lanky young man who had perfectly placed hair and looked as if he were barely eighteen years old looked over the crowd. "There's already not enough food and shelter, so what's going to happen to us?"

Another one shouted, "Miss, I know you from the dormitory. I heard you say that the first seal was broken. I hate to tell you this, but we've been at war for years, we've already had economic collapse, and we're already starving. Are you sure you know what you're talking about? Look around, girl. We've been in tribulation for years!" He turned briefly toward the crowd to find support. "I mean, these are our eternal souls this little girl is playing with here. Maybe someone else should be in charge! Someone older than her."

An elderly man who was barely able to stand up straight looked over at the grumbler. "Why don't you just shut up, ya darn fool! Why are you here? How did you know where to come?"

The man replied, "I heard the voice. God told me to seek his beacon, the one named—" he stopped midsentence and looked at Alijah.

"He told you to seek his beacon, the one named Alijah, right? The good Lord sent the same message to all of us! She's the Lord's choice, so give her some respect, all of you." He looked back at Alijah. "Go on now, young lady."

A frustrated Alessio barked back at the man who was confronting Alijah, "This little girl is a woman in her forties who's demonstrated more physical fortitude and spiritual resilience over the last forty-eight hours than most of us will ever have in a lifetime." Alijah placed her left hand on his shoulder and shook her head. He growled like a bear. "Forgive me, it's just, how dare he speak of you in such a way."

The crowded clinic became silent, and all eyes were directed toward Alijah. She looked to her closest friends for help and rested her eyes on Michel. He quickly took her hand and rubbed it, offering only the reminder that he could help her understand the Scriptures, but she was the one chosen to lead. She breathed deeply to calm herself and collect her thoughts while the crowd waited. She gave a nervous smile before she offered what she could.

"First, I want to say how happy, truly happy, I am that we are all here together. But everyone must remember that no one but our God above knows the day he will send his Son back for us. I didn't say there would be a second rapture. Our Lord, for a reason I will probably never fully comprehend, chose me to be his beacon. I'm a sinner, and I've faltered in my faith too, but if we are going to accomplish what our Lord is asking of us, we must *all* learn to throw away our bad habits, our self-indulgences, and our doubts, and focus on the task he has presented us with.

"You, sir, ask why you should follow me. Well, I'm not asking you to, but our Lord and Savior has commanded me to help those who truly want his forgiveness and salvation. I most certainly intend to honor that command. Another thing I do know for sure is that he brought us here for a reason, and we darn well need to start opening our ears, eyes, and minds." She fidgeted and looked at the ground.

A young Asian woman squeezed through the swarm of people and approached Alijah. She was obviously unnerved and confused. She wore a pink knit sweater and blue jeans. Her eyes were so brown that they were almost black. The young woman, who looked to be in her early twenties, came close to the bed on which Alijah was sitting. "Excuse me, but how do I know you? I've never met you, yet I feel as if I have known you all my life."

Alijah felt everyone's tension and hoped to ease some of their concerns. She rested the change of clothes on her lap. "I can't explain it. I'm only beginning to understand the idea of being this beacon. How about this?" She reached out her hand. "What's your name?"

The young lady blushed and offered her hand in return. "So sorry. My name is Umeko. I am from Soma, a city within Fukushima, Japan."

Alijah shook her hand with a smile. "Umeko? Well, Umeko, it's a great pleasure to meet you. I'm from much closer, here in Washington State, actually. Umeko, do you know how all of us are alike here?"

She shook her head to say no.

"We're all feeling a combination of fear and uncertainty, just to start with, and on top of all that, we have an overwhelming anticipation for the second coming of our Lord."

The rest of the crowd stepped closer. Alijah continued, "You all are wondering what is to come? Michel, if I'm wrong, please correct me. I believe this is the first half of the tribulation period. I do understand that a few things might be happening a little differently than what many of us were brought up believing. But I don't think we should dwell on the intricacies. We shouldn't be worried about semantics or order of events. We need to focus on what God has commanded in his Word, which is to stay faithful and help others find Christ before it's too late for them." Pain gripped Alijah, causing her to wince.

Before she could continue, Doc squeezed between Michel and Alessio. "Okay, everyone, it's getting late, and these three need their rest. Emil had them starved, beaten"—his voice sharpened in anger—"and even tortured." Gasps came from the crowd. "Alijah needs a day or two to recover. As soon as she is up to it, she will tell us more. I know everyone is excited. I sure am, but we have to give her some time."

Robert chimed in, "Now I need y'all to get rest 'cause there are other believers comin' soon, and we've got a lot of preparin' to do. We're gonna need all your help to get ready for them. So, everyone, get into our prayer circle. Michel, would ya mind?"

After Michel gave a quick prayer, the crowd slowly dispersed. Robert, Alessio, and Spencer spent the night in the clinic to help Doc take care of Alijah. Chante and Michel offered to take turns, but Alijah shooed them off so they could have their first night back together alone.

* * * * *

Alijah woke up midafternoon the following day. Doc had been giving her fluids and heavy doses of antibiotics all through the night. Chante sat close to keep a motherly eye on her. As soon as she noticed Alijah opening her eyes, she called for Doc.

He performed a quick checkup on her. "You gave us a scare last night. Your blood pressure kept dropping, and after that, you decided not to breathe—three times! After we finally got you stable, you didn't want to wake up. You gave me a run for my money, honey!" He chuckled nervously.

"You know me. I like to keep people on their toes." She smiled at him. "So why did all that happen?"

He listened to her heart once again. "Alijah, it's only by the grace of our dear Lord that you are here. The three of you are malnourished, dehydrated, and sleep-deprived, and you were tortured. Your body was horribly weakened prior to the arrest, and then the trauma of the burn and the shock that followed, you should have never made it through the forest. The weather dropped below thirty degrees over the last couple of nights, and you three surviving that long trip through the forest overnight had to be through divine intervention."

Alessio stood up and moved quickly to be by Alijah and Chante. Alijah stared at them. "I couldn't have done it without you both. Through all the madness of the last few years, it's because of you two and Michel that I'm still around. There are not enough ways to express how much I love you both."

Alessio threw his arms around Alijah. "*La mia ragazza pazza.*" He reached for Chante and hugged her. "Both of you."

"Hey now, I want in on some of that!" Before Alijah knew it, Michel, Doc, and Robert were all part of the group bear hug.

Lunchtime came quickly. The camp was bustling with people making preparations for the meal. Alijah watched from her bedside while Doc and Meg cared for people's bumps and bruises. Robert and Martha worked at a makeshift workbench in the corner of the clinic, diligently making plans to expand the camp.

The camp had grown tremendously. A number of new wooden buildings stood within the perimeter. Each one was nothing extravagant, but together, they were enough to keep the growing community dry and warm. The gardens were looking full and green, and the animal pen housed a new herd of cows and chickens going about their business.

Not wanting to burden anyone, Alijah quietly stood up from the gurney and grabbed the clean clothes they had brought to her the night before. She hid behind a blue sheet that masqueraded as a curtain to quickly change before she gathered her IV and headed out to the courtyard.

She was surprised to see so many people in the camp and to see such a diverse group. The new residents came from different backgrounds, religions, cultures, and ethnicities as well as different age groups, yet they worked in unison with one another. There were no tempers flaring or people yelling at or hating each other because of their differences. It was as if they were all a part of a performance in which the cast was in perfect harmony with one another.

Alessio snuck up behind Alijah to give her a peck on the cheek. "What are you doing out of bed?" His lilting accent had smoothed out since things had calmed down, which made him easier to understand.

She smiled and took his hand. "Look at them, Alessio. There's no bickering of any kind, and no one hates others because of race or religion. They're all just people being kind to one another."

"Sì, it is because there's no reason to hate each other anymore. We are united by a common enemy, no?"

"Yeah, but it's a shame that it took the Lord kicking us in the behind to wake us up."

He rubbed her shoulders. "You should lie down. Doc wanted you to rest."

Alijah suddenly felt a wave of familiar peace consume her body. As she searched the edge of the woods, she spotted Mavet in the distance. He kept out of sight so the camp's residents wouldn't see him.

"Mavet!"

"Mavet? The angel is here?"

She turned to Alessio. Unable to contain her joy, she explained, "I have to see him. Tell Doc I'll be back soon." She kissed him on the cheek. "Please don't tell them who's here. Remember, no one is suppose to know about him."

"Wait, wait, wait." Alessio wrapped a small blanket around her shoulders. "Keep warm and keep the IV up so it does not back up. Be safe."

Alijah moved quickly through the camp. She tried not to be too conspicuous as she ducked between people while they worked. After stubbing her toes a few times on little rocks, she realized she had forgotten to put on her shoes before she left the clinic. But she was determined to reach Mavet as quickly as she could, barefoot or not.

"Alijah." Mavet's gentle voice called to her from behind one of the great trees. In her excitement, she dropped both her blanket and IV to leap up into his arms, and she repeatedly kissed his cheeks. The warmth of his embrace triggered feelings of what heaven might be like—no pain, no sorrow, no hunger, just pure joy and the purest of love.

When she realized she hadn't stopped kissing him, she blushed and released his neck. "I'm sorry, Mavet. I'm just so happy to see you."

He gently lowered her and placed her feet back on the ground. "You needn't ever apologize for your affections. I too am quite joyful to see you." He looked down at the bag of fluids that was still attached to her arm. "What is this?"

She let out a noise as she scrambled to pick up her IV that was now backing up with blood. "This thing is an IV. Doc has been giving me fluids and medications. I'm supposed to be keeping it up." She stood too quickly, lost her balance, and fell against Mavet.

He caught her and then helped her sit down on a rock that was nearby. After dusting off the blanket, he wrapped it around her shoulders and sat on the ground close to her. "I have been watching." He took her right hand and tenderly touched the top of her bandaged hand. "I believed you would triumph over the false prophet."

"How did you know?" She forced a brief laugh. "I certainly didn't believe I could."

Mavet looked deeply into her eyes. "I had faith." He offered the sweet smile she had loved since the first time they met. "Your pain deeply troubles me."

She blushed, quickly saying, "I'll get through it, so you shouldn't worry for me." Regaining her composure, she smiled. "The voice I heard in the woods, was that you?"

"No, your Messiah spoke to you. He speaks to you often. It was he who led you through the darkness. He has always been with you."

"It's pretty amazing to know that the Lord would speak to me. To me. I mean, who am I to deserve to hear his guidance?"

"You are his child. He who is and always will be has a grand purpose for you."

"Do you mean the beacon thing? But it's not in the Bible."

His eyes shifted up from her hand. "No, the beacons were not foretold. However, it is the Fathers divine choice and right to call his children to service. Yes, you are among those who have been chosen to be a beacon for his children. Those such as you will aid in saving many—that is, those who are truly faithful."

Mavet looked to the heavens as if waiting for an answer from someone. Warmth flowed through her hand as he held it.

"Mavet? Is everything all right?"

He didn't respond but instead continued gazing at the sky. A few minutes passed before he refocused his attention on Alijah. "Forgive me for the delay in response."

"Is there a problem?"

He just smiled. "In your world, much is wrong."

She continued to question him, hoping to gain a better understanding of what was to come. She still did not fully understand the tribulation period or all the punishments that would come and why so many believers were still left in the cities. She asked question after question, but Mavet remained vague on many of her inquiries.

He held both of her hands and listened to her heartbeat. "There is much more to come. Each judgment poured onto your world is done so with a great sadness. El Shaddai will cleanse this world of the evil that has consumed it. Many of your kind claim to follow Christ, but they do it with a false heart. They are the ones who cannot hear his voice. They are the ones who do not seek the beacons and will be deceived when the final Antichrist takes his place." He released her hands.

Shocked, she looked from her hand to his eyes and back again until she finally formed words. "My hand?"

"It is a gift from Lord Jesus."

> *For we know that if the earthly tent we live in is destroyed, we have a building from God, an eternal house in heaven, not built by human hands.*
>
> —2 Corinthians 5:1

CHAPTER 29

People from all walks of life gathered close to one another, and silence overtook the entire camp. Many sat on the ground, while others rested on the collection of camping chairs and remnants of logs that had been used for building materials. They waited like little children at story time, ready to hold their breath so as not to miss a single word.

Michel started the afternoon with another prayer. He prayed for the people who had not yet found God, and he prayed that the wicked would be able to find the Lord. He prayed for the believers who were still in search of the beacons throughout the world. Michel begged for the Lord's mercy on all who were left behind. He asked for special guidance for Robert, Doc, and Alijah, whose tasks were daunting. Most importantly, he gave praise and worship to the Lord God Almighty, who had begun the cleansing of the earth to make it new again. Before he backed off to give Alijah the stage, he placed his hand on her chin and softly touched his forehead to hers.

Alijah sat down on a narrow stool in front of the curious believers and prepared to answer as many questions as she could. After surveying the crowd, she began talking. "Many people still only see the fulfillment of end-time prophecies as God's wrath. We should never forget that our own sins caused the people of the world to fall. By our own stubbornness, we chose not to see the truth. However, our God is nothing less than amazing! Even with all of our craziness, he loves us enough to give us another chance. Now we wait for his glorious return, but he has given us a task."

Her closest friends moved to sit with the others who were silently listening to the information Alijah provided.

Alijah filled her lungs and exhaled through her open mouth before continuing her speech. "My brothers and sisters, what's past is just that, the past. Up to now, the Lord has tasked us with having faith in him and his glory. He led us to one another here in Robert and Martha's home camp, which they've graciously turned into a safe haven for us." Cheers and clapping came from the crowd for a few seconds. Alijah thanked the couple before continuing. "Our Lord tasked us with building our faith so we may be strong for what the future holds. It's not just the judgments, my family. We have to be strong for the many who are still lost and unsure."

A young voice questioned, "Are there others coming here to camp?"

Alijah glanced down at Martha and Robert before she answered, "Yes, we believe so. Other believers heard the command too, but they're coming from greater distances."

A man in the back of the crowd loudly asked, "I don't mean this badly, but where are we going to put more people?" Other voices echoed his question.

"All right, everyone, hold on." Alijah looked at the man who happened to be the same man who had challenged her the previous night. "Look, no one said any of this was going to be easy. Actually, the days to come will probably be the hardest days of our lives, but let me ask you all this: Would you allow other children of God to perish in the city? Would you allow them to starve because we are too crowded? Should they be left to suffer the judgments because it's uncomfortable for us?" She tried to change her serious tone of voice with a short chuckle.

He looked down in shame. Chante stood up and went to him to offer support. "What's your name, brother?"

"Trevor." He smiled at her and offered his sincere apology to Alijah. Chante sat next to him and held his hand.

"I know, everyone. I know it's scary, and I don't have the answers to make anyone feel any better about it. I don't know where everything we need is going to come from." She paused to smile at Trevor. "I know it is in our nature to question and to protect ourselves and our family. I wish I could reassure everyone, but I can't. The one thing I know for sure is our Lord has a plan. I know he hears us and will answer us when we call. It may not be the answer we're looking for, but he knows what he's doing, and I most certainly know he will provide."

The crowd erupted into applause once again. Alijah lifted her hand to quiet them. "Fear will make us all question our faith at some point during this tribulation. What we need to do is hold tight and support one another. When one of us stumbles, we need to pick him or her back up. Now "— she let the word remain on her lips as she scanned the faces of those gathered—"I was told that we have chosen to call our little camp the Ark. I like it. For now, we are going to focus on the basic needs of the Ark and prepare for others to come."

Before ending the camp meeting, Alijah shared many things that Mavet had taught her. She emphasized the importance of offering aid to those who were still of weak faith.

As the day continued on, the camp leaders split the residents into groups. Those with planning and architectural skills gathered with Robert. Those with farming skills went with Meg and Martha. People with crafting knowledge assembled to create needed items. Those with medical experience came together with Doc and Alijah, and finally, those who wished to minister to the believers still in the cities gathered with Michel and Chante.

* * * * *

The day came and went quickly. Early the next morning, a group of about thirty people emerged from the woods. Shortly after their arrival, two additional small groups straggled in. People throughout the Ark greeted everyone with open arms. Robert, Michel, and Spencer helped the new people become acclimated to life in the forest community.

In the last group was a woman who came forward to speak directly to Alijah. "I have news." Alijah's companions gathered around them. "My name is Samantha. I'm a high school astronomy teacher. I made a detour before coming here. My friends over there"—she pointed to a small group of women—"left with me when we heard God call, but we each knew others who lived near your dorms. We stopped by to talk to them because we wanted to check to see if they heard the call."

Robert was the first to speak up, "Where did you tell them you were going? Could they track you here with soldiers?"

She shook her head rapidly. "No, of course not, but we tried to open their eyes. They claimed to believe in God, but they didn't hear the voice. When we questioned them, it became clear."

Alessio asked, "What is clear?"

"Well, isn't it written in the Bible that believers will be fooled?"

Alijah sighed. "Yes. The first seal was broken, and the angel must have started."

Samantha tilted her head and squinted her eyes at Alijah. "It was? When? What angel?"

"During the first blood moon, the first horseman was released."

Samantha looked at the gentle faces around her before she spoke again, "Do you know that there are people who believe the four horsemen of the Apocalypse are the embodiment of Satan?"

Alijah smiled. "Yeah, I've read that. It was an interesting theory some people came up with many years ago, but I don't believe that's true. The horsemen are angels of God who were created for that purpose. The first angel in white brings deception, and he will help the final Antichrist deceive. Even some of the followers of Christ who are weak in faith will follow the one who claims to be the returned Christ. I'm pretty sure it's Tony."

"I wonder if you are right because something big is going to happen tomorrow. Emil and his brother—"

"Tony is not Emil's brother."

Samantha pulled her head back. "How do you know that?"

Alijah glanced at Alessio. "We knew Tony before he was chosen."

"Well, we are on the brink of war with Israel. Emil and Tony are going on a mission of goodwill to Israel. That itself is a joke. They plan on broadcasting their speeches from the Western Wall of the Temple Mount of Jerusalem—the Wailing Wall, I believe they call it. Emil is claiming he is the real Jesus, and he intends to prove it. There's something else."

Alijah stared off and tapped her finger against her lips as she listened. "Emil's been claiming he's the messiah for about two years now, but to actually call himself by the name of Jesus and at the Wailing Wall in Jerusalem? What's the other thing?"

"They're anticipating another blood moon. Do you think it would tie in?"

The group looked at Alijah. "I would imagine so."

More people continued to gather behind Alijah until almost everyone in the camp was listening. She asked everyone to settle down and sit. She reviewed the previous conversation quickly to catch everyone up on what was happening outside the camp. As Alijah spoke, they seemed to hang on every word.

"The first four judgments, in my opinion, are the worst because they are intended to completely separate the truly faithful from the followers of the beast. For friends and family still out there, they're in danger."

An older woman spoke out, "I have a dear friend named Millie in Seattle now. I don't understand why she's not here. Do you think she's been injured, or maybe..." A tear slipped down her cheek. "Do you know if she's been hurt or captured?" Someone sitting next to the woman held her close and attempted to comfort her.

Alijah glanced at Alessio and Michel in hopes of quick words of wisdom, but neither man spoke up. "I don't know. I wish I had an answer for you, but—"

"But you are the beacon!" the woman said in a louder voice. "Doesn't God talk to you? Can't you ask him? Millie is like a sister to me. I need to find her."

Alijah shook her head as she searched for words. "It's not like that. I so wish I could ask questions and he would just give me the answers, but he doesn't talk to anyone like that. What I can tell you is that if she hasn't given her heart and soul to the Lord, then she won't hear his voice." She looked at the rest of the crowd. "Do you all understand the purpose of the first four horsemen?" Her eyes pleaded with Michel, and she asked him to join her and give a good explanation, but he shook his head no.

People were hungry for knowledge. They had become dependent on Alijah, and if she couldn't explain things, they became desperate. They begged for answers, direction, and promises for the future.

Another voice stood out from the crowd. "Okay, we understand that only believers who have fully committed to the Lord are here, but how many out there will be deceived? What did you mean? Are we still in danger?"

Alijah made several attempts to make them understand that she could share only what she had learned and believed to be true. "I'm not sure if we'll be safe from everything here, but just like all of you, I was called here." She lost her train of thought briefly as the crowd kept murmuring. "If you remember what Michel and Chante taught us, God has instructed his angels not to harm those of us who have the seal of God upon them. Remember, everyone, the seal is on our souls. Now, who is the first angel called forth?"

A young man who looked to be in his twenties was the first to chime in, "The conqueror."

"Yes. And this is what Revelation six has to say about him." She cleared her throat and held her Bible up where she could easily read it. "I watched as the Lamb opened the first of the seven seals. Then I heard one of the four living creatures say in a voice like thunder, 'Come!' I looked and there before me was a white horse! It's rider held a bow, and he was given a crown, and he rode out as a conqueror bent on conquest." She looked up before continuing, "From what I was taught, he comes here to help the final Antichrist deceive all people, even God's children. So those who have not given themselves to Christ can and probably will believe it when the Antichrist tries to reveal himself as the messiah."

The crowd grew restless, and many questioned why Alijah didn't recognize Emil as the Antichrist. She put her hands up in an effort to silence them and then explained what she had learned from Mavet and how the final Antichrist had not yet revealed himself.

"Please, listen. There's more to the chapter. Verse three says, 'When the Lamb opened the second seal, I heard the second living creature say, "Come!" Then another horse came out, a fiery red one. Its rider was given the power to take peace from the earth and to make people kill each other. To him was given a large sword.'"

She stopped to catch her breath. "The second horseman will come to take this false peace from us. There's a war brewing, my brothers and sisters. The false prophet Emil is certainly false. He would have us believe we have peace, just the way we have made an idol of him and built a false religion around him. He didn't end wars any more than he was able to bring the world into perfect harmony." She waved her arms through the air as if she were a passionate pastor speaking to her congregation. "That creature was only able to subdue the ugly dragon that is war, and I'm tellin', you my friends, the only being who can truly slay that dragon is the Good Shepherd above."

She had to raise her voice to be heard above the cheers that erupted from the people. "And as sure as I am standing here right now, you had better believe the very nations that are united under Emil will rage and strike out against us. But they will also strike out against each other."

The excited crowd begged for more. Alijah wasted no time getting to the third rider. "Revelation six, verse five, 'When the Lamb opened the third seal, I heard the third living creature say, "Come!" I looked, and there before me was a black horse! Its rider was holding a pair of scales in his hand.' This horseman represents famine. Now those of us who have lived in the cities after Emil came into power have experienced hunger. We have a good idea what it feels like. We've gone without fresh food for over two years now. All of us have struggled to survive on what few cans of processed food we could get our hands on, but once the third horseman rides, not even Emil's followers will have food. Everyone is going to suffer."

Many people jumped up, yelling out their fears. "What about us? Are we going to starve?"

"I thought God would protect us from his wrath!"

Alijah did her best to calm them. She too worried about what would happen to the faithful, but she reminded them—and herself—that everyone needed to keep their eyes on God and their ears opened. "We are his children, and he will not forsake us. I believe Christ will hear our prayers and lead us to what we need for survival. But we have one more to talk about, the fourth and final rider. 'When the Lamb opened the fourth seal, I heard the voice of the fourth living creature say, "Come!" I looked, and there before me was a pale horse! Its rider was named Death, and Hades was following close behind him.'"

Silence fell on the camp, and Alijah looked out at many fearful eyes. "This is the one some think is disease or pestilence, but in the end, he simply represents death. He has been given the authority to bring sickness, plagues, and death to living things. Behind him will be the angel who was cast out of heaven, the beast. Hell will be on earth as the other seals are opened and the final judgments come, but"—she smiled happily—"that also means our Lord will descend, banish the beast, and claim the earth as his own once again. How incredible is that? The Lord is coming back."

Don't let anyone deceive you in any way, for that day will not come until the rebellion occurs and the man of lawlessness is revealed, the man doomed to destruction. He will oppose and will exalt himself over everything that is called God or is worshiped, so that he sets himself up in God's temple, proclaiming himself to be God.

—*2 Thessalonians 2:3–4*

CHAPTER 30

Residents gathered around a television that Robert set up when his family first built their camp. With a large antenna, the set was able to pick up UCNN, which was broadcast across the globe. Robert and Doc regularly watched it to keep track of what was going on in the cities. On that day, the room was filled with people waiting to see what would happen at the temple in Israel, where Emil and Tony were being filmed.

UCNN started the broadcast with their usual nonsense of how grand Emil was and all the wonders he had performed, but the scene abruptly changed to show Jerusalem. The cameras panned over to Emil and Tony, who stood at the Wailing Wall. Protests could be heard from behind the camera crew, but the people were never put into view.

Emil and Tony were dressed perfectly. Their suits, hair, and makeup were impeccable. They both looked handsome and spoke clearly with stern but gentle voices. Tony reached out and stroked the wall, running his fingers over several of the limestone blocks. He stopped to remove a handwritten prayer on a small yellow piece of paper that had been placed between the blocks just above his head. He read it and then placed it in his pocket.

The Israeli prime minister stood nearby, dressed professionally in a black suit and surrounded by many heavily armed soldiers. Emil motioned to him and started another one of his long, meaningless speeches.

"Mr. Prime Minister, I have tried since the creation of our unified community to gain your approval and support. I have wanted Israel to stand strong, together with the world, in peace and harmony. You, however, refuse to bring peace to your country. You are the one who chooses to stand alone against the world. Your decision to live outside the unified community has not been without devastating consequences to your countrymen."

The prime minister shook his head rapidly and pointed his finger at Emil. "Your lies have blinded the world to your wickedness. You have forced nations to pledge their allegiance to you by starving their citizens and abusing them."

Tony shouted his retort, "You have lied to the good people of Israel." The protesters were outraged by that statement and screamed out, begging God to expose Emil and Tony for what they were.

The prime minister motioned to the angry mob to quiet down before he said, "How dare you stand near our temple and declare peace and goodness when you threaten to destroy my people and the holiest of places. Your propaganda cannot sway the truly faithful." To the crowd, he said, "We have stood against evil before. We have triumphed over persecution before." He turned back to face Emil and Tony again. "We stand firm against your oppression. We will rise against you and defeat you, demon, for our Messiah comes!" The crowd behind the camera crew cheered. They sang for their country and sang praises to God. Their leader sang with them while two rabbis by the wall recited from the Torah.

All the while, Tony had his head turned to the left as if he were listening to someone speaking. Emil quietly leaned over to Tony and whispered something to him, but it went ignored. Instead, Tony mumbled softly to the air. Only Emil heard him say, "No one shall take my place." Out of nowhere, Tony walked off camera. Emil looked confused but continued speaking to the people.

"Dear people, you have been lied to by your prime minister. Your government is withholding so much from you." Emil's face displayed the same condescending, arrogant look he had whenever he addressed people who refused him. "It is those whom you have placed into power that deny you all that you pray for. They are the ones who have denied you your choice. In their foolishness and stubbornness, they have refused my aid. People of Israel, you are hungry, but it is I who have offered you food. You go without adequate medical care because your government refuses medical supplies. New clothing, homes, and other necessities await you."

Emil pointed at the prime minister as if he were scolding a naughty toddler. "They have them, my lost children. There is food and supplies for all. You needn't go without. Your government has all the things you need locked in warehouses. They selfishly hoard them for their own use. I will care for you and provide for you, not them! Can you not see they bring you only suffering?"

The prime minister tried to cut Emil off. "Lies! Do not believe the demon, my people."

Emil bullied his way back in control of the speech. "You are the liar! I have come to stand before you as a gesture of goodwill, to show you I am the merciful one. I will welcome any Israeli citizen into my grand unified community. People of Israel, I long for you to be with us. Come to me, and I will set you free. I will help you build a fruitful new life anywhere you wish among the people of our community. All I ask is that you pledge your allegiance to me"—he raised his arms toward the sky—"for I am your messiah!"

From the left, Tony walked up to the wall once again, but this time, he had an object in his hand. Emil looked over and spoke to Tony but got no reply. Emil extended his left arm and touched Tony's shoulder. He repeated himself. "I am your messiah, and you will worship me!"

Tony signaled to three of the soldiers standing nearby. In an instant, the two rabbis witnessing to the crowd were executed by a firing squad. Immediately afterward, Tony's hand came up to reveal a 9-mm gun.

Emil could only watch as Tony placed the gun to his own temple and pulled the trigger. The people gasped in horror as his body fell to the ground, but no one ran. Emil and the soldiers went to Tony's body to render aid, but it was too late. Emil ordered the cameras to continue filming while he struggled to regain control of the situation.

He threatened violence to get everyone to quiet down. His words came out in the typical Emil way, spinning the event to his advantage. "Do you see, my children, that even my most faithful brother was willing to sacrifice himself for my glory? By this act, he has demonstrated the type of devotion all should have to the community and, most importantly, to me. As a citizen, you must have devotion so strong that you would be willing to give your life for the greater good. I am that greater good."

The commotion suddenly came to a halt. No one spoke or moved. They stared in astonishment as Tony's body stirred. Even Emil's eyes widened as he stepped back and watched as Tony slowly sat up and moved to his feet. He remained silent for a few moments and searched the crowd of people before offering a smile and turning his attention to Emil. He reached into his pocket to retrieve the folded prayer he had taken from the wall earlier. "This is a prayer of one of your own, my faithful children. 'Adonai Shalom, the Lord of peace. I plead for your mercy upon not only the sons and daughters of Israel but also all who believe in you, our holy God. I pray you send the Messiah to us. I beseech you to save us from this evil.'"

Tony dropped the prayer note to the cold ground. He offered a smile that resembled a little boy's coy smirk. "My people, the time has come. You have listened to Emil speak. You have watched as he ended wars, fed you, loved you, and gave you all you needed. He gave you tranquility and harmony, but at what cost? Sovereign Overseer Emil fed you lies that you believed because you were lost and alone. You were desperate for relief from your own humanity. I understand, my people. You thought that your Creator abandoned you and left you to suffer and die at the hands of evil. But once again, you were wrong! The one you elected is not who you thought he was. No! He is not."

Emil began breathing harder and took a few steps toward Tony. "This is my time. Do not continue."

Tony looked at Emil and shouted, "The cost of your allegiance was your very soul. Now I say away with you, demon! Return to where you came from—hell." At that moment, Tony lifted the gun and shot Emil point-blank between the eyes. In a second, Emil's body twisted and dropped to the ground. Screams of anguish and torture came from his mouth. From out of his body came a glowing figure. It stood above the corpse that once was Sovereign Overseer Emil. Its wings were spread wide as its mouth uttered abominable sounds and screeched at Tony in a language no one understood.

People from all around cried out in horror. In that instant, Tony levitated a few feet off the ground, extending his arms and proclaiming, "I am your messiah. Kneel before me!"

A UCNN cameraman dropped the video equipment to run for his life, but his camera continued to record. The earth quaked beneath Tony as lightning consumed the sky. It struck the earth mercilessly and destroyed almost half of the Wailing Wall. Tony smiled and laughed out loud as people ran in fear.

He pointed his hand toward the two executed rabbis as they rose up. "There! Do you see? I resurrected my children!"

A fissure opened beneath Emil's body. The creature that hovered over him shrieked a final time before it flew down into the pit that devoured the body of the former sovereign overseer.

* * * * *

The people in the camp were stunned by the broadcast. Alijah was the first to speak out. She asked the group watching, "Did anyone see the angel that was talking to Tony?"

Doc looked over at Alijah and hollered, "Angel? What are you talking about, Alijah? Didn't you see what happened? What was that thing that came out of Emil?"

Alijah took hold of his elbow and pointed at the screen. "The angel that was talking to Tony before he killed Emil—that was him. That was the first horseman."

People cried out in fear. "What's happening?"

"What happened to Emil?"

"Was that thing the horseman?"

At that moment, the earth shook violently. A noise came from outside that sounded like two planes colliding midair. Everyone ran out of the room.

The day turned quickly to night, and as the moon appeared, it darkened to the color of blood. Lights fell from the heavens and bombarded the earth. Everyone living at the Ark had run into the central gathering area to watch the sky.

A single word thundered from above, "Come." A light blazed like fire and sailed through the sky for everyone, everywhere, to see. It called out to the earth in a booming voice. "Let there be no peace."

Alijah yelled out to everyone, "Don't run! We're God's people, and we have nothing to fear from his judgments. Quickly, take hold of each other." The commotion sent the animals into frenzied stampedes in their pens. The earth continued to rumble and knocked everyone off their feet. The believers grabbed one another and circled around Alijah as deafening sounds filled the dark skies.

Chante shouted the first Bible verse that came to her mind. "The Lord is my shepherd, I lack nothing. He makes me lie down in green pastures. He leads me beside quiet water. He refreshes my soul. He guides me along the right paths for his name's sake. Even though I walk through the darkest valley, I will fear no evil, for you are with me."

The lights fell from the sky like meteorites and crashed into the ground in what seemed to be a purposeful formation. Several fell close to the camp, not far from the believers. Chante's eyes filled with tears, and her voice trembled as she continued to shout out the prayer again.

As far as the residents could see, the earth around their camp was pummeled from above. They were still on the ground when one of the lights crashed into the ground just a few feet from them. Many people had been knocked to their sides or backs. They lay across one another and gripped each other with white knuckles. The light that had fallen near the group slowly stood up and revealed itself.

The brightness emanating from it faded enough for the being to expose its true identity to the people. It stood tall, appearing to be a giant to the people on the ground. Its form was that of a mighty angel dressed in blue armor with the words of God seared into the thin metal. His long white hair framed piercing eyes that were dark as the night. His shoulders were broad and strong, but the details of his face and hands were impossible to make out because he still glowed far too brightly. He had a mighty sword sheathed by his side.

Three other angels came into the camp and stood at arm's length from one another. Each one was dressed similar to Mavet, robed in long white garments that ended just above their knees and partially covered their pants. Each one had a midnight-blue sash wrapped around his waist. The four angels stood in silence while looking the group over.

From her knees, Alijah sat up as high as she could to quickly unravel from her body the sash Mavet had given her. Her hands juddered as she tried to wrap the sash around them a few times. She lifted her trembling arms and revealed the blue material to the angels. "Please, don't harm us. We too are faithful servants of God. We're children of Christ...," she tried hard to continue but couldn't get the words past the knot in her throat.

The first angel turned and spoke in what Alijah quickly recognized as the language of God. All four beings turned and walk away but not before the first angel looked back. "Fear not, beacon, for ye have yet to be summoned home. The good work he has tasked you with is not complete." He lifted his eyes to the rest of the group. "His glory shines upon you all."

No one moved or spoke, not even Alijah. They all watched with wide eyes as the angels walked away. The silence in the camp lasted until the angels had disappeared from sight. The moon shed its unnatural color, and the heavens quieted down. The clouds assumed strange formations, but the sky returned to its usual blue, yellow, and white hues.

Sometime during the event, Michel had held his breath, so the first sound coming from the group was his loud exhalation. Chante followed by shouting, "Sweet Lord our God Almighty, those were his angels!"

Laughter and cheers erupted from the crowd. "Do you believe that?"

"Angels! We just saw angels!"

"Oh my gosh!"

"The Lord has forgiven us, and he protected us from his wrath!"

"Hallelujah!"

"Alessio. Alessio!" Alijah said.

"Sì, my darling."

She smiled toward the sky. "Alessio, I love you, but could you please let go of me? You're cutting off the blood supply to half my body." Laughter erupted once again.

"Oh, sì! Forgive me."

As he released her, the rest of the group sat up. No one rushed to get to their feet.

Alijah snorted and shook her head. "Well, okay then. Um, I'm at a loss for words."

One of the cowboys questioned her, "What do ya reckon that was all about?" A low rumble of questions from others in the group followed his words.

Alijah explained that she had witnessed the first of the horsemen near Tony and that she believed he had completed his duty to bring deception. "A lot of people will now be fooled into believing that Tony is the true messiah."

Another in the crowd spoke up, "What were the red light and those voices? One of the voices said there would be no peace."

Alijah held Mavet's sash close to her heart and took a deep breath before she spoke, "That was the second horseman. He comes to steal the peace from us." She turned in a circle slowly. "War is coming, war unlike anything any human has ever seen."

Doc followed up with a distinct new fear in his voice, "Next is famine, right?"

Alijah took his hand and looked right into his eyes. "We'd better start storing whatever food we can get our hands on. We should ration in case we will be affected." She tried to gulp down the lump in her throat as she struggled to speak honestly. "We've got to save more people. We've got to convince them that Christ is the only way."

> *Nation will rise against nation, and kingdom against kingdom. There will be famines and earthquakes in various places. All these are the beginning of birth pains.*
>
> —Matthew 24:7–8

CHAPTER 31

At the Wailing Wall in Israel, the first horseman, the one sent to deceive, spoke to Tony. He had manipulated the powerful figure by instructing him to slay Emil and take his place so that the gates of hell would open. Tony, desiring not only to raise the one he called father from the depths of hell but also to free his brethren, was more than ready. Hell was to be unleashed onto the earth, and all who followed Tony's path would become souls won over to the evilest of beings.

Once again, the world was in torment. People were more confused and lost than ever. Tony demanded that UCNN broadcast the execution of Emil over and over again. For two weeks, his act was openly displayed on televisions around the earth. The network twisted the event to create a story that left people astounded by Tony's deeds. Individuals everywhere watched as he took the glory for resurrecting the witnesses, and his believers took to the streets to joyfully exclaim that the Antichrist had been slain, and a messiah had risen. The people had been deceived.

UCNN displayed Scripture verses during each newscast, further cementing the idea that a messiah had risen. The network showed interviews of people crazed with joy, saying God would renew the world, and Tony's followers would be the only ones to live in the new Eden.

But the joy didn't last long. The execution of Emil frightened officials from every country. They became confused and uncertain of the unified community's future, and before long, a new war broke out. Nearly everyone believed there was a god, but that wasn't good enough. It started in the Middle East, since Israel was God's promised land, and people everywhere believed it should belong to the world, not just to the Jewish people. National leaders cried out that it was time to take Israel. They demanded the land belong to the unified community and petitioned Tony to exile all who were not a registered part of it.

Over the weeks that followed, the Israelis fought valiantly to keep their land, but with the majority of the world rising against them, victory seemed unattainable. But they refused to trade their beliefs for Tony's lies, and God intervened. A natural disaster blocked every strike that was made against them. Unable to overtake Israel, the unified community was furious; after all, God had promised that the land of Israel was for his people, and followers of Tony believed they were the chosen people. They desired to have dominion over Israel.

It didn't stop there. With the continued failure to overthrow the country, the unified community divided into factions, and each party felt more entitled to Israel than the next. Riots broke out in every corner of the earth. Factions pointed fingers at one another and cast blame on each other for not vanquishing the nonbelievers from the nation.

Tony held fast and did not lash out in anger. Instead, he begged for a publicized conference with the Israeli prime minister. Once on the air, he pleaded with people to remember that he only wished peace for his people. "My precious, precious children. You fight to restore a land that was once promised to the Hebrew people. It was promised then to my first children just as it is still promised today. I will not allow anyone to take the land from them as you have witnessed. I have performed wonders to prove to you that overthrowing those cities will not be permitted."

The prime minister all but shouted into the microphone. "The true Messiah would never laugh while his children ran in fear. We do not believe you, and I implore all who believe in God not to be deceived."

The cameras panned back to Tony, who was skilled at crafting his words in situations like this. He stood, pulled his chair beside his opponent, and attempted to diffuse the situation. The prime minister leaned to the other side, creating more space between them.

Tony's voice stayed soft. "I understand your consternation." He looked at the camera with a smirk. "Almost all of you have been confused. You believed in Emil, and you took his mark in hopes of a brighter future, but you were fooled. The Antichrist did what was once prophesied, and now, you are lost once again. But I am your true savior." Tony stood and held his hands out toward the camera.

The video zoomed in to focus just below his wrists. Under each one were markings that resembled puncture wounds. Tony stepped back to show the prime minister before he sat down. "My dear children, do the scars not prove anything to you? Do you not see the wounds I was afflicted with by the crucifixion? I gave my life for you then, and now, I return to you."

Personnel in the room clapped and cheered. Tony smiled and waved to them, but the prime minister remained unimpressed. He stood up before he faced the camera to speak. "Has this creature performed wonders? It would seem so, but is he the Messiah? I do not believe he is. For centuries, people of varying beliefs have quarreled among each other. People throughout the world believe there is only one divine God. All of us seem to believe we alone have the precise understanding of his Word and others are wrong. Many believe the Messiah has yet to come, while others believe he was crucified and will return. If there is one thing we must believe, it is that those differences no longer matter, my brothers and sisters. We must cease our arrogant ways and beliefs. The Word of Elohim is no longer open to our earthly interpretations. Regardless of your faith, there is only one God and one Messiah, and he is coming. Do not be fooled by the son of the beast!"

The crowd in the room booed. The camera crew watched Tony for direction, but he gave none. Instead, he stood up beside his opponent with a look of disappointment on his face. He motioned to the group to quiet down.

"The prime minister and the lost souls still roaming around our fine cities are simply misguided. Those children have grown leery of the deception brought by Emil. They all fail to realize that everything has happened just as the apostles foretold."

The crowd cheered once again. Tony beamed and raised a hand toward them. "Yes, yes, my people. The apostles foretold the end-time events, and those warnings were passed down to future generations."

"What of the mark of the beast? Why are those who have been in league with the beast still here? There is no forgiveness once the mark has been—"

"I turn away none who seek me!" Before the prime minister had a chance to rebut the comment, Tony took control of the debate. "Even though I have ended the tribulation, evil still exists. There are those who will seek to deceive you, to turn you from me, and though many of you chose to accept the mark, I will forgive you. I will make righteous what was once malevolent. I will make what once was the mark of the beast into the mark of my father, the creator!" Tony moved to draw the camera away from the prime minister. "Heed my warning, children. Until now, I have allowed you to deny me. I have tolerated your disobedience, but I will do so no longer. As of today, everyone must prove their love for me."

Silence fell around the room. "I say to my people everywhere, all must take the mark of the ruler of this world. If you cannot prove your love for me, then I will not prove my love for you. There will be no place for you in my kingdom. I will not feed you, even though you are hungry. I will not care for you when you are ill. I shall not keep you safe." He stopped to quickly change the mood. "I love you, my people. I desire none of you to fall. Love me, and in return, you will not go hungry for as long as you live. You will not suffer in sorrow for as long as you live. You will not live in loneliness and isolation. I will give you all that you ask of me if you just show me you love me. I offer you a gift of freedom, and all I ask is a gift from you. A gift for a gift. Won't you prove to me I have a place in your heart?" His eyebrows rose together toward the middle of his forehead as he reached out to the camera and offered a mournful smile.

Sounds of approval filled the air. Tony's new followers expressed their elation every time he spoke. His reign was different then Emil's. People loved Tony, but they had feared Emil from early on. People felt a connection to Tony and were compelled to follow him. In conjunction with the wonders he performed at the Wailing Wall, people were positive there was a god, and Tony was their direct link to him.

The Israeli leader stood in silence, clearly outnumbered by Tony's supporters. Before Tony ordered the cameras to be shut down, the prime minister leapt in front of the closest one. "Since humanity's beginnings, we have been foolish and prideful. Even though we are all children of the one and only Creator, our differences and the weaknesses of our flesh and minds have spawned separation from and anger toward one another. We label other believers as sinners because we cannot see beyond our distinctions. But here and now, we, as a people, stand at a crossroad. I make a promise to all. Regardless of our differences, if you love and serve the true God of Abraham, Isaac, and Jacob, do not feel alone. Come to us! Come to Israel for refuge, and stand with us as we, the children of God, stand against the greatest evil and wait for the mighty Messiah to come!"

Laughter and jeers came from Tony's followers. A man from the crowd called out to him, "Our lord and savior, why do you allow this talk? Why do you allow him to cast doubt on your holiness?"

Tony grinned and signaled to him to quiet down. "I allow this because I am a patient and loving messiah. I will not stifle his fear. Instead, I will give him the opportunity to renounce his false beliefs. Is not benevolence and tolerance what you expect from your messiah? I offer sanctification to you all, my little children. Delight in me always." He motioned for the cameras to shut down and then ordered everyone out of the room.

Only Tony and the prime minister remained in the war room. Tony lifted his imposing frame out of the chair and approached the man. He spoke no words but backed the prime minister up against the cold wall and said in a whisper, "Believe what you wish, but in the end, you will burn just as every other feeble mortal will. We are angels and we will be the rulers of your kind forever."

"Why would you abandon the love of your Creator?"

"He rejected us by creating sinful, meaningless creatures like you. He vaunted his love for you. He adored you more than any of us. Ignorant little creatures like you should have never been placed above us. Your kind needed to be ruled, and he banished us for doing so. We were and are the ones who should hold dominion over you."

"Sin afflicts your kind as well, but he forgives."

"Sin? We are not capable of sin, simpleminded parasite!"

"Like a small child who becomes angry when a sibling gains the attention of his parents, you covet the love he has for us. All of you fell from grace because you lusted for power. Your kind became prideful and bitter. You speak of arrogance in my kind, but I see there are few differences between us."

Tony lashed out with a yell and struck him across the face. "We have started the end of your time." His voice grew louder and was accompanied by a low growl. "I control the little lost sheep, and I will raise the one I now call father. Lucifer and his hoard, my brothers, will reign forever!"

The prime minister shook off the slap and did not appear to be afraid. "Elohim will soon send the Messiah. He will defeat and banish all of you."

"He will fail—"

"It has already been prophesied. The Messiah's army will slay you."

Tony backed off, clenching his fists. "We will see." He bellowed for the soldiers. When they ran into the room, he commanded them to remove the man and send him back to Israel. The prime minister was ordered never to return, but before the soldiers escorted him away, Tony looked over his shoulder and scowled at him. "Yes, let all of the Creator's people travel to the Holy Land. From the four corners of the earth, let them gather there." He sneered and turned to walk away.

Do not tremble, do not be afraid. Did I not proclaim this and foretell it long ago? You are my witnesses.

—Isaiah 44:8

Chapter 32

For weeks, the people of the Ark worked tirelessly to prepare for what was to come. Small groups ventured out into the cities to evangelize to anyone who had not yet gone for assimilation into the unified community. Testifying God's Word was dangerous, and even though they feared arrest, the groups persevered to save as many as they could. Their only goal was to cultivate faith in anyone who would listen, and even though the number of people left in the dormitories was minimal, none of the believers wanted to give up.

It was no easy task, either. Those still in the dormitories were frightened of being dragged off for assimilation or worse. As Tony decreed, anyone caught engaging in worship of anything but him would be arrested and imprisoned. Furthermore, the teaching of God's Word was punishable by immediate execution.

But the courage of the groups was paying off. They reached people from the neighboring towns, and new believers flocked to the Ark and expanded the population more quickly than the settlement could grow. All were welcomed wholeheartedly, and each new resident was swiftly put to work doing whatever his or her skills and capabilities were. The newbies were overjoyed to be in the company of fellow disciples and were eager to participate in the daily duties.

Alijah wished to reach out with the others, but the core Ark members—Chante, Michel, Doc, Robert, and Alessio—encouraged her to stay. They feared for her safety, but they also impressed upon her the importance of the beacon being at the Ark. She stayed and continued to aid Doc at the clinic. Much to the dismay of her friends, she continued to take frequent private walks into the forest in hopes of finding Mavet.

Early one morning on a walk, Alijah felt the familiar tranquil presence of the angel. She had visited with him several times over the last few weeks, but this morning, his presence felt different. His greeting was also dissimilar from his usual warm hello.

Something was clearly troubling his mind. Alijah stood nearly toe-to-toe with the angel and looked up to catch a glimpse of his face. After a brief awkward moment, he looked at her with great sadness. She offered him a childlike smile.

"My sweet guardian angel, what's wrong?"

He whisked her in a hug, and his arms and wings engulfed her. He lifted her high off the ground but remained silent.

While she knew he was unable to feel love as a human would, she couldn't help but feel great delight every time he was near. "Why won't you speak to me?"

Mavet gently placed her on the ground but held her hand as he led her deeper into the woods. They walked in silence for a few minutes until they arrived at a small clearing. The vivid forest was alive with the smell of fresh mountain air.

She tried to urge him to speak. "I love the forest. It's spectacular all throughout the year, but the majesty of winter is just amazing. Isn't it a captivating sight?"

They both sat down under the winter sun that was shining down into the clearing. Mavet remained close to her and looked up at the sky. "The Creator made a perfect world for his children. The sun and the moon move in perfect harmony to nourish the earth and your people day after day." He looked over at Alijah.

"Mavet, what's bothering you?"

He didn't speak.

"I know you, my friend, and I know something is weighing on your mind."

He finally spoke up, "I grow weary for your people."

"It's more than that, isn't it? I know you are sad for us, but I feel like this is different." She cupped his hand with both of hers.

He smiled sweetly before he spoke again, "How do you know so much of me in such a short time?"

She tried to be playful and coy with him to lighten his mood. She moved to sit in front of him and said, "Well, unlike angels, we humans have short lives. We have to move fast to get to know each other, ya know." She forced a laugh.

"My time will come soon. I will not be able to visit you once the Lamb breaks the fourth seal."

She stared at him for several seconds. "Why?"

"All angels will be called to the east to stand beside the Lamb of God when he descends."

Alijah tried hard to fight back the tears. "What's going to happen to all of us? Will we be around to see his return? Mavet, I still don't understand a lot of what is written in the book of Revelation. Who's rising from the dead?" An obviously fake smile accompanied her questions, but it faded when she came to a sudden realization. "Mavet, will I be around to see the Lord's return?"

He reached up and wiped away a few tears that snuck out from her eyes. "Sweet Alijah, you are his beacon. The Father chose you to gather his people and to steady them until he returns. Not everything is for you to understand."

"Try telling that to a mob of frightened people."

"The one thing the human race has never been able to do is accept the Word of God for what it is, not what humanity chooses it to be. His good words need no human approval." He lifted her chin with two of his large fingers. "You asked of your fate. Please understand that only he knows your future, but if it is death you fear, you needn't ever fear it. The Messiah overcame death and gave you salvation. It was a gift to your kind. Now tell me, do you remember what is next? The next judgment."

She struggled to move on as his words loomed in the back of her mind. "Oh yeah, we've been busy trying to hoard food. Everyone at the Ark—that's what people call the camp—is gathering supplies and food. But I'm scared. I mean, our numbers have grown exponentially. I don't know how long the food is going to last. Do you think the faithful will be affected too?"

"Those who pledged their loyalty to the beast have lived with the physical things they desired. The items they lusted for, they received. They have lived in a false state of peace. Each judgment is meant to bring suffering upon them. Worshipers of the beast sinned, causing the Fathers people to suffer while the deceived enjoyed all that the false god offered. They were fooled into believing they were at peace, never realizing that false gods offer nothing less than fallacies. The peace they experienced is no different. The horseman you referred to as war intends to remove peace from them as we speak."

Shivers ran up her spine, but she begged him to continue.

"Their false god offers food to some but not to all. God's people know hunger, and now, people of the beast will know it in a way that none of your kind has ever fathomed. It is why my brother is depicted with a scale. All who had will be equal to all who had not. Until now, the Creator allowed the beasts of burden and livestock to remain. Once my brother who brings famine rides, those animals will be gone as well. Other consumables such as vegetables and fruits will spoil. Nothing edible will remain."

"And you?"

He looked down again and sighed. "Many of your kind will fall to pestilence. Death will come to them." He glanced back at her. "The great deceiver will rise and follow me."

"Hell will be unleashed?"

"Yes. From every corner of the earth, the hounds of hell will be set free."

"Mavet, it's not your fault. It is what you are supposed to do."

"How can you pity me? I will bring absolute evil to your people."

"We've done some pretty evil things. Christ forewarned us. He told us this would happen, but like insolent children who refused to listen to a parent's warnings, we ignored him. We ignored God, and it is time for us to answer for the dirtiest of our deeds."

He shook his head from side to side. "These are horrible things happening to your people, yet you speak so lightly of them. I am confused."

She leaned back. "I'm sorry! You don't understand. These are the end-times for us. It's the end of everything I know. I lost the only family I had—my mom and my dad. Do you have any idea how much pain I'm in, emotionally and physically? I lost everything I owned—everything, Mavet! For as long as I can remember I wanted to help people and even save them. I spent years learning and working to build a secure future for myself. But everything I did was for a future that's—that's just gone. If I stopped to really think about what is happening here, I would drop to my knees and never stop crying."

He tilted his head. "Alijah, I only wished to understand. I do not pass judgment—"

"And it's not that I don't have heart for anyone, but at some point, we have to own up to what we've done and the consequences that have followed. I mean, I watched for the last ten years as our society plummeted into darkness. People everywhere did anything they wanted, anything they pleased, with no thought of how it affected anyone else. I saw children mercilessly beat other children because it was fun. I saw parents maim and murder their own flesh and blood. People everywhere didn't want to take responsibility for anything they did. Television and movies did nothing but encourage narcissism. Some people claimed to be spiritual leaders but did nothing but breed hate and violence. People arbitrarily assaulted others because someone had something they wanted. What's more, people abandoned babies in trash cans and used abortion as a means of birth control! If you didn't agree with the government, they labeled you either part of a hate group or a domestic terrorist. Please don't think of me badly for it. I hate, absolutely hate, that I can't save people and make them understand. I never meant to sound cold or smug. It's just my way of dealing with all of this."

Mavet reached out to take her hands. "Alijah, these things began long ago and will remain so until the time of cleansing. The Creator and the Son have always known of these days. They forewarned your kind. And do you not realize that you have saved many? By your obedience, you have drawn numerous people out from the cities and to your—what name did you say—oh yes, to your Ark. With the aid of your companions, you give them food, clothing, shelter, discipleship, and guidance."

He paused for a moment to lift her chin. "Think of the sacrifice the Messiah made to give your people a way to know the almighty God once again. Because of sin, humanity was separated from the Creator. Lord Jesus offered humankind the hope of salvation, but it came at a tremendous price. On the cross, he took the burden of all sins to reunite the Father and his children. You say you have lost everything when you have not. Your parents simply traveled home before you. They are not lost. And many of the physical items you desired were nothing more than cruel taskmasters that kept your eyes turned from the Father and His Son."

"I can't help but be scared. Famine is coming. What will happen to us?"

"You must always remember that he is with his disciples. Pray and then listen. The Christ Jesus does hear you and will lead you to what you need."

Mavet still had Alijah's hand in his own when he jerked his head toward the sky. In an instant, a crimson moon rose and chased away the sun from the sky once again. The sound of shofars echoed through the forest as if the sound were bouncing from tree to tree. They both jumped to their feet and looked up. Mavet wrapped his large wings around Alijah's body.

They looked at the trees around the edge of the clearing when they noticed movement, and Chante, Michel, Alessio, and Robert emerged.

"We've been searching for you! Didn't you hear us calling your—"

Chante stopped speaking, and all four turned and backed up close to Alijah as they stared at the sky. A deep voice boomed the word, "Come." Another voice followed, saying, "The sting of hunger shall enslave ye," and a crimson flame burned brightly while thick, black smoke stretched around the earth. Thick smoke spread like the fingers of an enormous hand that grasped the earth. And then the crimson light was quickly extinguished before the sun crept back to its previous position.

Mavet released Alijah and folded his wings behind him, and the four friends turned to look at Alijah again. She watched as shock spread across their faces as they each looked up at Mavet's face. None of them spoke. Alijah took a step to the side and smiled first at Mavet and then at her friends.

She clasped her hands together and looked at them briefly before opening her mouth. "Well, I guess our secret is out." She looked at Mavet. "May I tell them your name?"

He dipped his head in approval.

"First, you can't tell anyone who you saw or who he is."

All four slowly nodded.

"His name is Mavet, and if you haven't guessed, he's an angel. He is the one who has helped me truly understand the Lord, as much as we are meant to understand him, and he has helped lead me to the path Christ had laid for me." One by one, she introduced her friends to Mavet.

They stayed in the clearing to discuss what had just happened and how they would be affected by the upcoming judgment. Mavet pleaded with Chante and Michel to continue to evangelize and impart the knowledge of the Word of God. He urged Alessio to keep close to Alijah and support her as she embraced the new members of the Ark. And he reminded Robert to keep his heart open and support all of God's children who came to seek refuge.

> *May God himself, the God of peace, sanctify you through and through. May your whole spirit, soul and body be kept blameless at the coming of our Lord Jesus Christ. The one who calls you is faithful.*
>
> —1 Thessalonians 5:23–24

CHAPTER 33

She had wondered how it all would happen. Alijah had thought for years the Bible was nothing more than folklore, so she never had much interest in learning about it. Her dad always preached the importance of believing in something more than science and the world. He spent countless hours trying to explain the book of Revelation but she could never get past the metaphors.

Her mom tried for many years to reason with Alijah's logical side by asking her to think about the human body. She challenged Alijah to explain how the body could be such a perfect mechanism if an accident in the universe or a tiny amoeba had spawned humanity.

The conversations usually stemmed from a comment like this: "Really, Alijah? In that scientific head of yours, you truly believe something can come from nothing? If that's the case, honey, why doesn't your father's bald head sprout hair?"

For years, her parents begged her to reconsider her harsh views about faith and give the Lord a second chance, but she always fired back with some other question, like, "How can you believe in something you cannot see or prove?" Of course, in the end, she learned how wrong she was. She now understood that the Bible was all true, and current events were playing out just as she had read in the book of Revelation.

She saw firsthand what the first horseman did. People changed dramatically in such a short time. Nonresidents flocked to assimilation centers to prove their love to the man they believed was the messiah. Fewer than ever remained in the dorms, and those who did, they stayed in hiding from the ever-increasing dangers.

The coming of the second horseman accelerated society's descent into madness. Civil wars raged more fiercely than ever because residents wanted more of what they already had. Tony provided everything they needed, but their desires were insatiable. Incidences of theft skyrocketed in cities around the world. People turned against one another and fought to take everything they could. In addition to the fighting within the cities, UCNN reported that countries throughout the world were poised for warfare against one another. The world was again at the brink of a global war, and people didn't understand why they were suffering when they were worshiping the so-called messiah.

The arrival of the third horseman was devastating. His words traveled to the farthest reaches of the earth and were heard and understood in every language across the globe. The black smoke that filled the atmosphere spread around the world, contaminating everything it touched. Every source of drinking water dried up overnight, crops shriveled away to nearly dust, and all of the remaining livestock died from disease. All marine life died, and their carcasses washed up on ocean shores everywhere. People ransacked stores to steal everything edible and drinkable.

At the Ark, food supplies were becoming slim. Every day that passed, Robert and the cowboys kept a close eye on the provisions. All residents received adequate nourishment, but the leaders rationed the food to be safe. The livestock at the Ark did not die, but only a few cows and a single bull were left. A steady stream of water came down the mountain and provided the only secure water source.

Chante took her place as teacher, just as Mavet had told her. Her beloved Michel continued to lead the evangelism groups into the cities. Over time, members of the groups were captured by soldiers and executed. Even though some did die, the rest refused to stop. They followed their leader to try to save as many people as they could.

Hearts were broken from the losses, but Alijah focused on lifting their spirits and reminded them that their fallen comrades had taken their places in heaven. Chante organized multiple prayer sessions daily and made sure everyone had ample time to worship. Alessio continued doing what he expressed desire to do—protect Alijah.

Over the next few months, he remained by her side as a dear friend and protector. They greeted new believers daily, and though their numbers were small, Alijah was grateful to see any new believers come into their little community. Alongside Chante, she encouraged people to learn and understand God's laws, grow spiritually, and never give up faith.

She stressed the importance of understanding and accepting one another so that everyone in the camp would feel a tremendous sense of community and goodwill toward each other. Alijah continued to learn from Chante as well. She wanted to understand all she could about God and the Messiah. Even after the things she had said and done in her past, Christ had given her love, redemption, and the incredible purpose of helping his people find their way.

* * * * *

The camp was bursting at the seams. Even though it was overcrowded, everyone there worked to help the camp function as well as support the outreach teams. The harmony was not always perfect, but everyone cared for each other.

Mavet's visits to Alijah became less frequent. She knew their time together was coming to an end. While it broke her heart to think she would lose him completely, she understood he had a much grander purpose than being her guide and friend. He was an angel, and the love she had developed for him was a love he could never return.

Alijah knew the next judgment had to be near, and she woke up one morning feeling a deep need to see Mavet again. She quickly dressed and wandered off from the camp for her daily walk through the woods.

She traveled deeper than normal into the forest. After an hour, she passed the small open meadow where she often spent time with Mavet. She crossed her arms on her chest and shivered. The morning sun had not yet burned off the mist hanging around the treetops. From where the camp was situated in the mountains, the sun at its peak was huge and golden. She often thought of it as the eye of God watching his creation.

Alijah smelled dewdrops all through the woods. As she strolled, she ran her hand along the bark of the trees that stood strong, unaware of the world's turmoil. The crisp breeze created a gentle song in the bending branches. Alijah stopped along the path to close her eyes and breathe in the fresh scent that permeated the air.

She didn't know what her future held or how many days she had left, but she no longer feared death or the emptiness she had once felt. She imagined what heaven would be like. Would there be streets of gold like so many people thought? Would she see her family again, and if so, would they remember her?

With her face to the sky, she sang a song of worship. After the closing note, she lowered her face and opened her eyes. To her surprise, Mavet was leaning against a huge tree not far from her. He had waited between the trees, watching and listening. She blushed from embarrassment and covered her mouth with her hands to stifle a giggle.

He smiled and walked toward her. When he reached her, he gently pulled her hands from her mouth. Alijah looked at the ground and apologized.

"Why do you apologize?" Mavet embraced her before he walked her to a nearby boulder.

A grin spread across her face as they sat down. "I sing terribly!"

Mavet shook his head. "You sing to the Creator. How can that be terrible?"

"I can't sing, so I usually don't sing at all. I guess I was caught up in the moment."

He brushed her hair back soothingly. "I am amazed by how your heart has grown and how close you have become to your Savior."

"Well, I am amazed that he still manages to love me after I've sinned the way I have. I'm so happy to see you. I was getting scared that the time had come, and I wouldn't get to talk to you anymore. You have been the light in my darkness. You led me to Christ. You are a part of me now."

He stared in the distance before he spoke, "The Christ is the light. I only helped you open your heart and mind." He slowly blinked, and in a soft voice, he continued, "But thank you. Please know you are a part of me always."

She dragged her fingers in the soft moss again and then held his hand and touched his smooth armor with her other hand. "Why do I have this feeling that today is the last time I will see you?"

He wrapped his wing around her to keep her close. He turned and kissed the top of her head tenderly and left his cheek leaning against her hair. "I believe this to be true. My deep desire is to return to you after the fourth seal has been broken, but the Lord Jesus granted me only limited time here with you."

She stayed still. "You never told me why Christ allowed you to help me. I mean, why me when there are so many others he could have chosen? So many people are better, stronger, bolder than me."

Only the sound of the wind through the trees broke the silence. "He often chooses the most unlikely vessels to deliver his greatest messages. Your soul is especially bright. There is such a goodness in it."

"Why? Why would my soul shine like that if I wasn't a believer?"

"You have a pure love for your fellow human beings. You wish to help them. You only lacked belief in Lord Jesus."

She glanced down. "But it wasn't strong enough to save me from myself. I failed to believe in God."

He lifted her head. "The spirit is strong, but the mind is weak. You fell in the same manner as many before you have and many after you will." He looked into her eyes. "The Creator knew you before you were born. He has loved you always, and as with others of your kind, he only wished for you to return to him. I was only a means to an end. I am most honored to have been chosen by Christ to aid you in your return to him. I am most honored to have become your friend."

The angel and Alijah sat in silence for almost an hour. They enjoyed each other's company and simply listened to the chilly breeze roll by like waves on an ocean. They watched the shadows creep along the forest floor. She contemplated what she would say to him.

"Mavet?"

"Yes?"

"What will happen to my friends Chante and Michel? What about Robert and Doc? And I hate to say this, but I'm most worried about Alessio. Do you know what God has in store for him?"

He stood, offered his hand, and helped her up. They began to walk in the direction of the Ark. "I know not his fate. Tell me more about him."

"Alessio? An angel once told me he was my protector." She smiled.

"I am aware, but tell me of him."

"Well, he keeps to himself a lot. He has never really shared too much of his past. He carries great shame, and he usually chooses not talk about it."

"His trial was great?"

"I know he was born and raised in Florence, Italy. Most of his family members were devout Catholics. I believe his siblings went into the service of the church early in their lives. Alessio was different. He never felt a calling for the church. He told me he could not understand why he could not just worship God for who he is and not have to worship under so many rules. So he followed his own way and grew distant from the church. He got involved with the wrong crowd and became an alcoholic, getting into trouble with his friends for many years. He spent time in jail for drunk driving a few times. His family rejoiced when he finally found a woman who changed his life."

"It seemed that his life had changed dramatically—that he had finally found a purpose. Things seemed to be going well. He found a job that turned into a career, and soon after that, he and his wife had a baby girl. But the pressure was building on Alessio. He didn't feel like he could handle a new family, a new house, and an incredibly demanding job. Not too long after his little girl began to walk, a new baby came along. Unfortunately, Alessio was laid off at work and could no longer support his family. It didn't take long for them to lose their home, which forced them to move in with his parents."

Mavet stopped to look at Alijah. "This troubled him?"

"Yeah, from what he told me, it's what got him started drinking again. He felt lost and inadequate. When his wife could no longer take it, she threatened to leave him, so he vowed to seek help. The night before he was to enter treatment, he picked up his wife and children to drive them home. He thought it was safe because he had only a few drinks, but it was enough alcohol to impair his judgment. When he woke up two days later, he found himself in the hospital with his parents crying. They told him he had lost control of the car and driven head-on into oncoming traffic. Alessio was the only survivor."

Mavet swung his head from side to side. "Such a pity."

"He was tried and found guilty for driving while intoxicated, but the authorities felt there could be no greater punishment than what he had already suffered. He couldn't forgive himself, so shortly after the trial, he attempted suicide, but it failed.

"He had shamed his mother and father over and over. He caused the death of his family, and God wouldn't let him die. So he left Italy and came to the United States. Sadly, the years went by, and he lost contact with his family. Then the rapture came, and there seemed to be no hope to see them again. We met in the dormitories six months later and have been friends since. I know he's a good man, and he has found faith again, but I still worry if he will be forgiven."

"Alijah, why do you think there's a chance he may not be forgiven?"

She didn't know how to respond. "I love him like a father, and I know it was an accident, but he chose to drink—to abuse alcohol—and in the end, he caused the deaths of three innocent people. I don't understand why a man who had so much to give would do something as destructive as drinking."

Mavet appeared disappointed. "There are times El Shaddai asks his suffering child to journey upon a raging sea. Only he knows why. Therefore, you should take caution not to pass a verdict on sins that a person has committed." He paused and drew his lips into a tight line. "The result was, as you say, an accident, a calamitous ending to a tormented existence. The regret that he lives with will follow him for all of his days. However"—he stroked her cheek—"Jesus offered him a new path and a renewed sense of purpose in you."

"Christ has forgiven him?" she questioned with a smile.

"He bears the mark."

Mavet stopped abruptly and looked up.

"What's wrong?"

His eyes returned to hers. She could tell something had suddenly changed. Mavet took her hands and lifted them to his chest plate. "The time has come, and I must return."

She took a gulp of air and tried to prevent herself from crying uncontrollably. "The fourth seal is about to be opened?"

"Soon. Alijah, do not mourn." He tried to wipe away her tears, but they fell too quickly. "I will see you again." He lifted her chin and touched her cheeks. "Listen to me carefully. Hell will be on earth, and you must stay faithful to Jesus Christ, and be strong, for the worst is yet to come." He squeezed her tightly and wrapped his wings around her once again. "May the love and blessings of El Shaddai be upon you always. May the light of the Father warm you and comfort you through this journey." He loosened his grip but did not let her go as if he wanted to steal her away from the world. Alijah was pushing up on her toes to reach up to him, so he pulled her up off her feet to embrace her a final time.

When he set her feet on the forest floor, he kissed both of her palms. "Good-bye, sweet child."

Mavet stepped back to spread his mighty wings and began his ascent to heaven.

> *Hear the prayers and petitions of your servant. For your sake, Lord, look with favor on your desolate sanctuary. Give ear, our God, and hear; open your eyes and see the desolation of the city...We do not make requests of you because we are righteous, but because of your great mercy.*
>
> —Daniel 9:17–18

CHAPTER 34

Her heart was broken, but she knew the time for emotion had passed. Alijah hurried through the forest under the midday sun to return to camp as quickly as possible. Her mind was filled with thoughts of what was to come.

When she came out from the trees and ran into the center of camp, she called out for her dearest friends between gasps of air. People began scurrying from all areas of the Ark to see what was happening.

Alessio was the first to arrive. "*Che cos'è?*" He threw his arms around her and nearly knocked her off her feet.

Her other friends ran to her soon after. Chante shouted, "What is it, baby? What's happened?"

Alijah's body trembled with fear, and she struggled to form words. "The fourth seal, the fourth seal is going to be broken!"

All of the Ark residents had circled around and began murmuring to each other. People shouted out questions and concerns.

Chante tried to regain control of the crowd. "People, please calm down. Everyone, take it easy."

"I'm sorry, I'm sorry, everyone," Alijah said as she finally caught her breath. "Listen, I think the next seal will be broken soon, and—"

"What's that mean?" Alessio looked into her wide eyes and took her hands in his.

Chante stepped toward them. "Alijah, you're freaking us all out. What's gonna happen?"

Robert blurted out, "You were in the forest. Did ya talk to that angel again? Did he tell ya that?"

"I'm sorry, everyone, I didn't mean to cause panic. Yeah, the angel told me."

Tensions in the crowd reached the breaking point. People cried and screamed for help.

Alijah raised her voice. "Stop it! Everyone! Look, I know this is frightening, but we've got to get ourselves under control. Robert, where are you?"

"Behind ya."

"Oh!" She reached her hand out to him and grabbed his sleeve. "Listen, how many people do we have out there? How many?"

"We have two groups that haven't checked in yet. Ya reckon they're in trouble?"

"Yes. The angel said the gates of hell are going to be opened in the next seal."

A man from the crowd grabbed her shoulder. "Wait a second, the Bible says that Jesus has the keys to hell. It's not time for him to come down yet, is it? I mean, I wish he would, but..." He uttered a laugh but his face remained void of anything resembling lightheartedness.

Alijah put her hand on his shoulder. "I know what the Bible says, and all of it is true, but we don't have time for this. Hades will ride in the wake of the final horseman, so I think Christ might have given him the authority to open the gates of hell."

The crowd closed in behind her, and many asked what they needed to do.

"When the horseman rides, hell's going to be unleashed on earth. And if we've all been called here to gather at our little Ark, then I can only believe there's a measure of safety here from the evil that's about to infest our world. We need to get the two groups back here quickly. Robert, do you know where they were going?"

"Dormitory four, for sure. We've been hearin' that a lot of people been headin' over to your old dorm because they hoped to find you. I'm pretty sure they were headin' there."

"Okay, what I want is for everyone to get into their groups and gather all the supplies you can. The new gathering room is the biggest, right?"

Robert nodded. "I reckon so, but it needs a bit of work to finish sealing the roof. We can knock that out in about two hours."

"Get it done right away. I want as much food, water, bedding, and whatever other supplies you think we need, and store them there."

"Yes, ma'am. Buildin' teams, get movin'."

"Doc, move the essentials from the clinic in there."

"Got it."

A man called to her from the crowd, "Alijah! Why do we need to squeeze in there?"

She looked solemnly into the crowd. "Because if hell is going to be on earth, God's people will be hand in hand, praying the whole way through it. If anything is going to come for us, it's got to get through our little army of disciples! I don't want a single soul left out."

Alijah quickly gathered two search parties together. She included herself in the group, to which Alessio protested, "No! Absolutely not! You stay here in the camp. No, no, no, no!"

She insisted that if people were at her old dorm looking for her, then she was going to go personally to retrieve them. She caressed his cheek and gave him a loving smile. "My dear, sweet Alessio, my great protector. I love you. But I'm going." She went back to packing her backpack.

"*La mia ragazza pazza.*" He shook his head. "How can I be your protector if you no listen to me?"

"What does that mean anyway?" She laughed. "Remember, I don't speak Italian."

He chuckled. "My crazy girl, I don't know what to do with you. If you must go, then I will come with you, and you will stay by my side."

Alijah leaned and kissed him on the cheek. "Like glue."

Before they left the camp, Chante gathered the residents together to pray for safety and strength. Everyone knew that Alijah leaving the camp was dangerous, but they all understood why she felt the need to go. As they left, one by one, they hugged each other and prayed quietly for everyone's return.

Chante, Michel, Robert, two cowboys, Alessio, and Alijah headed off to her old dormitory. No one spoke much, but Alijah sensed they felt dread of what the soon-coming end would bring.

* * * * *

The dormitory looked as if it had been deserted for months. It was a disaster area. Doors had been ripped off their hinges and personal belongings of former residents were thrown into the hallways. Every room had been ransacked. Clothes were emptied from the closets; furniture had been broken; and sheets had been shredded. Bullets were lodged in the walls, and where there were no bullets, chunks of drywall were torn and strewn all over. There were bloodstains on the doors and floor.

The men continued to check each room on the first floor, peeking around each doorframe first and staying in front of the women. Lines of blood stretched down the hallway like the lines on a highway. When the group arrived at the end of the corridor, they opened the only room with an intact door. They all gasped at the same moment.

"*Madre di dio!*"

"Sweet Jesus in heaven, what happened here?" Robert was visibly overcome by emotion and turned his eyes away.

Chante grabbed Alessio's arm. "It was a massacre."

Michel's jaw hung low as he looked back down the hallway. "The doors, they must have been looking for something. But what?"

Alijah's body trembled, and her voice shook as she said, "Me. They were looking for me. Oh my Lord in heaven, it's all my fault."

"Alijah, no, you don't know that." Robert put his arm around her shoulder.

"I know them. Mrs. Kozlov, Ellen, Joshua." The pain echoed in her voice. "I'm so sorry. Tony must have been searching for me." Her legs gave way, but Alessio caught her. "Oh God, please forgive me. I caused their deaths. I'm so sorry...I should have been here. I shouldn't have run. They paid because I was a coward and ran." She sobbed hard.

"No, no, no. You are no coward any more than this is your fault." Alessio's words were choppy and high-pitched as he wiped the corner of his eyes.

"The smell." Michel plugged his nose and curled his upper lip. "It's gonna make me vomit. They must have died some days ago."

Robert gathered their little group and encouraged them to focus on finding the others. "If they're here, we've got to find them."

From the stairwell on the fourth floor, the group could see a light. They silently made their way down the hall and listened at the door for any voices. Without warning, the door swung open. A familiar face stood in the doorway.

"Holy—Alijah, Chante, you scared me half to death!"

In front of Alijah stood Spencer, who had headed up one of the two recent outreach groups. They all hustled into the room and took turns hugging Spencer and the four other members of the little missionary group. Spencer told them they had found a small bunch of people still hiding in the dorm. He tried his best to share the gospel with them and was surprised to find such eager people left behind.

From out of the crowd that stood on the other side of the room, low voices repeated Alijah's name. One by one, they stood up and went to her. Each of them took a turn touching her and asking for forgiveness.

"Wait, everyone, just wait. I'm just like you, just a person. Please don't ask me for forgiveness because only our Lord and Savior can forgive you. I'm just a calling card of sorts. He's using me to gather his people. " She faked a big smile. "But I am so happy to meet each of you, and I pray you come with us now."

Michel asked, "What happened here?"

One of the guys from the pack of new believers stood up. "This is my dorm room. I was in the bathroom down the hall when it happened. Soldiers came, knocked down doors, and dragged people out. I could hear the screams from below." He looked up at Alijah, who encouraged him to continue. "Tony himself was here. The soldiers searched room by room. They rounded everyone up like they were nothing more than cattle. When they couldn't"—he looked down—"find you, Alijah, they began to interrogate people and beat them horribly. Then they forced everyone to take the mark and microchip. Those who resisted, were lined up and systematically executed. They treated them all like trash. One by one, they took the bodies to Frank's room and threw them in."

Alijah covered her face and cried. Alessio wrapped his arms around her and rocked her gently. "Oh momma, do not blame yourself. This is not your doing."

Michel rubbed Alijah's back and asked, "Why didn't they kill you?" Everyone looked at the man.

"Because they didn't find me. When I heard the screams, I shut off the light, opened the door, and laid down in the tub. They didn't see me. Once everyone was on the first floor, I snuck down and watched from between the bars of the banister. Once the soldiers all left, I ran to my room and hid for two days. I hear they cleared out dorms all around the city."

"But I escaped months ago. Why now? Why would they do this now?"

"Baby girl, think about it. With so much time passed, you'd feel safe comin' back. Tony knows ya, and he knows you'd come back for the rest of them."

Chante rubbed Alijah's shoulders and kissed her head before she stood up. "Brothers and sisters in Christ, soon the hardest days of our existence will come, and there is only one way to get through it. There is only one way you can find redemption, and that is through our Lord. Do you want it? Do you want that glorious love and promise of new life away from all of this?"

The man who witnessed the tragedy stood up and pronounced, "I didn't believe you, Alijah, but I didn't believe Emil or Tony either. After everything I've witnessed, though, I know this for sure – there are demons here on earth, and if there are demons, then there has to be a hell and a devil. And if there's a devil, then there is a God. So you tell me, how do I get on his good side? How do I ask him to save me?"

Everyone stood, grasped hands, and prayed to accept Jesus. Tears flowed from every eye in the room. Everyone's faces showed a peace and joy that hadn't been seen for a long time. But just as everyone was rejoicing, the sound of the shofars bellowed through the sky.

"We've got to go." Alijah grabbed the arm closest to her and started to pull people out of the room. "Come on. We need to head to the forest now!" They jogged two by two down the stairs quickly and ducked out the front door.

Before they could get halfway around the building, the clouds began to swirl, and the sky turned gray. Deafening thunder rolled like a drum. Bolts of lightning decorated the darkening sky with glowing stripes.

Chante pointed to the sky. "Look, it's different this time. Where's the moon?"

This time, the moon didn't come out and mask the sun. It was completely gone. Instead, the sun turned bright white and then slowly dimmed. At first, there was a blue haze to it that quickly changed to shades of green and gray. Then a red haze slowly rose up as if a cup were being filled. When it was complete, the sun was the color of dried blood.

The earth quaked and trembled beneath their feet, strong enough to topple over buildings. The group ran into the street and out of the way of the crashing debris. They huddled in a group, but they were knocked to the ground. They held tight to one another and looked up.

Once again, they heard a single word, "Come."

Crashing sounds came from below, and an explosive noise rose up from the ground. Then the earth split apart.

> *They will be tormented with burning sulfur in the presence of the holy angels and of the Lamb. And the smoke of their torment will rise forever and ever. There will be no rest day or night for those who worship the beast and its image, or for anyone who receives the mark of its name.*
>
> —Revelation 14:10–11

CHAPTER 35

The earth shattered and cracked like fragile glass. Gassy fissures opened all around them and cut off their route back to the forest. From out of the fissures, darkness crept out in waves of smoke.

The group ran furiously along the forest edge, looking for an entrance. They ran for blocks and ducked behind the slowly crumbling buildings. Through the twists and turns, they lost their way and ended up on the edge of a cliff. They stared out into the ocean with no idea what to do. The earth rumbled again and brought the city to its knees.

A pale light beamed down from the heavens and stopped in the middle of the sky. A thunderous voice came from it. "Covetous angel, filled with lust and greed, ye were cast off from grace by the great I AM. You were doomed to burn in the pits of hell, and the time has come. By authority of the exalted Creator, the Alpha and Omega, I command you, Lucifer, to come forth and do his bidding."

Alijah called his name softly, "Mavet."

"The angel from the woods?" Michel said. "He's the fourth horseman?"

"Yep."

"Holy, we've got to go!" Robert pulled on Alijah's arm.

A noise came from the ocean like the roar of a mighty lion. They all turned to see. From high up on the cliff, they watched the water retreat from the shores and disappear.

Suddenly, a massive wave came rushing from the center of the ocean as if an enormous hand pushed it toward the city. When the wave hit, the coastline was saturated with seawater. Screams of terror came from people in the city as they tried to run from the wave. Alijah and her friends could only stand and watch from a distance as the raging waters silenced the people below.

Aftershocks rumbled underneath their feet, crumbling part of the cliffside. The group was knocked off their feet again as they attempted to flee from the reverberating quakes that seemed to stem from the sea. From as far in the distance as they could see, fireballs erupted from the ocean and launched high into the sky.

"It's coming, isn't it?" one of the new believers questioned.

At that moment, a creature shot up into the air behind Mavet. It was an exquisite being with six long elegant wings. It had the head of a lion, the body of an ox, and the talons of an eagle. It made a horrible metallic screaming sound as it breathed in the earth's atmosphere. It followed Mavet across the sky and down toward earth, trailing black smoke behind it.

The sky turned a greenish-gray color with hints of the red beams of light from the darkened sun. Ghastly noises came from the fissures beneath as the gates of hell opened and the dogs of hell poured out.

Alijah jumped up and instinctively ran toward the city, leaving the group with no choice but to follow her. The only thing on her mind was to reach Mavet. As the group ran, they saw creatures ruthlessly crawling over one another like ants to get out of the crevices.

They had tortured dark eyes and could not stand up straight or run. Each one looked as if its bones had been broken long ago and had healed horribly out of place. Their spines were twisted, and their skin was charred. A putrid smell dripped like liquid from their bodies.

As Alijah and the other believers ran through the city, they witnessed an incredible but frightening sight. Alessio began to pray and threw his arms around Alijah to hold her as tight as he could. Chante and Michel took Spencer's hand and began to pray. The others took hold of each other and repeated the prayer Chante was leading. Citizens of the unified community were being captured by the demons and dragged down into the cracks in the earth. They cried out in horror and tried to escape, but no one could save them.

Angels had arrived and were poised to fight. Mavet was in the center with his hood raised over his head and his sword drawn. Tony, who stood just a few feet away from Mavet, laughed out loud to the heavens. "Come, my brothers. Kneel before your master!" Demons came forward and knelt down before Tony and the creature that had come from the sea.

Then the hideous beast changed to reveal a new self. There, standing beside Tony was an angel more beautiful than anything Alijah had ever seen. His face was divine, smooth, and captivating. His large frame stood taller than Tony, but the long wings he extended were soiled and broken rather than white and smooth. His hands and feet were bare and scorched. His gown was dilapidated, torn, and singed. His deep metallic voice was familiar and spoke the language of God as the angel raised his arms to heaven and shouted, "Kneel before me, human creatures, for I am Lucifer and your god! On this day, I shall sit on the throne of the Creator. Heaven is mine!"

Ear-piercing screeches erupted from the demons as if they were cheering in joy. Panicked, Alijah turned her head to see they were completely surrounded by the foul creatures. She knew that not making it back to the Ark in time had left them in peril.

Lucifer spoke to Tony before he shot back up into the sky and flew away. In one command, Tony ordered the demons to take the conquered humans and destroy the angels. A war unlike any other unfolded in front of Alijah's eyes.

A demon ran straight to Alijah, but an angel of God struck it down with an arrow and told her, "Run to the safety of the forest."

She begged for answers. "Where did Satan go?"

"He travels to the east, where the Son of God will meet him in the heavens, where all of the earth shall see."

At that moment, Tony noticed Alijah's presence, but Mavet blocked him as he went to charge her. The group ran and ducked between the battling creatures. Fear fuelled every step they took. All around them, those who had taken the mark were grabbed and dragged into the growing abyss.

Just as Alijah's group thought they were getting closer to the forest edge, another earthquake shuddered through the earth and knocked everyone down again. More demons erupted from the depths and tried to reach Alijah.

One of the new believers yelled out, "They want her! We need to get away from her!"

Spencer shouted, "No, stay with us!" He tried to grab the woman, but she squirmed out of his arms and ran off with the other new believers in tow. It wasn't long before Tony's soldiers gunned them down. Even the soldiers were on their own and terrified, and they shot at anything that came at them. They too were cut off from safety.

Alijah and the others continued to run and did their best to get back to the woods. With people and soldiers running wild all over the city, they had to fight their way through the crowds. Alessio fought hard to protect Alijah and the others. They all combated evil valiantly as they made their way through the city.

New sounds of mighty shofars bellowed through the sky. The sun that burned red suddenly turned nearly black. Another great earthquake opened more gaps in the earth, but this time, a nearby mountain split open, and the skies darkened even more with ash. Fire spewed from the mountaintop and turned the sky red. Fire scorched the buildings throughout the city.

The evil that came out of the crevices was only matched by the putrid sulfur smell that oozed from below. Everywhere they turned, the faithful group of disciples was surrounded by evil.

Michel held tight to Chante. "Oh no...no, no, no! How can this be?"

"Oh, hell no!" Robert couldn't help but shout his disgust.

Alijah grabbed Chante's and Alessio's hands. "We must have made a wrong turn."

"We're back where we started from." Spencer covered his face with his hands.

As they looked into the town, they witnessed Mavet and a band of angels fighting furiously against the evil. The once-beautiful city Alijah called home was in fiery ruins. Demons lay destroyed on the grass next to the bodies of countless community citizens.

People everywhere ran crazed in the streets. The air was thick and hard to take in. In an instant, a scowling, frightening creature appeared in front of the group. It stopped just in front of Michel. As it tried to grab him with its boney, twisted fingers, it snapped its arm back as if it had been shocked by something. It screeched and showed its teeth before running off and killing a nearby citizen with one swipe of its sharp fingers.

"Why didn't it take me?" Michel said in shock.

Alijah's eyes were almost as wide as half dollars. "They're collecting souls—the ones who carry the mark of the beast. They can't take us into hell because we belong to God."

At that moment, another earthquake rattled the ground. It split an opening between the group, leaving Alijah and Alessio on one side. Robert tried to jump over the fissure, but the scorching heat seeping out of the fracture scalded his right hand. The group charged forward hoping to reach each other.

But mere seconds later, Alessio and Alijah ran straight into Tony. In front of their eyes, Tony changed into his true form. They witnessed the creature that had stolen Tony's soul and taken his place—the creature with a lion's head, ox's body, and the talons of an eagle.

Alijah screamed in terror as Alessio jumped in front of her to block the impending attack. In one swift swing of the creature's talons, Alessio was struck to the ground. The beast let out a fearsome growl and lifted its talons to strike again, but a sword penetrated its body from behind.

Alijah threw her body on top of Alessio and tried to spare him any more pain. She cringed in fear, believing there would be a final blow from the creature that once had the form of Tony. But the creature's body fell limp and laid lifeless beside them.

Mavet was at their side, holding the sword used to destroy the fallen angel. He touched Alijah's shoulder as she wept over the lifeless body of Alessio.

"No! It's not fair! I didn't get a chance to say good-bye. It's not fair..." Her words became inaudible from her weeping.

Chante and the others cried for Alessio. He had been a part of their family for nearly three years. Chante dropped to her knees and whispered over his body, expressing her sorrow over losing the man who had been through so much with her and Alijah since the time of their capture.

After several minutes of mourning, Robert and Michel struggled to lift the ladies to their feet. Michel finally yelled, "We have to go now!"

Spencer pulled Alijah up. "Come on, girl, we've gotta go."

She tried to push away. "No, I'm not leaving him here! I won't let those things take his body!"

Robert whispered in her ear. "Baby girl, he wouldn't want this. Alessio wanted ya to live, so much so that he gave his life for ya. Come on now."

The group tried to make it through the city square, but chaos was all around them. There was nowhere to go, no way to escape.

"Alijah, what's going to happen to the others in the forest? And all the other believers around the world?" Chante grabbed her arm and huddled close to her.

"I don't know. We were told to stay in the safety of the forest. I can't imagine our Lord leaving them to die up there."

She paused as the sound of another shofar thundered in the sky. At that moment, complete silence fell. The winds stop blowing, the mountains stopped burning, and all that walked on the earth stood still and looked toward the sky.

Alijah stepped away from the group to walk toward Mavet, and then the sound of a single gunshot pierced the air.

Chanted screamed out, "Alijah!"

> *What no eye has seen, what no ear has heard, and what no human mind has conceived—the things God has prepared for those who love him.*
>
> *—1 Corinthians 2:9*

CHAPTER 36

She laid on her back, unable to move. Alijah watched the world change as the stars rose in the night sky. Each one danced ever so gently, moving slower and slower until they stopped all together. They watched her from above.

The cries around her faded into nothingness until all she heard was the slow, low beat of her own heart. She felt the caress of Mavet's mighty but gentle wings as they snugly engulfed her. He cradled her in his arms to keep her safe from any other harm. Chante, Michel, Robert, and Spencer knelt beside her to say their good-byes.

They jerked their heads up when they heard four massive shofars roaring in harmony in the sky. Once again, all creatures looked toward the heavens. Not a single breeze blew.

The translucent, bronze-colored sky became void of any clouds. A full moon appeared, and Chante said in a whisper, "Another blood moon?"

Mavet spoke loud enough for all of them to hear, "He prepares."

The stars that were watching over Alijah suddenly hurried across the sky and began to take on a new formation.

Alijah tugged on the fabric under his armor. "What's going on?"

Mavet briefly returned her glance. "He dons his armor."

Michel asked, "Who?"

"The Son of the Creator prepares to come."

The shofars blew four short bursts. The sound seemed to come from the four corners of the earth and consume the air. The stars suddenly dropped from the sky and smashed into earth. As they crashed into the ground, the beings of light immediately knelt and bowed their heads. The heavens ripped open, and a blinding light shot out. A mass of angels descended from the sky and prepared for the Lord's descent.

Mavet looked out at the crowd and commanded, "On your knees. Bow before the King of all kings. The Lord God, your Creator, looks upon you."

Everyone dropped to their knees and held tightly to each other. Spencer asked Mavet, "He's comin' now?"

Mavet looked back down at Alijah and caressed her cheek. "The Lamb awaits."

Chante reached over Mavet's wing to touch Alijah's forehead. Her hand was trembling. Eye to eye with the mighty angel, she cried, "Why does he wait?"

"The beacons have fulfilled their purpose, and he calls them home first."

Robert scooted up behind Chante, who was on her knees. He did not speak. He too reached past Mavet's wing to quickly touch Alijah's head.

Alijah knew she was dying and did not have much time to say all the things she had wanted to say. "Don't be sad for me. I'll see you soon. I love you so much."

They could no longer contain their tears. Chante and the others sobbed heavily.

"It's been a long and hard journey, Mavet. I'm not going to escape this one, am I?"

"There is no need to escape this time."

"I'm scare...d." She struggled for breath.

"There is nothing left to fear, child. Nothing at all."

"Mavet?" She tried hard to focus her eyes on him.

"Yes?" He brushed the blood from the corners of her mouth with the tips of his fingers.

"I love you. I can't ever tell you...how thankful I am...to you for coming for me. I don't think I could've...done this alone."

"Shhh, quiet your mind. With or without me, you were never alone."

Soft lights grew around the believers as they looked back up at the sky.

"What...," her voice trailed off as she gasped her last breath of air.

Mavet leaned toward her ear and whispered, "Such a marvelous creature. You have taught me so very much, and it is I who should give you thanks." She felt the warmth of his breath on her cheek as she listened to the last of his words. With the final beat of her heart, darkness fell.

* * * * *

From out of the darkness, a door opened. She slowly walked through it to find a bright green meadow that went on as far as her eyes could see. She searched for any signs of life but there was nothing—nothing but emptiness and silence.

The vivid green grass caressed the soles of her bare feet. Each little blade was soft as silk. A warm smell filled her nostrils and reminded her of sweet pea flowers in bloom. The inviting scent was carried on a cool and calm breeze that seemed to be guiding her somewhere. Although she could not find the sun, the sky was unusually bright and nearly glowed with hues of blues, greens, pinks, and various shades of white. Small gatherings of puffy white clouds performed a graceful dance across the sky.

Alijah had no recollection of the garment she was wearing. A soft blue-and-white gown fluttered across her body as she walked through the meadow. Around her waist was a deep blue sash that was tied in the back and cascaded down the length of her gown.

She wandered for what seemed like hours. *It's beautiful here, but there's no one, no sign of life. Is this some kind of purgatory, or is this hell?* she thought *Am I doomed to be alone for eternity? Is that my hell? Did I displease the Lord that much?*

A soft voice from beyond one of the rolling hills called her name slowly. "Alijah."

She sprinted toward the voice while her mind raced with thoughts of what she would find. Would it be a gateway to heaven or a gateway to hell? Or even worse, would all the loss, pain, and suffering she'd endured be nothing more than a dream?

When she arrived, she saw two figures by a large fig tree. It was an odd tree, tremendous compared to the fig trees she knew. She focused first on the tree and noticed that each branch had ribbons in varying shades of blue, white, and yellow dangling on them. Each ribbon had a single word written on it in a language Alijah could not understand but had seen before. Underneath the tree was a simple white book on a pedestal that was adorned with gold and silver.

Beside the tree, a painfully bright light shined into her eyes. After a moment, she was able to focus slightly, and two figures came into view. One of the figures raised his hands and slowly pulled the hood of his robe off his head to reveal his face.

"Mavet!" Alijah grinned and placed both hands over her heart, doing all she could not to run to him. She breathed in deeply. "Mavet, what is this place? What's happening to me?" She took a step closer and continued to beg for answers.

Then he raised that subtle smile she had come to know and love, but oddly, he did not respond to her. Instead, he turned his head toward the second figure. The light slowly dimmed enough for her to make out the face. She had never seen the face before, but no words or pictures could ever have described him.

She saw no distinction of race or any of the differences humanity had viciously fought over since their creation. It seemed all of it had no meaning or place anymore. The creature who stood before Alijah was a pure, perfect being. He was a pure, perfect angel of light, strength, hope, shelter, forgiveness, and love. The being who stood in front of her was the Son of the Creator of everything. The being who stood before her was the Father of every human being and Creator of every creature that slithered, crawled, walked, or flew. There in front of her was a Father who did not abandon his children, even though they had long since abandoned him. He was the Father who, even at the end of times, would give his wayward children one last chance to come home. Before her was the Son of God, Christ Jesus.

Her knees buckled from under her, dropping her quickly to the ground. Alijah felt no pain; instead, she extended her hands forward. Mavet dipped his head slowly toward his master as if he were saying, "As you wish," and turned his glance back to Alijah.

Christ smiled and came forward. Mavet followed close behind. There was so much she wanted to say, to tell him how sorry she was for all her choices and to beg him for forgiveness for the ugliness of her sins and thoughts, but she could not utter a word no matter how hard she tried. Tears fell from her eyes while she laughed uncontrollably.

In an instant, she felt as if a cloak of pure love and absolute peace, unlike anything she had ever known, wrapped itself around her.

In front of her, the meadows changed. They revealed an odd type of cityscape that seemed to erect itself in the distance, like pieces of an old celluloid film being placed back together after being spliced apart. It grew brighter, as if dawn was approaching. She could see other people waiting in the street and looking at her. They smiled as if they had been waiting for her arrival.

He placed his warm hand on her forehead and bent to the ground. Christ wiped away the tears from her cheeks.

With a deep breath and a shaky voice, she said, "I'm so sorry."

He offered a warm, loving smile. "Why do you feel such shame?"

Overwhelmed with joy and fear, her jaw trembled as she searched for the words. "I've been weak and unworthy of you. I've said such terrible things to you."

He smiled and shook his head. "It is for those sins I gave my life. I am most joyful you have returned to me. Dear child, you see iniquities, but through you, I have worked wonders."

Alijah's mind was wild with thoughts she desperately wanted to speak. She wanted to ask what was going to happen to the others, but she could only say, "I don't deserve your love."

"Oh, my precious child, I know your heart, and I am most pleased." He lifted her chin to see her tear-filled eyes once again. "Welcome home, my sweet daughter. Welcome home."

Look, I am coming soon! My reward is with me, and I will give to each person according to what they have done. I am the Alpha and the Omega, the First and the Last, the Beginning and the End. Blessed are those who wash their robes, that they may have the right to the tree of life and may go through the gates into the city.

—Revelation 22:12–14

REFERENCES

Scripture quotations taken from the The Holy Bible, New International Version®, NIV® Copyright © 1973, 1978, 1984, 2011 by Biblica, Inc.® All rights reserved worldwide.

About the Author

Victoria Garafola is a veteran who traveled from coast to coast but considers Colorado her home. Presently, she resides in Florida with her family.

She holds a Bachelor's degree in Human Development and Anthropology in addition to a Master's degree in counseling Psychology. Victoria is an active member of her local Baptist church and enjoys studying the Lord's Word.

A few of her favorite pastimes include kayaking and hiking. She is an avid reader and a writer, with *Covenant Kept* being her first novel. She is a certified diver and US Navy veteran.

Victoria can be found on covenantkept.com or twitter/covenantkept.

CPSIA information can be obtained
at www.ICGtesting.com
Printed in the USA
FSHW02n0033210918
52226FS